SHOOTING THE BREEZE

SHOOTING
THE BREEZE

ANTHONY SATTIN

JONATHAN CAPE
THIRTY-TWO BEDFORD SQUARE LONDON

FOR MONA AND GERALD

First published 1989
© Anthony Sattin 1989
Jonathan Cape Ltd, 32 Bedford Square, London WC1B 3SG

The lines from *Cat on a Hot Tin Roof* quoted
in the epigraph are reproduced courtesy of
Tennessee Williams Trustees, Lady St Just
and John Eastman

A CIP catalogue record for this book
is available from the British Library

ISBN 0–224–02724–7

Phototypeset by
Computape (Pickering) Ltd, North Yorkshire
Printed in Great Britain by
Mackays of Chatham PLC

BRICK (*at the liquor cabinet*): Big Daddy, you sure are shootin' th' breeze tonight.

(*There is a pause and voices are heard outside.*)

BIG DADDY: I been quiet lately, spoke not a word, just sat and stared into space. I had something heavy weighing on my mind but tonight that load was took off me.

Tennessee Williams, *Cat on a Hot Tin Roof*

I

One night, a while back now, I dreamed I was walking down a long, dimly lit arcade where my footsteps echoed around me. I had a cheque-book and wallet in my hand, the most expensive shops in front of me; I searched their windows for something to buy.

I could give him that, I thought, or that. No, he wouldn't really want it.

More windows, more possibilities.

There – that's it. I went into a shop and bought a black leather wallet. How right, I thought, and how very expensive.

'My brother is emigrating to America,' I told the elderly shopkeeper.

'Really, sir?' he replied without interest, slipping the wallet into a little blue and gold plastic bag.

'Yes . . . he's going to play jazz trumpet in New York, so I thought a wallet was probably the right thing to send him off with . . . There's money to be made in the music business.'

'Absolutely, sir. Perhaps the gentleman would like a credit-card holder to go with it?'

'Well, perhaps, but if he does I'll come back for it.'

I stepped into the arcade again and closed the door behind me. Then I hesitated; maybe a wallet wasn't enough. It had to be absolutely right, no matter how much it cost. I thought about going back into the shop, but the man was watching me, his old face filling the window; I carried on down the arcade, intent, searching.

I was considering an automated display of penknives in another window, their blades flashing in the electric light, when a hand touched my shoulder. It was my brother Alexander, smiling at me, pleased to have sur-

1

prised me. He stared at the bag I was rolling up in my hand.

'I took the day off work to drive you to the airport,' I told him.

'Thanks, brother,' he said, still smiling.

We turned and walked in silence along the arcade and out into the sunlit London street. Alex was taller than me, and walking beside him I noticed again that his height gave him an air of superiority. I felt we were very close as we made our way through the crowd. I was aware of each of our movements, of every muscle; I never once doubted that Alex felt the same way too. I could have hugged him then.

I drove him to Kensington to collect his luggage and then we moved slowly through West London. The traffic was heavy and held us firmly in its centre, oppressed our thoughts and conversation as well. We didn't mention Caroline, his wife, who had already left for New York, or the arguments that had accompanied her departure. Instead we talked about cars and clothes, and I wished then that I had bought him the credit-card holder. As time passed I became dark with disappointment, thinking that we might continue like this until we reached the airport, and that then he would just say goodbye and leave me. I didn't know what else could happen, but I wanted something more from him. I needed Alex to do something brotherly.

Finally, when we left the city, we brightened a little.

'You must try to come and see us,' he said, as he must have said to so many people those last weeks. 'Of course, it'll be strange for a while – we'll have to settle in first. But we'll be open for visitors before too long.'

Open for visitors. Those words echoed quietly in my head. 'It's not quite like dropping in for tea, though, is it? I mean, you'll be thousands of miles away.'

'I know, I know. It's sad, isn't it,' he said flatly. 'There's just you left with the parents now.'

'Somehow I always thought I'd be the one to go. It just never occurred to me that you would even want to . . . '

When we arrived at Heathrow, Terminal Three, International Departures, I told him I would miss him.

'I will miss you too. Whatever has happened, or will happen, we're family. Always remember that.'

As he said it, there were tears in our eyes, and we looked away towards the sign flashing CHECK IN — CHECK IN. 'Come and help me with my luggage,' he suggested, handing me the case that contained his trumpet, which we were sure would bring him success.

When we had heard the murmur that was the last call for his flight, we both moved towards the departure lounge, but we had seen too many movies to be able to say goodbye. Instead, in front of the barrier, we looked at each other for the briefest moment and hugged, clumsily, wished each other good luck and hurried off in our separate directions.

It was dark when I got back to the car. As I reached down to clip in my seat belt my hand touched the blue and gold plastic bag, and I woke up with a start.

I was young, but old enough to make my own decisions. I don't think I realized then that their consequences would affect my chances of happiness, of success and love — what some of my friends referred to as sex and money. Sometimes, after a few bottles, we used to argue about which one we could live without, if we had to choose between money and sex, success and love, wealth and family — we didn't have to consider disease or death. Mawkish with wine, haunted by the memory of our empty beds, we always decided that love was the most valuable.

I loved my family. I was a son and a brother and I hoped, one day, that I would also be a husband and father. But my expectations were not always fulfilled — what happened on the day that Alex left for New York, for instance, was a little different from the dream. I did take the day off work to drive him to the airport, and I did buy him a leather wallet in the Burlington Arcade, but I didn't find him. Instead I got a farewell phone-call from Heathrow just before he boarded the flight for the States to join his wife. He was going to 'make a big noise', with his talent for the trumpet and with her money and connections, and nothing I could say added to that. It was a long time before I heard from him again.

3

Before his wife left him there were a couple of brief phone-calls. Then she took up an offer of work in Hollywood – something to do with film promotion. It was, of course, too good to turn down and he told me they had both thought it best for him to stay on in New York, to make the most of their new contacts, to wait for her there because she would come back just as soon as the job was over.

Months went by. It became clear that this was one job that would never end, and in the mean-time, still waiting for her, he was rather lonely. When he came back the following summer he was on his own.

He arrived at Heathrow on a Sunday, a bright blue day early in July when the city was hot, unhealthy and as still as the failed breeze. Around mid-morning I left the flat I rented in Camden Town, partly asleep, mostly drunk from the night before, and unlocked my car. This was my pride and joy, an Austin Healey 3000 Mark III, an ice-blue, wire-wheeled, boys'-own dream, a convertible sports car with the right amount of chrome, a walnut dashboard and a thin wooden steering wheel. It sat low on the ground and made enough noise when I revved the engine for heads to turn. All in all it gave me enough pleasure not to grudge the fact that I would be repaying the bank loan for a few years to come. It had become my security – if things got too bad I could always drive away in it. But when I drove out to Heathrow that day I didn't think about the car. I turned the radio up as loud as it would go, and as I sang along at the top of my voice I caught a glimpse of my face in the mirror: it was hard and set, my eyes sunken and staring wildly. When I smoked a cigarette I took short, nervous drags, and when I closed my mouth I found myself clenching my teeth. I breathed slowly and deeply to calm myself and drove with the window wide open. When I pulled over along the motorway, to roll back the roof, I was surprised by the countryside, deep and green, the fields already rich with growth, the air heavy with the smell of cut grass and manure.

At Heathrow I left the Healey on the third floor of the car-park and walked through a glass-sided passage to the arrivals building, along a carpeted upper gallery – a glance

4

at the screens flashing flight details — and down on to the floor of the arrivals hall. Airports are contradictory places, always in motion but never changing. People were walking around, leaning against pillars or sitting at an open-sided coffee bar sipping pale liquid from pale plastic cups and reading the Sunday papers. Others, three and four deep, lined the metal barriers and defined a gauntlet for passengers to pass through when they emerged from Customs. They faced a board which told them that the flight they had come to meet was expected, or that its baggage had not been unloaded, but they stood there all the same, idly watching passengers from another flight, who came in packs, pushing trolleys, bags over their shoulders, tans smooth and still glistening with sun-cream. Some smiled emptily and walked straight on, while others, with set faces, searched the crowd for someone they knew. Lucky ones were picked out straight away — just a name called or a hand waved — and were embraced by eager arms. Those who failed to see the friendly face or waving hand walked more quickly as they went along the line, and it was only when they reached the end that they were surprised by the person who had been waiting there. Or they carried straight on, to the telephones and a taxi or tube train. As I watched them I became nervous about seeing Alex again; I wondered how we would act together, what we could say now.

The expectation of a flight from Tel Aviv was replaced by that of others — from Abu Dhabi, Moscow and Mexico — but the Los Angeles–New York–London flight was still way down the board so I walked across to the news-stand and bought a Sunday paper, ordered a coffee and dough-nut from the bar and tried to occupy myself. But I had had one whisky too many the night before and was distracted by never-ending messages for people meeting friends who would not now be arriving, or for people who had just arrived who were not going to be met. The paper drooped in my hands and I stared blankly across the floor at the other people passing time.

As a family, we were never very good at travelling. The first time we went abroad, when Alex was seven and I was five, we were so sick on the flight to Naples and so scared of the flight home that it was decided in future we would stay on land. The following year we drove across Europe, and although we resented such a long confinement in the car it was worth enduring it. Once we had arrived we were very good at being away – with Dad's fluency in French and Italian, and with Mum's Mediterranean looks, we were able to pass for locals as long as Alex and I kept our mouths shut and we were out of sight of the racing-green Jaguar with its chrome GB badge.

Alex used to look after me when I got into scraps with other boys playing football on the beach or polo in the water. He was already tall, and had presence, despite being so skinny that he looked frail. I thought he conducted himself like a divinity. Then, one year, at a place called Camaiore on the Italian Riviera, where we had stopped for lunch and a swim, Alex got into a fight. The beach was hard and we were annoying the other bathers lying in the sun by kicking a ball around. 'Why don't you kids go and play somewhere else?' Dad suggested, so we moved around the headland, to where the beach was covered with a fine shingle and larger, rougher stones. A group of Italian boys about the same age as us – eleven or twelve years old – came down to the beach and suggested that we get up a game of five-a-side football. We removed the larger stones, used T-shirts to mark out a pitch and then Alex and one of the Italian boys chose the teams. I played behind Alex, as I was used to doing, passing him the ball and watching his delicate legs move out of the way of tackles, his ragged, salt-stained hair bobbing as he ran. He was a better player than the others and we were going to win easily, until the Italian boys started going for him. When he was tripped and grazed his knees on the pebbles in the sand he said nothing, and played on. The next time he had the ball he was pushed and punched. They bruised his shins and he banged his head as he fell. I could see what they were doing, but there was nothing I could do to help him.

'Let's not play with them any more,' I said, but Alex brushed that idea aside. He would show them. We would still win. The next time I tackled one of them, a tall, powerful, dark-skinned boy, I landed heavily on his ankle.

6

I knew I had hurt him, but far from stopping them this violence raised the tension of the game. The next time Alex had the ball three of them went for him together. They tripped and kicked him, and when he didn't get up they ran along the beach and disappeared up on to the road.

I helped Alex on to his feet, brushed the sand off the cut on his cheek and pulled little sods of hot, hardened oil from his leg. He was pale, silent, as I put his arm around my shoulder, unaware that the tears I was crying were not for his hurt but for the belief that something, now, had changed between us. He had been bettered and I had witnessed it. He spent his time with girls after that and I, too young to follow, was left alone for the first time in my life.

Alex had never got used to the idea of flying. He had backed out of returning from New York on three occasions on the grounds that he could not face the seven and three-quarter hour flight, and I pictured how, when he had finally boarded the plane, he would have sat by the window, lifeless eyes staring out on to the sunlit tarmac, and prepared himself for the dead hours ahead of him by slipping on the headphones of his Walkman and closing his eyes as though deep in concentration. Maybe his lips would have been shaping some notes. The person next to him would have taken one look at the figure hunched in the corner and asked the stewardess if there was a seat elsewhere on the plane. But someone would have sat there and watched with concern or annoyance as, just before take-off, he began fidgeting, picking up the emergency procedures card and studying it carefully, switching the light above him on and off and ringing the bell for attention. Then, somewhere over the Atlantic, the tape he was listening to would have ended and his Walkman would have slipped automatically to OFF.

I broke into a sweat when I saw that his flight had landed. I had so many memories of Alex and me, of our childhood together, our youth and manhood. I could see so many faces of Alex too – when we were very young and he was fast and cheeky, bright and intelligent, and always in trouble. Alex at school, with his individual interpretation of the uniform, his long curling hair tied up to look as though it was the regulation length, slipping out at night, eyes wild, my money in his pocket, off to meet a girl in a dark corner of her school and, later, eyes red with alcohol and exhaustion, dragging himself back up the last of many stairs, reaching for a hand to help him into bed. He always got away with it, though, because everyone could see that there was something about him – he had talent. And then there was Alex, poor and stylish, at music school and after, playing in bars and out of the way clubs, doing it his way, always pushing, always pushing too far, but making it work for himself and then also for his wife.

I had always been just one step behind him, still very close, so I had known that something was wrong the last time I telephoned him in New York. But when I called Dad afterwards he insisted that Alex was fine.

'So what are the long faces and lowered voices for, if everything's so perfect?' I asked.

'I'll have to call you back,' he said abruptly, and hung up.

Later, his voice was shrill and hard.

'Alex is in trouble,' he told me. 'He's coming home.' Then he stopped, as though that was all he had to tell me. 'I just don't know how to say this – I don't want to . . . I don't want to upset you.'

He told me that Alex had been ill, and so many thoughts rushed through my mind at once, the names and images of diseases and afflictions, but never, not once, did heroin ever occur to me. When Dad explained that Alex was a heroin addict I didn't really understand. It didn't make any sense.

'What do you mean?' I demanded. 'Alex? An addict?' That sounded stupid, so I said, 'How? When? For how long?'

'It's all over now,' he told me, still grave, breathing heavily down the phone. 'Some time ago he told us he desperately needed money, so we sent him some. But he wouldn't tell us what it was for. Later, he said it was for a methadone cure. Then he decided that he wanted to come home again for a while, just to sort out his thoughts, get his life back into perspective. You know we said that if either

8

of you were ever in trouble we would send you money to get you home.'

He was silent for a moment, and then said, 'You won't tell anyone, will you? I wouldn't want anyone to know.' The shame he felt because of his son hung like a pall over his words, while in my mind I could see another face of Alex, created from images glimpsed in nightclubs and London streets, from AIDS posters and late-night movies. I had never known an addict before, although I had heard plenty of stories. This new photofit face seemed to have no relation to the one I remembered from our youth and childhood, but it suited the deadened voice I had heard over the phone from the States.

Alex didn't see me when he came through from Customs – he didn't even turn his head to look – and when I saw him I kept silent, suddenly needing a little more time before I greeted him. I crouched down behind the metal barrier and the people who separated us, and hurried along to the end of the line to wait for him there. He was huddled in a crumpled brown overcoat, with a pair of tortoiseshell light-sensitive glasses over his eyes, head-phones over his ears and his head mostly covered by a black woollen beret. He was bent double with the effort of pushing his trolley, as though it were an enormous weight running on rusted wheels. His head was pointing straight ahead, though, and he seemed to be looking at the EXIT sign at the far end of the hall. Other passengers from his flight passed on either side of him, pushing their trolleys as though there were a race to be won, but Alex paid no attention, either to them or to the people in front of him who stopped half-way along the barrier to lean into reach-ing arms, hands and lips.

When I stood out from the barrier, waiting for him to come up to me, he still didn't appear to see me. Instead he walked on slowly, although his head was twitching occa-sionally, as though he were now going to have a quick look around. But when he saw me there was no recognition on his face, no smile or quickening of pace as I had seen from others that morning. When he reached me he just stood up straighter, taller than me, shrugged his shoulders and pulled back the strands of hair that had slipped out from beneath his beret. 'Brother,' he said, sighing, and then smiled, the flesh loose near his mouth, his cheeks hollowing in under the bones as though he no longer had any teeth. He slipped the sunglasses into his pocket. His brown eyes had sunk too, and his face was given definition only by the outline of his skull. When he talked the skin on his face was pulled tight, and when he stopped it fell loose again. He was only twenty-seven, but suddenly he looked so old. I never felt further away from him than at that moment.

Alex put one arm out to embrace me and we held each other without moving. He smelled of must and yesterday's sweat; with both arms around him I could feel the little skeleton inside his coat. He pulled away and stepped back, looking me in the face and then down at the ground. People stared at us as they passed. I said, 'How was the flight?' 'At least you weren't delayed!' and a few other platitudes that pass for conversation when you won't tell the truth and can't think of anything else to say.

'Fine, fine,' he replied, holding his briefcase close to his chest as though it contained the most valuable thing in the world; he used to hold his trumpet that way, but I noticed he hadn't brought it with him. He followed me as I pushed the trolley towards the escalators and out into the July-bright daylight.

We drove out of the airport and back along the motorway into London. Alex kept his coat on, although it was even warmer in the car than it had been outside. Behind his glasses, he searched for familiar things, to reassure himself, and when he asked me to confirm his memories I told him he was right, even though he had it all mixed up. He seemed to relax after that, and wound down the window so that he could rest his elbow on the sill.

'I feel so out of it,' he said casually. 'It was the drugs I took before I left New York that did it – slept the whole way across.' I said nothing, but drove more slowly, scared and upset. 'You should've seen the looks I got from the stewardess when she finally managed to wake me as we came in to land. It was good of the doctor to give me sedatives . . . '

'Oh,' I said, and looked at him quickly, almost smiling, 'I thought you meant that – '

Alex stopped me with an expression I was often to see during the following months, a look which reproached me for wrongly accusing him and forgave without any more being said; he never forgot, though.

'He was putting his career on the line, prescribing drugs for me,' he explained, 'but he knew that there was no other way of getting me on to that plane.'

When we came off the motorway and drove through the Sunday-still streets in Chiswick, everything slowed down and seemed to close in on us. Alex watched the patchwork houses, red, grey, black and white, and became sombre.

'Jesus,' he said after a while, 'it's so solid.'

'What do you mean?'

'Just look at these buildings – they've been here for hundreds of years. In New York, no sooner has someone finished putting up a block than someone else comes along with a new plan to develop the site – cheaper and more lucrative – and down it goes.' He stopped for a moment, his eyes caught by a large, red-brick house.

'That's like our old house,' I said, nodding towards it, but he ignored me.

'It's not surprising they're all neurotic over there. How the hell can you be sure of anything if your neighbourhood changes every day? That's why the English are so well-adjusted. These buildings were made to last. They've been here for generations – people are born in them and die in them and still they stand, strong, solid.' He thought for a moment, and said, 'The Americans have no respect for a place. If you told them you were born at home they'd laugh and assume that your family couldn't afford the hospital room. It's just the same with dying.' Still looking at the houses, he was biting his lip now. 'They can't imagine anything worse than dying at home, can't conceive of that moment because they don't think of their homes in the same way as the English, not in any permanent way. They've probably got some scheme to knock it down or to expand, improve, alter . . . God, that's why they've got such reverence for our history, our buildings

11

with date stones on them. They're strange that way.' He was scornful but then, very quietly, added, 'I want to die at home.'

There were beads of perspiration on his face now, and veins stood out on his neck and forehead.

'Take your coat off if you're hot,' I suggested, but he said he was OK, really, that it was quite cool after New York, that maybe it was just a side-effect of the drugs he'd taken before he left. Then he began wringing his hands, slowly and rhythmically massaging his legs. I thought it might be something to do with his addiction.

'Are you sure you're all right?' I asked again, because I felt awkward and didn't know what to do. He nodded now, took off his coat and, folding it in half with great care, put it on the little bucket seat behind him.

'I bought this coat after I lost the old one – woke up in the park one morning with dogs sniffing at my face, licking me. When I sat up and felt in my pockets, everything had gone, money, lighter, cards, keys – the lot. It wasn't till later that I realized the coat had gone too. And however hard I tried, I just couldn't remember who I'd been with the night before, what the hell I'd been doing or how on earth I'd got there . . .

'One day, when I was going through a really bad time, I found myself in a public lavatory with a whole load of junkies. Jesus, those people were taking water out of the toilet bowls for their fix – and for mine.' He shuddered and, after a moment, perhaps guessing my thoughts, added, 'Thank God my HIV test was negative . . .

'One night I was invited out to a real smart Manhattan party,' he said, now with an East Coast twang to his voice. 'I used to deal to the biggest of them there. I remember walking into the bathroom and there was – no, I shan't tell you his name. Anyway, there are people, well-known people, some real big-shot record producers lying on the floor in there trying to put needles in their arms. It's hip to use heroin there, you see. Of course, I had to join in, and we got friendly, and that's when I told them I was in actual fact a jazz trumpeter, and they said, "Al, boy, if you come on down my office in the morning, I might just have something you'd be interested in." But when I turned up

12

there they didn't even know who I was, not even my name, and I never got past the reception desk . . .

'When I think of what I've seen and done – what stories! And it's all stored away in my head, just waiting for the right time. I've got enough ideas for a life-time of music. Did I tell you who was at the clinic with me, coming off, in a much worse state than I – '

'Don't brag,' I told him. 'I don't want to hear you talk like that.'

He was silent for a few minutes and then started rolling up his shirtsleeves. 'There's something I want to show you,' he said angrily. 'Something I think you should know about – I'm sure you want to see it anyway.' When he had rolled his sleeves right up over his biceps, he held out both arms in front of me.

In the soft, hairless creases of his arms there were a number of marks. I looked up at the road again, but he held them there for me to see. A line of marks ran down from the creases towards his wrists, and there were a few marks higher up, nearer his biceps. Some were older and had more or less healed, leaving his arms badly scarred. Others were fresh, with little dark scabs. Some were the mid-points of large bruises where he had bled under the skin, and these were still slightly raised, like extra muscles bulging out beyond the natural contour of his arms. The skin around them was like rotting fruit, variegated from yellow to black. Although both arms were covered with these marks, the left was worse than the right.

He put them down when I no longer looked at them. 'I'm showing them to you,' he said, tenderly now, 'because I don't ever want you to do what I have done. It's such a waste, too high a price to pay for anything.'

I couldn't think of a reply, but he was waiting for me to say something.

'Don't worry,' I told him, and tried to laugh it off, 'I've always been terrified of needles.'

'Huh,' he sneered. 'That's what they all say, but you soon forget that. It gets to be worth the pain.'

'But I'm not going to get into it,' I insisted. 'I don't want to. Look, this is ridiculous.'

He laughed at me, sadly. 'You're naïve if you think

13

people set out to be addicts. They don't, I can assure you. But I don't want to talk about it, anyway. I just wanted to show you so you'd know. Because you're my brother, my little brother . . . I won't show anyone else.'

Alex rolled down his sleeves, methodically, buttoning them at the cuffs, and didn't speak again until we passed Baker Street. Marylebone Road was empty, but we got caught at the traffic lights the whole way along, and each time we stopped he seemed to become more edgy. 'God!' he said scornfully, nodding towards a new development. 'Will you look at that. They're so far behind the States here – they were putting up buildings like that years ago. This is old-fashioned in New York now, but I suppose it's new here.'

'You haven't been away that long,' I reminded him. 'It was almost finished before you left. Remember?'

He didn't remember, and he began sighing as we drove up-hill towards Highgate. He put on his coat with some difficulty and then sat flicking his fingers through his hair, pulling down the visor to look at himself in the mirror. He put his wool beret back on, slipped on his headphones and left them dangling around his neck, and then pushed his heavy tortoiseshell glasses back up his nose. He looked absurd, but it seemed to make him more confident and he sat upright and alert as I parked the car outside Mum and Dad's house.

This was not the house we had grown up in. It wasn't till I left home that they moved to this symmetrical, four-storey Victorian town-house with its white-painted stucco front and the heavy, black railings that led up to the front door. Despite the heat, on the day of Alex's return the windows on each floor were closed, the curtains arranged perfectly in front of them, the shutters pulled to as though the house was shut up and the inhabitants gone away.

Alex went to the back of the car, expecting me to unlock the boot. 'Let's go in first,' I suggested. 'I'll bring your bags later.' He insisted that he needed his briefcase at least, and with that in his hand, his coat buttoned to the neck, he stepped across the empty street.

Alex hesitated on the steps and leaned against the

14

railings. I could understand why he wouldn't want to go in. Mum and Dad used to shout at us or at each other when they were angry or frustrated, and it was clear that they would be upset now, for they had tried to dissuade Alex from going to New York in the first place; when they failed they were silent, but now that they had brought him home again they would be loud in their disapproval. He seemed to be expecting it, and when I unlocked the door, waiting for him to go in, he waved his hand to usher me in first. I hung back, and after a moment he sighed and walked past me.

He saw Dad almost as soon as he got through the door, and Dad saw him; I'm not sure who was more shocked. Alex, standing against the open door and the sunshine, looked exactly as Dad had imagined a junkie would. Dad, tall, still slim, and as imposing at fifty-five as he had been at thirty, was standing in the shadows of the hallway. He looked menacing.

'Hello, Alex,' he said as calmly as if Alex had never been away. Alex just looked at him. Then Dad said, 'How are you? How was the flight?' and stepped forward to hug him, holding him protectively, almost covering him with his own body. Alex relaxed into his embrace.

When they broke away, Dad didn't move back but stood close to him, looking him in the eyes and then ushering him into the darkened sitting room where the shutters muffled all but the merest glimmer of brightness from the street.

'Let's have a drink,' I suggested.

Dad walked over to a cupboard in the corner, surrounded by shelves filled with law books and with his collection of antique silver – a Victorian silver travelling clock, a Georgian silver and glass inkwell, a small rectangular snuff-box amongst a number of small pieces.

Alex sank back into the large leather sofa in the centre of the room. Behind him a massive gilded mirror reflected the gloom. In the silence he leaned forward towards a low table just in front of him to peer at the silver-framed photographs of the family, and of Dad outside the High Court in his barrister's robes. Then his eyes moved around the room till they reached me, flicked back to a photograph taken a few years before and settled on me once again. He smiled.

Dad carried Alex's tomato juice with both hands, as though he needed to steady himself. As he leaned forward to place it on a silver coaster he said, 'There you are, young man. That'll make you feel better,' in his most conciliatory manner. He poured me a whisky, neat, to revive the ones I had drunk the night before, and filled up his own with soda. Then he stood by the white marble fireplace, one elbow on the mantelpiece, cut-glass tumbler in hand, with the air of a gentleman at home, but unshaven, wearing creased trousers and a plain blue polo shirt open at the neck. We didn't know what to say and were silent, sipping our drinks, smoking, looking at each other with the awkwardness of strangers. Then, seizing on an idea, Dad said, 'I don't know where your mother is. I'll go and see what she's doing.'

When Dad had closed the door behind him I gave Alex the packet I had brought for him, the wallet I bought before he left. He unwrapped it and said, 'Thanks,' putting it into his back pocket and smiling. I wished he wouldn't smile at me, for when he did his face appeared to be so full of pain, the flesh sinking around his temples, the shape of his skull showing around his forehead, its hollows looking deeper in the dim light. I turned quickly, afraid to show my feelings, wishing that I too could go away. If he had been anyone but my brother I would have left him, but I stayed and observed, thinking how like an animal he was now, one that had been caught in a trap and was no longer able to struggle.

Through our silence we heard sounds from upstairs – Dad's raised voice, Mum searching for the courage to come down and greet her son. Then they too were silent and we heard footsteps on the stairs. Alex sat up, pulling his straggling hair from under his collar – even his hair was changed, thinner and more lank – and flicking strands off his forehead that were mostly illusory.

When she came in, Mum had the impress of sympathy on her face that I, as her younger son, had known all my life. She usually looked quite youthful, was still attractive and always elegantly dressed, but her sympathy face admitted to each one of her fifty-two years of age. She hadn't made herself up as she usually did and the lines were deeply scored around her eyes and neck. She stooped as she walked, as though in pain, or trying to hide herself.

As Alex stood up the expression fell from Mum's face and she looked behind her to make sure that Dad was there. When she looked back she seemed angry, as though she was going to say, What have you done to yourself? How dare you have done this? Alex saw this happen, just as he was stepping forward, now with tears in his eyes, to embrace her. Nothing was said as they stood together, arms around each other, but Mum kept her head well away from him and shook it gently from side to side.

Dad handed her a glass of dry sherry and she crossed the room to sit on a straight-backed chair, while Alex returned to the sofa. She looked around her, lost and very distant; Alex, unable to look at any of us, leaned forward with his hands between his knees, watching the ice melting in his glass, swirling it a little from time to time.

'Did you eat on the plane?' Mum asked him at last. This was the first thing she had said to him. Alex looked at her and laughed, saying, 'Oh, Mum, you don't change, do you,' and before she had time to look hurt, he said,'No, I didn't get to eat before. I'd love something if there is . . . '

Mum now smiled to comfort him. Her voice was soft. 'Do you think I'd let you come home without organizing something? We'll have lunch as soon as your grandmother gets here.'

'So how does it feel to be back?' Dad asked. 'Have you missed England?'

'Of course,' Alex told him sadly. 'I have that White Cliffs of Dover feeling. I have missed the smell of the air, the sound in the streets, the shades of green. The thing is, though, that you never realize just how much you miss it all until you're back.'

'You've picked a good day to come home – ' Mum started, but Alex interrupted her. 'I'm not home,' he said. 'My home is in New York with my wife.' She looked at him blankly. 'Oh, you know – of course this is home, but it's not where I live. That's what I mean.'

'Well, you're here now,' she said, smiling slyly, 'and

you'll remember that in this house we clean the basin in the morning, the bath each time we use it, and if you're staying for any length of time you can also clean your room. That means once a week.'

Her humour, if this was humour, was wasted, and Dad frowned at her.

'It's just as well that we get it straight from the start,' she told him; Alex's silence implied agreement.

When the doorbell rang, both Mum and Dad stood up.

'I don't want you to mention a word of what's happened to Alex – either of you,' Dad said as he went to open the door for his mother. 'She doesn't know a thing about it. OK?'

I could never imagine what my grandmother was like as a young woman. I could see a young woman doing the things Eveline described when she talked about her past, but it wasn't her. Eveline was seventy-nine and her small, fat body was storm-struck – twisted and bent over. She had almost no money left now, and no companion either. In her mind, as in her life-time, these two things were linked, for she had had both money and the love of a husband, and had lost them at the same time: my grandfather died suddenly a few years ago and left her with nothing but debts, memories and their collection of paintings. Occasionally the sudden change in her life became too much for her, and at family lunches, when she had drunk too much, she would lean across the table, still chewing on a mouthful, to grip someone's wrist with her fleshy fingers, staring through the thin slit between her eyelids, and say over and over, 'I just want to die. Oh, God' – glancing towards the ceiling – 'just let me die.' However, her doctor insisted that she would live for a long time yet, although she was suffering from a number of disabilities and was completely deaf when it suited her.

Most of the time, though, she was an indomitable woman, fiercely protective of her independence, living in a small flat in Hampstead which my father had bought for her and where she entertained at least once a fortnight, even though it took her three or four days to prepare a simple dinner for her friends. Apart from food, she was passionately fond of Art, and was now expected at the openings of most new exhibitions in town, although she made it clear that she had no time for abstracts. Renoir, Cézanne, Van Gogh – these were the sort of painters she admired, for the sound reason that in their work she recognized the world she had lost.

'You're ill, my child,' she told Alex as she held his lowered face between her hands. 'What have you been up to, eh?' She patted his cheek, as she would have done twenty years before, and left him for a hard-backed chair. 'And why is it so dark in here? You know your pictures are beyond protection.'

'Alex is tired after his flight – we thought this would be easier on his eyes,' Dad explained, although in truth they had closed up the house because a friend had informed them that junkies, like vampires, could not stand the light.

The dining room was in the basement of the house and looked out on to the garden. It was a small, low-ceilinged room, warm tobacco in colour, easy to heat in winter and cool throughout the summer, although it wasn't the temperature that made Alex shiver. I could see him massaging his legs under the table.

'Would you like a sweater or something?' Mum suggested before she sat down. Alex shrugged his shoulders and said it would pass in a minute.

In front of him the mahogany table stretched across the room; the carefully pressed white linen cloth was almost covered with plates and bowls of food – little Italian loaves and New York bagels, French tomatoes, English cucumbers and peppers, cold sliced meats and spreads of Norwegian herring, of cod's roe and of mashed egg and mayonnaise, arranged around the table for colour and size. There were sprats and marinaded mackerel and a large platter of smoked salmon – oily slivers swung from the edges and touched the cloth – and at random around these dishes were others with wedges of lemon, a variety of olives and pickles, butter and cream cheese. Red napkins were folded into triangles on the side plates, and in front of each plate there was a slim, tulip-shaped glass of chilled '86 Chablis. Alex looked across the table, took a Dunhill from the porcelain pot in front of him and smiled to acknowledge the holiday which had been declared for his home-coming.

He was sitting between the curtains, with his back to the garden doors, and all I could see of him was his silhouette against the sunlight; he could have been a mysterious narrator in a black-and-white movie. Mum and Dad deferred to him and passed him dishes before they helped themselves, but Alex was selective, arranging just a couple of small piles on either side of his plate and placing half a buttered bagel between them.

'Is that all you're having?' Mum asked, unable to disguise her disappointment.

'For the moment . . . '

'Why don't you leave the boy alone?' Eveline told her.

'I might have something else in a minute,' Alex suggested.

Our hands criss-crossed the table – a forkful of salmon, a layer of cream cheese and a sprinkling of red pepper and lemon – we reached and passed, more polite and careful than usual.

'Some more wine?' Dad offered, and I held out my glass while Alex, who hadn't even tasted his, watched me with amusement.

Before long Alex stopped eating and began massaging his legs and arms again, pretending to listen to the conversation. Mum didn't notice at first – her mother-in-law was talking about the numerous women in Renoir's life – but when she saw what he was doing she frowned at him.

'Are you OK?' Dad asked, and when Alex said, 'Yes,' so dismissively Mum looked upset and sighed a little, saying quietly, almost to herself, 'What a waste.' She hooked another forkful of salmon and pulled it forlornly back to her plate.

'Really?' Dad asked again.

'Really,' Alex told him firmly.

'So what did you take in New York before you left? I know you've had something – I can see it in your eyes.'

'I don't know what it was,' Alex said, off-hand. 'Something the doctor gave me,' and then, as though he suddenly saw a way out, he said, 'But I do feel rather sleepy. I hope you don't mind. I can see you've gone to a lot of trouble, but I think I'd better go upstairs and rest for a while.'

'Yes, my dear,' Eveline agreed, 'you go and lie down.'

With heads turned away, bowed with disappointment, Mum and Dad watched him walk slowly, sheepishly, out of the room.

'I know how you feel,' I told them, breaking the silence, 'but it doesn't help acting like this. You've got to give him some space – it's only food . . . '

And it was only food, but it sat neglected on the cloth, which was now covered with breadcrumbs and spots of lemon juice, specks of ash dotted across the crisp whiteness. It looked as though the party was over and, unable to eat more or to speak, we sat in the dimly lit room, smoking without enjoyment.

Before I left Dad asked me if I would go upstairs with him to speak to Alex; we found him awake, lying on his bed.

'How are you feeling now?' he began, innocently enough. He was just being a father, but he couldn't help repeating the questions he had asked earlier – Which drugs had Alex been given? How much sleep had he had on the plane? – and more: How long was he staying for? How long had he been off heroin? What was his wife doing? Did he have any money?

'I've just got here and you're starting already.' Alex's hand shook as he lit a cigarette, and he tried to flick ash from it before any had formed.

'Have you brought any drugs with you?'

'This is ridiculous,' Alex shouted.

Dad stood over him, talking in his calm, courtroom voice, scratching the bristles on his chin. 'We need to know. Can't you tell we're worried?' he pleaded. 'We don't want to see you like this . . . Just look at you – ' He stopped, as though he knew he was going too far, and stood by the bed, breathing heavily. After a moment he shrugged his shoulders – he didn't know what more he could say now – and went back down to the kitchen.

Mum and Dad came out to watch me leave and I kissed Eveline goodbye in the hallway.

'You enjoy yourself, my boy,' she said. 'Life's too short.'

21

'Oh, I will,' I assured her. 'Partying tonight.'

'On a Sunday?' she said, a little surprised. 'With work tomorrow?'

'You just told me to enjoy myself.'

I kissed my parents goodbye on the steps. 'Call me if you want,' I told them as I walked over to the car.

Before I drove off I turned to wave at them. Mum and Dad were standing in front of the shut and shuttered house, waving at me, not smiling, but frowning, even though the sun was low and the deep shadows from the house fell across them. Upstairs, in front of his bedroom window, Alex stared at us without waving, with neither a frown nor a smile.

Eddie Mackenzie lived in a small room which his estate agent had called a large studio. It was within hearing distance of Stamford Bridge, the Chelsea football ground, and was a good place for parties if you were unsure how many people would turn up, for the place was soon filled. But Eddie, whom I had known from school, made friends with the same appetite as the Spanish bankers he worked for in the City acquired companies. He seemed to believe that social mobility was power, and in a peculiar way it was, for him. His guests, standing glass to glass on the narrow staircase leading up to his stippled front door and across the teak floor of his flat, were as different in accent and dress as they were in financial and political outlook.

Eddie was near the door when I climbed up, the entry-phone in one hand and a portable telephone in the other. He had grown a narrow, bushy moustache since I last saw him, presumably in an attempt to hide his blunt upper lip. He did not wish to appear blunt – he would have liked to be thought of as amiable – but the moustache made him look even more severe.

'Darling,' he called out, brushing my cheek with his bristles as though we were old lovers, 'you look awful. Go to the bar at once and tell Miguel to pour you a nice big special. I'll come and find you in a minute.'

It took five minutes to make my way across to Miguel, a gay Catalan who worked in Eddie's office. I had met him once before, when he and Eddie were lovers. Not that

Eddie was gay; he just enjoyed sex and was unable to resist a new experience.

Miguel poured me a special, a mixture of dark rum, sparkling wine and lemon juice, and we raised our tumblers in an unspoken toast. The music was loud and everyone seemed to be talking to the beat, a fast, South-American-style mambo which was entirely suited to the atmosphere of smoke and sweated perfume. I laughed and told Miguel I thought it was indecent that it should take so much effort and money to re-create the sound and smell of a sleazy back street in Rio at carnival-time.

'You have been there at carnival?' he asked admiringly.

It was hot; sex shimmered between bodies like a haze; and it seemed not at all absurd that Carlos, to whom Miguel introduced me, explained from the start that he preferred to make love when he was sober – if possible, a couple of hours after eating.

'It is no good with a full belly, or at three in the morning with a headful of drugs,' he explained. 'You cannot tell me that you are as good in the middle of the night as in the evening. No. *Alora* – you must choose your time. You owe it to yourself, and the girl.'

Carlos, a short, dark-skinned man in jeans with a leather jacket the colour of ten-pound notes, came from Madrid, he told me, where he had an apartment overlooking the Plaza de la Independencia. He seemed a man of some extremes, tired or uninterested until I mentioned something that concerned him – money and sex. Yes, he explained, you have to start in London or New York if you want to get anywhere in the financial world – the accumulation of wealth is a matter of art more than intelligence; if you are smart then you can get rich, but if you have the temperament then you will know what to do with the money when you have it – the English climate has created a temperate people. 'It is like purgatory here,' he complained in all seriousness, 'like something I must pass through before I can return to my own country and live as I wish to live. Like your sun, your girls have no fire in them. I get no warmth lying beneath them.'

Carlos smiled at a girl he had been talking to and winked at me. 'This is Katie,' he said, pulling an attractive redhead over by the wrist, 'who, I guess, is a good English girl.'

'And you're a good English boy?' she asked me, smiling sympathetically and shaking my hand. Her eyes were dark and bright, searching my face. They were large enough to make everything else around me disappear, and for a moment it felt as if we really were alone. Her hand was warm and moist as she slid it out of mine.

No longer the centre of attention, Carlos excused himself. There was someone he had to talk to – he winked at me again – but he would return. 'And then maybe we will get out of here and go to a club I know,' he suggested.

'Is that reptile a friend of yours?' Katie asked as I mixed us another special.

'He's my best friend,' I told her. 'I love reptiles. But they can be a bit of an embarrassment when you take them out.' She watched me, unsure if I was serious.

'Actually,' I explained, 'as with all snakes, I like to keep him at a distance.'

There was too much noise for us to talk, so instead we exchanged comments – about the music, the people, of whom she, like me, knew very few, and the heat. I had assumed that Katie worked in banking, but I was wrong. She was a production assistant in current affairs TV at the BBC. She undid another button on her thin white blouse. Between comments she looked across the room, and I looked at her. I thought she was beautiful.

When Carlos came back with a tall blonde girl, whom he did not introduce, he suggested that we should leave. I wasn't sure what to do; the room was hot and crowded, but I didn't really want to go to Carlos's club – at least, not with him. When Katie suggested that we should leave, either with Carlos or without him, the four of us forced our way across the room and past Eddie, still near the front door, still holding his portable phone. 'Darling,' he complained to me, 'the trouble with having your own party is that you never get to talk to anyone. But you do look much better now . . .'

It wasn't until I got into fresh air that I realized I was drunk. The sky was completely clear and it was cold after

24

the heat of Eddie's flat, so when I staggered I tried to disguise it by huddling into my jacket. 'Brrr,' I added.

'Let's take my car,' Carlos said, pointing across the road to a gold Rolls-Royce.

'Jee-sus,' the blonde murmured and held his arm more tightly.

'How old are you?' Katie asked him.

'What has that to do with anything?' he replied, puzzled.

'How old are you?' she repeated, angrily this time.

'Twenty-four,' he said with pride, 'but I made my first million dollars a while ago.'

'Still old enough to know better,' she told him bitterly. I thought for a moment that they were going to have a fight, but Carlos just laughed at her.

Before he started the engine Carlos switched on a CD of Serge Gainsbourg and unlocked the glove compartment. He took out a small glass phial with a chrome stopper and, giving us his broad, matinée-idol smile, said, 'Cocaine?' He looked absurd.

He handed the phial to the blonde first, but she didn't know what to do with it, so he took it back and showed her, pulling out a heaped shovel of white powder with a steady hand and snorting it up into each of his nostrils in turn. He handed it back to her with another of his smiles — he intended to be in bed with her before the night was over — and, after the phial had been passed around, we laughed ourselves away from Eddie's flat and over towards Knightsbridge. Katie and I didn't say very much, but Carlos talked quietly to the blonde, below the music. I stretched an arm across the back of the seat, near to Katie, and caught a whiff of the dark scent she was wearing. She was looking forward, past Carlos, almost laughing now, an aura of street-light diffused through her ruddy-brown hair. She had broad, strong shoulders and I could see her raised collarbone through the open neck of her blouse. When she turned towards me I kissed her, pulling her nearer, hungry, not even thinking of holding back, and she kissed me too. Through our clothes we began exploring each other's bodies, and I ran my fingers through her fine, curling hair as she laughed again.

By the time we arrived in Soho, outside the club Carlos

wanted to go to, the blonde seemed a little uneasy – she had turned once as we stretched out noisily over the cream leather seat – and Carlos was terse. But Katie and I were together on a cocaine high, my front teeth still numbed by the drug, neither of us with even the slightest interest in Carlos's objections.

'Let's not go in,' Katie whispered. 'Let's go back to my place.'

What I remembered most, as we climbed the stairs to her first-floor flat somewhere beyond Notting Hill, was the depth of Carlos's annoyance, the yellow light of the taxi, the dull street-lights which still showed up the gleam in Katie's eyes, the softness of her breasts, the brightness when we got out to pay and looked up at the perfect crescent of moon and at the stars which had spilled out like powder across the sky.

Her flat was an empty stage. Two bedrooms leading on to a small balcony, a bathroom and kitchen on one side and a sitting room on the other, all littered with boxes and tea-chests and cartons and bags, some still neatly tied up, others ripped open, things spilling out over the floor in front of them.

'I've only just moved in,' Katie explained, 'and what with work and going out in the evenings, there hasn't been time to get this place sorted out . . . I have found the kettle, though,' she said as she saw me looking around, 'and more wine.'

We went into the kitchen and she reached up to get the coffee out of the cupboard, but I put my arms around her, pulling her away, and kissed her. She began unbuttoning my shirt, dropping the coffee on the counter, and we were both naked before we got to the bedroom, in a hurry, pawing each other like animals, falling on to the mattress on the floor, on to the white sheets, the duvet thrown back, a dim light turned towards the bare wall giving a sheen to our nakedness, the cocaine in our heads, alcohol in our veins and no one else to consider, nothing in the whole world but ourselves and the pursuit of an exquisite moment.

We found ourselves lying on the hard bed, aware of everything around us, familiar and now transformed. Languidly we stroked each other, stretched out side by

26

side across the soft white sheet with Katie's breasts against my chest and my face in her hair. We were warm and tired, empty, feeling our hearts beat. Words passed between us to fill the silence where, just moments before, there had been a sound in our heads like ocean waves breaking on a shore; we did not wish to hear that it had gone. We talked until our words made no sense any more, trying to hold on to that moment, whispering so softly now as to be almost inaudible. But there was no holding it that way and we lay back to sleep. I put an arm around Katie and she rested her head against my chest, but we were still strangers in bed so there was no holding on in our sleep either. When I woke, excited, in the night I found that we were lying on opposite sides of the bed.

We had intended to embrace Alex on his return to London, to hold him firmly and allow him to feel the strength of the family. This was something we believed we could do, but we failed even to touch him. It was Alex who chose the direction in which he went, and all we could do was follow him.

I was working as a junior account handler at a new advertising company called *The* Agency, a refuge for burnt-out managers and defunct equipment brought in from competitors. The juniors and trainees were the only fresh talent in the place, and some days, when things went very wrong, we felt like new cement trying to hold up shattered old bricks. It was the start of our careers and we all believed we deserved better. But we were young and hungry and the company was paying us more than its competitors would have offered, so in a way we were caught, for we had already begun to make plans with that money. On the days when advertising jobs appeared in the papers, though, we pinned the relevant pages on the wall and stared at them as though they were windows through which we could look out on to the other, better world we knew existed.

Into this atmosphere of hung-over mornings and interminable afternoons, the office littered with out-of-date campaign schedules and the previous day's plastic cups, came the telephone-calls which followed Alex's return.

Dad called me early one morning to explain that, 'We tried talking to him after you left, only he said that he was too jet-lagged and more or less went straight back up to his room. But for hours afterwards we could hear him walking around up there, very late into the night. Listen – he has refused to talk to us about what has happened to him, so we're going to send him to a psychiatrist, an old friend of mine from Cambridge – ' .

'He's agreed?'

'I haven't even asked him yet, but I assume that since he took up our offer of coming back to London and staying with us, he'll do everything he can to get going again.' He was insistent. 'Christ, we're only trying to help, you know. This man, Simon Blake, is in Harley Street – he's going to cost us a great deal of money. But that's all right. You know there's nothing we wouldn't do to help Alex.'

'So why don't you leave him alone and see what he's got to suggest? He's twenty-seven years old, and he's not going to like being told what to do.'

'I'm hoping that this way we'll find out what the problem is – I don't want Alex to know that Simon is a friend of mine. I need to know what he's taking,' he explained.

I told him I thought he was making a mistake. 'If he hears you repeat something he said to the psychiatrist then he'll know what's going on – he's very quick.'

'I know,' Dad agreed, 'and I don't trust him because of that. But if he doesn't go and see Simon, and if he won't talk to us, then we'll have real problems.'

On another morning, when I came out of a client meeting, there was a message to call Mum. The phone rang only once before she answered, and without asking who it was she said, 'Thank God you called – you've no idea what he's done.'

'What who's done?' I asked.

'Alex – who else?'

'What's wrong?'

'I just don't know what to do,' she complained. 'So far he's broken my waste-disposal unit and my washing machine . . . ' She was close to tears. 'He's been in the

28

bathroom now for over an hour and your father's in court all morning.'

'How did he break the machines?' I asked, aware that sometimes she remembered the spirit rather than the facts of an event.

'I don't know, but he has. And now he's been in the bathroom for so long and every time I call him he just says, "I'm coming". What can I do?'

'Wait till he comes out?'

'Oh very funny.'

'What else has happened?' I asked.

'So much . . . I don't know if I can take more of this.' She was silent, and then continued more slowly. 'He's such a disturbing influence, and he's wearing your father down. I just don't know what to believe any more. I don't know whether he's on drugs or off them . . . '

'Listen, I've got to go now,' I apologized, 'another client meeting – but if I were you I'd let him do what he wants, because he's going to do it anyway. You just have to put up with him. I'll come and see you one evening this week.'

We were having a heatwave, and on the first sunny days the parks and city squares were filled with girls in bikinis and G-strings taking their lunch-hour: some of them made it on to the evening news; others just got accosted. The bus I took to *The* Agency carried people in cut-away holiday clothes, and for a day or two everyone seemed so happy; people smiled; one evening someone leaned over – unprovoked – and talked to me on my way home. But the camaraderie and good humour began to fade when it became clear that the sun was here to stay. This was no longer fun. Conversation on the bus was now all about how much longer we would have to put up with it, and people played one forecaster off against another like greyhounds at the track, weighing up past records against their latest forecasts that the rain should arrive before the drought. Office workers no longer took sandwiches into the park at lunch-time, but sat in cafés and talked about skin cancer and the new anti-wrinkle cream they had bought in the Body Shop. Everyone knew a story about someone who had died because the heat had got too much for them; or someone whose freezer had packed up – the food inside had rotted, maggots had taken over the kitchen floor and men from the council had been called in – something like that.

On one of these hot days, Alex came to meet me for lunch. He had never been punctual before and I didn't expect him to start now, so when I arranged for him to be at my office at midday I was allowing plenty of time for him to be late and still give us a chance of eating when he did arrive. I don't know why I was so upset when I was still waiting for him at a quarter to one.

I phoned my parents and Mum answered.

'Don't tell me he hasn't got there yet. He left an hour and a half ago.'

'Well, I don't know where he is,' I said, controlling my voice with difficulty, 'but it's OK – I'm sure he'll turn up soon. If he's not here in the next hour I'll call you back.'

'OK,' she said, 'because I worry about him. Yesterday I know his appointment with the psychiatrist ended at four, and he wasn't back until just before seven. And when I asked him where he had been he said he'd gone to sit in the cemetery because the dead, at least, would leave him alone. Can you imagine that?' She sighed. 'I tell you, I worry about him.'

'Yes, I know. But try not to. He's got a lot on his mind at the moment and he probably just needs space to think it all through. I'll speak to you later.'

Those were some of the most difficult days, for none of us knew what Alex was going through; he kept it as a secret to be shared only with the psychiatrist. He spent hours sitting in Highgate Cemetery, he told us, or went to see a matinée at a West End cinema. He knew these were things we could not check up on, and they made us suspicious. I found it difficult not to take it personally when he didn't call me or kept me waiting – it felt as though he was leaving me again. Mum and Dad also became defensive – early one morning Dad called to ask me if they had been hard on us when we were children, if they had been particularly unfair as parents. They had, of course, made mistakes, but I didn't believe these were intentional or malicious. But they now blamed themselves for Alex's problems, and when he threw a phrase like 'elder-child syndrome' at them they felt that this, like his addiction itself, was something of their own creation.

At about half past one the internal telephone rang and the receptionist said there was someone to see me. 'He won't leave his name,' she complained.

I found Alex talking to the girl on the reception desk as though he was in New York and she had access to a recording studio. He was ready with a list of explanations of what had happened to him on the way and of why my instructions were inept; I noticed from the sheet of paper in his hand that he had written the address down wrongly.

'Do you remember Lerici?' I asked him as he followed me out into the sunshine. 'Do you remember?'

'Oh yes,' he said slowly. 'North Italy – we went there. I must have been ten or eleven years old then. It was a fishing village, wasn't it?'

'That's right. We stayed in a *pensione* on the front, just where the fishermen sold their catch in the morning. The noise they made used to wake us up early. They stored their nets below our room and we could hear them talking down there.'

We went to a cheap Italian restaurant named after this village, where we were greeted by an energetic Italian waitress. Most of her regular diners had eaten quickly to get back out into the street. Inside it was hot and smoky and the old box air-conditioner above the open door made a lot of noise, but little difference to the temperature. In spite of the heat, Alex was wearing a heavy cotton shirt, with loud checks, which he kept buttoned at the cuffs. He was carrying his briefcase, which he placed with care beside him on the seat.

'What's in the case?' I asked. He had no business affairs here, no assets or money, so I was curious that he should need to carry a case at all – it made me suspicious.

'Would you like to look?' he said aggressively, as though he had been expecting the question; it was probably one that each of us had asked him sooner or later.

'No,' I lied. 'You can tell me.'

There was his passport, address book, the wallet I had bought him, his plane ticket back from the States, a Sony Walkman and headphones, a couple of tapes and a few other bits and pieces. It still didn't satisfy me. There was something about the case that invited suspicion, something about the way he carried it and always kept it locked, making such a show each time he opened it, pulling it up on to his lap with care and staring at the ceiling as if the sequence of numbers to the combination lock were written up there.

I pointed to the tapes. 'What sort of music are you listening to? Still the same jazz?'

He looked uncomfortable sitting on the red plastic bench. His face glistened with perspiration; he pulled a couple of tissues out of the chrome dispenser on the table and wiped his forehead. 'No, I can't listen to that stuff at the moment. I play pop music.'

'But you always hated it.' He nodded, not looking at me. 'So have you given up on jazz? I see you didn't bring your trumpet back with you . . . '

He looked up, perhaps surprised that I had mentioned it after so long. 'No. I had to pawn it in New York.' He looked back down at his hands. 'I think I'll go and have a wash.'

When the waitress came over, I explained that I would wait until my brother came back before ordering.

'I knew you were brothers.' She spoke with a strong, sing-song Italian accent. 'I knew it at once. I'm never wrong. Ah, here he is again.' She watched him coming back. 'I was just saying, I knew you were brothers. And you are the older, eh?'

'You're right,' Alex said with a smile, 'but I bet you can't guess how old I am.'

'Oh, now, let me think.' She stepped back a couple of paces to look him up and down, one hand on her hip, another raised to her mouth. 'I say you're nineteen.' She winked at me.

Alex, not realizing that she was joking, said, 'Well, you're wrong. I'm twenty-seven, and happily married.'

'You never!' the waitress said with a laugh. 'I don't believe you.'

Alex was happy to pass for nineteen. He unlocked the briefcase and pulled out his wallet to show her a picture of his wife. He looked relaxed.

32

'If I was you,' the woman said, picking up her notepad, 'I'd stick with her. You'll never do better. Now, what would you boys like to eat?'

Alex ordered a plate of antipasto, some pasta and salad, and asked the waitress to bring it all at once. She took the order and shrugged her shoulders as she went out back into the kitchen. Alex sat with the photograph in his hand.

'Do you miss her very much?'

He stared at the picture as though there were just a thin strip of film between him and the smiling face. 'My wife,' he said, his head still down. He put the photograph back in his wallet, locked it away in his briefcase, sucked in a deep breath between his teeth and said, 'And what about you, brother?'

'Do you remember Lerici, on the day of the fair? I think it was a saint's day or something, and there was a procession with jugglers and acrobats. And later there was a street race . . .'

'Oh,' he said, rolling his bottom lip between his fingers, 'was there?'

'Yes, you and I entered the race and you ran on ahead of me. You were fast then, running past the local boys. Some of the streets were cobbled . . .'

'Yes, I was fast then.'

'Too fast for me.'

'Yes, I was, wasn't I.'

We sat in silence, turning over our memories, until he stood up and said, 'I must make a phone-call,' and left the restaurant. I thought about going after him, to make sure that he was all right, but I assumed that since he had left his case behind he would come back.

When the waitress brought the food, all at once as he had ordered, she looked surprised that he had gone again. She shrugged her shoulders at me.

'He is coming back this time?' she asked, not sure whether to take the food back to the kitchen. 'He's all right?'

'Yes,' I told her without conviction, 'I think he'll be here in a minute,' and just then Alex did come back in.

'What's the matter?' he asked. 'You look surprised.'

'I didn't know where you'd gone.'

'Oh, now come on!' He was annoyed. 'Don't do this to

33

me. Do you really think I'd just walk out on you like that? What do you think I am?'

'OK. OK.' I was annoyed too. 'Just drop it.'

We had our meal in silence. Alex ate everything very quickly, and when he'd finished he sat back on the bench with his head down. His left hand, holding a cigarette, sank lower and lower as he relaxed; his eyes fluttered and closed; then his head jerked up and he smiled at me with his thin smile, with too much effort.

He apologized. 'The heat must be getting to me. And,' he added as an after-thought, 'Mum and Dad never go to sleep until way past one. They keep me up, wanting to talk – they always want me to tell them things.'

'I know,' I told him. 'They're worried about you, about how much money you owe.'

'Mmn,' he muttered, chewing his cuticle. 'I am as well.'

'Is it that much?'

'Well, apart from the money I've borrowed from them, there's quite a few thousand dollars I owe dealers in New York. But I won't worry about that just now. They can't get me here.'

'Is it really that much?' I asked again.

'Yes,' he grinned, 'it really is that much. But there's nothing I can do about it at the moment, so there's no point in even thinking about it.'

We were the last people in the restaurant and I had to get back to *The* Agency, so I paid the bill and left the waitress a few pounds as a tip; she gave us an expression of gratitude and the most peculiar looks as we left.

Outside, squinting at me in the sunshine, Alex suddenly became formal.

'Goodbye, sir!' he said loudly in a Brooklyn accent, no longer breathing through his nose. 'And thank you so much for your kindness' – we shook hands vigorously – 'it really has been most enjoyable. We must go there again some time.' He was sweating heavily, although it was cooler outside than in the restaurant.

He must have known that I didn't believe he remembered Lerici. The recollection of it was in there some-where, but the faces of his more recent past stood in the way and blocked it out. I wanted him to remember,

34

though, and would have asked him again, but as though he knew what I was thinking he suddenly said, 'Bye!' I watched him run across the road and disappear into the Underground.

My love for Katie was obsessive, uncool and lustful. I recognized her, wherever I turned, as the one clean thought in my head, and for that reason I decided not to tell her what was happening to Alex.

At night I went back to my flat to change after work and then drove over to see her. We sat on packing cases and ate the ragouts and Caribbean stews she prepared so well, and later, with a bottle of cheap white wine, we would go out on the balcony, our backs against the railings, and watch people passing in the street. We would talk about ourselves – Katie was an only child and her parents now lived in Barbados. Her father worked for the Foreign Office and had been posted from one foreign country to another all her life, so that she had been put into a boarding school in Oxford by the time she was ten. Having her parents abroad made her holidays exciting, but she missed having a family and a home; it was the one thing she wanted now.

We used to walk around the flat while she told me what she planned to do with it. 'I think I'm going to paint the walls blue,' she would tell me, her eyes bright with enthusiasm. 'I've got so many *objets* from the places I've been to – junk, most of it – that I suppose I'll have to try for an eclectic look. You know the sort of thing . . . ' She would rush around, pointing out where she wanted cupboards and shelves, where the chest of drawers and bookcases should be. 'And then that'll be that.' She would laugh, knowing that nothing was ever so simple.

It was strange to be in her flat. She was independent and entirely capable of looking after herself, but she wanted a man to be there with her, someone to help her paint the walls and put up pictures, to open bottles of wine, someone who knew how she liked her whisky – one ice cube and a dash of soda – someone she could be a woman for, as though she wasn't one without him. I wanted to be that person, but I also had a feeling – a premonition, perhaps – one I could not explain at the time, that made

35

me hold back a little. It was only when we were in bed that I didn't feel this way. I was obsessed by her body. It contained me whether I was watching her moving around the flat, imagining her beneath the clothes, or, later, lying on top of her, naked.

One hot night, as we lay with the duvet thrown back, idly touching each other, looking through the open window at the yellow-black London sky, Katie propped herself on one arm, clay-brown hair falling over her shoulder, and said, 'Why are you so silent? Something's wrong, isn't it?'

I thought about Alex, but I didn't want to tell her about him. It wasn't that I didn't want her to know, only that if she didn't then I could pretend that – with her at least – no such thing existed. But she knew me well enough now to see that something was upsetting me.

'You don't have to tell me,' she said, stroking my hair, 'but if I can help in any way, if it will make things easier, then you should tell me.'

She put her arms around me and held me for a while, and after that I told her everything. All of it. Right down to my earliest memories of Alex and drugs, of how he sold me dope when we were young and how I believed he'd given me heroin one night without any explanation when I had thought it was cocaine, although all I had known for sure was that it wasn't cool to ask. I told her how worried I was that Mum and Dad knew so little about heroin.

'Well, if you're worried,' she suggested, 'why don't you phone them?'

It was strange to call Mum and Dad from there, to say 'Hi Mum,' from Katie's bed.

'Thank God,' Mum said. 'Where are you?'

'What do you mean?'

'Alex . . . ?'

'No, Mum. It's me. It's not Alex.'

Dad picked up the phone – Mum was too upset. 'Listen,' he said, 'I got a call from Alex a few moments ago. He was in a phone-box near here, but he wouldn't tell me where. Anyway, I made him promise when he first came home, and thank God I did, that if he ever got desperate and wanted to take drugs again, he'd call me first, before he did anything. And he was tempted tonight,' he said urgently. 'He wanted me to go and fetch him, but he didn't tell me where he was. So what the hell am I supposed to do? He's asking me for help, but he's not letting me give it. How cruel.' I could hear his laboured breathing. 'If he's taking it again, I won't have him in my house. And I won't lift a finger to help him.'

'Calm down,' I said. 'This isn't helping. If he comes back tonight then he comes back, but there's nothing that either you or I can do about it. If he does show up, then call me on this number.' I gave him Katie's. 'And don't jump at him and expect him to thank you for it.'

'I just want to say, just so you know, that there's nothing I wouldn't – that I'm not doing for Alex. Nothing. If he wants to reject it, well, that's up to him, but he won't get it twice.'

I wondered why he was saying this to me. Why not to Alex? I remembered that a long time ago he had said to Alex, 'If you are ever really stuck, if you need help, or money or something, you know you can count on us. Always.' We had come a long way since then.

'I know, Dad,' I reassured him. 'And I know how you must feel. But what's wrong with Alex isn't something you can kiss and make better. It'll take a long time.'

'Yeah,' he murmured, a long way away. 'I know that.'

'Is there nothing we can do?' Katie asked when I put down the phone. 'Couldn't we go and look for him?'

'No, really,' I said, holding her, 'he could be anywhere. And if he wanted to be found then he would've made sure that he could be.'

I didn't know what was going on then. Everything changed from moment to moment, and in the centre of it all Alex did whatever he was going to do, seemingly unaware or unconcerned about anyone else.

'Well, we don't even know that anything's happened yet,' Katie reminded me. 'All we do know is that he called your parents – he could just be getting them worked up. I know that under the circumstances – under *his* circumstances – there's good cause for alarm, but perhaps nothing has happened. What's going to happen if he really does go overboard, with your family running around shouting at each other every time he's late for something?'

She was right that my parents were over-reacting. 'But, you see, they don't understand Alex. They were wrong to think that all he needed was a good dose of home cooking and family love to get him going again. It was stupid to think that he would fall for the patriarchal act. But they've done it now and they've got their necks stuck out . . . '

'Very eloquent,' Katie said, laughing at me. 'Have you finished now?' She got out of bed and turned on the TV.

It came as no surprise when the phone rang around midnight.

'He's back,' Dad said, his voice still strained. 'He's just phoned to say he's round at your grandmother's.'

'I'll go and get him.'

Eveline charted her life through successive movements in painting, just as other people remember the changing fashion for clothes or music or interior decoration. She was born, she would explain, at the end of the age of the Impressionists; she was married at the time of Surrealism; produced her children during the Modernist movement; had grown old with post-war despair and fragmentation; became disillusioned with psychedelia; and was now at a loss what to make of contemporary experimentalism, of abstracts. She never explained whether she believed that art had influenced her or whether she had had an influence on art, but perhaps, like leaves on a tree, they had just been exposed to the same elements.

A few years ago she took me to the private view of the Royal Academy Summer Exhibition, and afterwards we went back to her flat for supper.

'It's so strange to see how things have progressed – we had no idea it would lead to this,' she said, tapping the exhibition catalogue sternly. 'I mean, if we had, I wonder whether we would have done the things we did do.'

She paused and leaned forward, straining to reach her cigarettes, which were next to the lighter and ash-tray – her essential supplies. I was sitting next to her but didn't offer to help. It was a ritual she re-enacted so many times each day. One day, I thought, she will no longer be able to reach that far and then she will fall over and die.

She sat back into a cloud of smoke and grinned an old grin.

'It's stranger still to think that we've lived a life you can never experience. That some things have passed for ever.'

'I suppose there will be things for me, as there were for you,' I told her, sliding the ash-tray nearer without her noticing.

'Ah, but I remember, oh, it must have been back in the thirties, going to the Opéra, in Paris. In those days, everyone dressed, all the men there in black tie . . . it was just as Lautrec or Renoir or Béraud painted it, so wonderful. And then to dinner somewhere and maybe to dance . . .'

I sat silently for a few minutes, trying so hard to find in this withered body some clue that would unlock visions of beauty and vitality, but it eluded me and I became even more aware of how old she looked. I stared at the sagging, wrinkled skin on her neck and hands, at her mouth moving as she continued to talk, her teeth irritating her a little. Her voice registered somewhere in the back of my head, but I was locked into my own vision and only the sharpest comment from her would have aroused me at that time. To me, she had always been an old woman.

But her vision gave her delight. It was her youth and her active life that she saw. She looked around, animation in her voice at least, and for a little while she could imagine that the empty seat beside her had been sat in again, that the bed beside hers was crumpled and warm, and that her life was not yet over. But I knew that no one had sat in that chair for a very long time, and that no one would ever sit in it again.

Sometimes, though, if she had that look in her eyes, I could imagine how wonderful it must have been, and I wished then that I could pretend that things were otherwise; but she was old and I was young and nothing that I could do would ever change that.

Eveline's one-bedroom flat, on the ground floor of a converted Victorian building, was a monument to her passion, where paintings were hung frame to frame across the walls. None of them was particularly valuable, but each one had its own story of how and where she and my grandfather had bought it. The mantelpiece in the sitting room was covered with photographs of the two of them with artists, mostly minor figures, and forgotten now, but well regarded in their day. The bookshelves were filled with art histories and biographies and dusty old exhibition and auction catalogues.

That night, when I saw Eveline standing in the hallway, which she always kept bare on the grounds that it was not a proper place to hang pictures, it struck me how alike she and my mother had become. But whereas my mother had her look of sympathy to put on and take off my grandmother's face was carved deep with lines: some for scowling, for expressions of disgust and annoyance, and others that came out when she grinned or laughed. When I saw her, her face was hard and disapproving, a look so clearly impressed on her skin that I thought it would never go away again. She stood in the doorway, shaking her head from side to side as Mum had done when she had first seen Alex. She was less than five feet tall, and I almost six; she waited for me to bend and kiss her soft, downy cheek.

I followed her slow progress into the sitting room, without either of us saying a word, her shaking head in front of me. Alex was sitting in an armchair beside her sofa and beneath a wall of portraits in oils. He had pulled up a battered antique side-table, and on it there were several plates of Indian food.

'Brother,' he said as he saw me. He was nervous. Perhaps he realized that he had gone too far this time. His eyes flicked from the plates, to Eveline, to me.

'I see you found the take-away.'

'Well,' he quickly explained, 'I was so hungry before I came here . . . but now we've been talking and it's ruined my appetite. It's always so morbid talking to you,' he told Eveline, who had settled back into her sofa with a cigarette in her hand, and an ash-tray on the table in front of her.

'Oh, stop it,' she spat at him. 'Just get on with your food.'

'Isn't it a little late to be out visiting?' I asked him.

'I phoned from the tube station to ask if it was all right . . . '

40

'But you were so long,' she complained. 'You were over an hour getting here – what were you doing?'

'I was getting my food.' He spilled Coke on to the table as he picked up the can. 'I'm sorry,' he said, and quickly put a tissue over it to make it disappear. The old woman peered over from time to time to try and see what he had done, but her eyesight failed her.

Alex looked as I had never seen him look before; he was wild and aggressive. The room was dimly lit, and he stared as though he couldn't quite see whatever it was he was looking at – just like the woman beside him – as though there was a filter in front of his closing and sunken eyes, which he could see through but which he couldn't ignore. He had pushed his hair back off his forehead and it stood up in all directions. The veins on his neck were raised and his shirtsleeves were rolled down and buttoned.

Eveline went out to make coffee, and the two of us were alone.

'What do you think you're doing?' I asked as soon as she had gone. 'What do you hope to achieve?'

'What do you mean?' he asked innocently. 'I just came to visit my grandmother.'

'At midnight? She's an old woman, remember.'

'I phoned her first.'

'I'm sure you did, but she hasn't seen you for so long, did you think she would say no?'

He dismissed this with a flick of his cigarette.

'And what about your phone-call to Dad, earlier this evening?' I asked angrily, hoping to provoke him into losing control.

'Oh, that,' he said, without a trace of emotion. 'I didn't think you'd have heard about that so soon.'

'Well I did. So you were tempted again, were you?' I said with bitterness. 'So you got the urge? And then what happened? I suppose you got over it and everything's all right.'

'I didn't take anything,' he insisted. 'I don't want to take any. Don't you believe me?'

'You're not doing anything to make me. We're all watching you to see what you will do next, and you're doing nothing to court our trust. Instead, you make us doubt and mistrust you more.'

41

Eveline came back into the room as I was shouting. She looked amazed, with no idea of what was going on.

'Don't look so hard done by,' I told Alex.

'What do you mean?' Eveline asked, putting the cafetière back on to the tray.

'I wish I knew,' Alex told her confidentially, not believing that I would drag everything out in front of her.

'Have you taken any drugs tonight?' I asked him calmly. He tried to pretend he still had no idea what I was talking about, so I said, 'Heroin?'

Eveline looked at me and then back at Alex – her head was moving very quickly – peering through her thick glasses into the dim light.

'What is this?' she demanded. 'I don't understand what you're saying.'

'The reason Alex is here, and not still in New York,' I explained, 'is that he's a heroin addict. He's supposed to be here to recover.'

'Is this true?' she asked him fiercely.

'It's not just me,' he snapped. 'You take drugs. You take plenty of drugs.'

Eveline, sitting between us, turned to me.

'Well,' I admitted, 'I have done.'

'When was the last time?' he demanded conclusively.

'All right,' I said, 'so I take drugs, so I smoke a joint, or take a line of cocaine when I'm offered it. So what? That doesn't quite match up to a heroin habit, now does it?'

As quickly as it started, it was over. We sat, slightly out of breath, with neither the energy nor the desire to continue. It was as though Alex had called another truce, had made another rule in the game I didn't understand how to play. He smiled at me.

Eveline lit another cigarette and sucked smoke noisily between her teeth.

'I don't know,' she said to Alex. 'I just don't understand.' In her voice there was anger and frustration. 'I don't see why you need to do this. What happened to the way we used to live? We didn't go running round the world living off someone else's money. We got on with our jobs, with our own lives. We were honest with each other, and hard-working, and maybe we didn't get everything we

42

wanted, but we had everything we needed, and the few luxuries we did lack were the things that kept us going, that made us try to do better. But you, you come out of music school with a fancy piece of paper that says you can play the trumpet, with a wife, and in one year what have you done? Nothing. You haven't worked once. You've just ruined your life. Where did you get lost?' She paused for a moment, and when she started again she spoke softly, as though she wanted to coax him out of his old ways and into something new. 'You know you're my favourite grandson, Alexander. You know that I love you more than anyone else. I can't talk for your dear grandfather now, but I know that when he was here he always said the same. So don't kill yourself with these drugs. For what are you going to do that?' She paused again. 'I just want to see your life working out, to see you happy. So please, just leave the drugs and the deceit and everything alone.'

Alex was playing with his lips again, squeezing them together with the thumb and forefinger of his left hand as though he was shaping a note, or words that his mouth did not want to utter. When Eveline stopped, he stopped, and they sat and stared at each other.

'Now get out of here,' she told him, and stood up to show him to the door.

When I followed him, Eveline waited for me to kiss her goodbye, as I usually did, but I walked past her, bitter that she had been able to acknowledge Alex as her favourite in front of me.

It was a warm night and I felt a trace of the soft breeze on my cheek, refreshing after the smoky closeness of Eveline's flat. Alex and I started walking along the road towards the car, but then he sat down on a low brick wall outside one of the houses and I sat with him. The brick was cold to touch.

We sat in silence for a few minutes and then he started talking with a clarity that I hadn't heard from him for a long time. 'How can she say those things?' he asked, looking down the road. 'Why can she say them? She has no right. Not at her age. It's past for her now and what does it all add up to? What has her life meant? Not a lot really.' He thought about it for a moment. 'I created freedom for myself — perhaps I created too much by going to New

43

York. Perhaps people shouldn't be allowed to do things like that. What's to stop me going anywhere in the world? Nothing. Just like nothing stopped me from going to the States. But should I have gone there? That's the question I keep asking myself. And what would I have done if I had gone somewhere else? Sure, I could have lived, and probably quite well, but there must be some meaning to it all. It has to amount to something or else it's just – just a waste of time. And staying where you are, where you come from, where your family and friends are and you belong – I suppose that has some meaning, the same sort of meaning as dying in your bed. Grandfather got it right. Life becomes more than just an existence.' Then he asked, 'Is that clear?'

'Yes,' I told him, 'it's clear.'

'Then?' he asked.

'Then what?' I snapped, still angry. 'You were the one who went away, remember. You were the one who was so sure that being here wasn't right, that it was dull and boring to stay at home. You made me feel stupid by going away so suddenly and leaving me behind. "Come and see us," you said. "Shake it up and come and live." But now that it hasn't worked out you've got nothing else to hold on to, so you come back and polish up these good old "traditional values" as if you had known all along that they were the only thing of any worth. Well it's not quite like that. Some people do make it by going to New York, or anywhere else – and with their families. What have you got to say about them, I wonder. It's not where you go that counts, it's what you take there, and if all you took to the States was one broken marriage, a drug addiction and a few shaky dreams, then I'm surprised you're in such good shape because you deserve to have killed yourself.

'And,' I told him, 'with your brave new knowledge, what will you do now? It's time to start being honest, Alex – time for us all. You can start by getting it right with your suddenly so important family, who are afraid that you're still a junkie, that you're going to kill yourself in front of them.'

Alex looked crushed, and I wanted to apologize as soon as I'd finished. I wanted to say, 'Listen, I didn't mean all

44

that − you'll be OK. You're fine − you've got it right.' I
wanted him to have got it right. But I didn't believe it and I
don't really think he did either. Anyway, he shrugged his
shoulders and said, 'Let's go and face them.'

As I was parking the car outside Mum and Dad's house,
he said, 'Just one thing. When we went to the States we
didn't know it was right or better or anything like that. It
just seemed like a chance − our chance to do something
better, to make something of our lives. We took it, and with
luck, if we had had luck, we would have come out of it in
good shape. But it didn't work out like that. And if you
were left for months in a strange city, with no one to talk to
except people's answering machines and no one to contact
except the drug crowd, who want to know you because
you've got money − then I think you'd go the same way.
And if you didn't hear from your wife, for whom you'd
given up so much and done so many things, if you didn't
even get a phone-call from one month to the next, then I
think you'd begin to falter as well. And by then your cracks
would've begun to appear. And on your own there's no
one to hide them from. On your own there's no one to hide
them for you, to cover them over and pat you on the back
and pretend that everything's OK when it's so patently
obvious that it's not. No − when there's no one but you,
what do you remember? What gets stuck in your mind?
Certainly not the happy times − certainly not. And not the
good things, either. No, you remember the bad times and
all the things you were ever scared of. All your weak-
nesses. All the things you took such elaborate precautions
to protect yourself from when other people were around
suddenly leap out at you in the darkness one night when
you're alone. And you say, "Hello, this looks like fun."
And for me, heroin was the weakness I'd tried to resist.
And then, some weeks, or months, or years later, the
person who dropped you in it comes back and says, "Hey,
what's going on? What a mess. What the hell have you
been doing?" and all you can say is, "I've been doing
without you."'

'So what will you do now?'

'Let's go in,' he said, and walked up the steps to the front
door.

45

Had I been in his position, I don't know that I would have gone in. But I think he really did want to try, then. He knew what was going to happen when he opened the door, and I believe that he hoped, for a moment there, outside, that he had explained some of the unmanageability of it all.

Although my parents' house was familiar as we walked in – the burgundy Liberty print wallpaper in the hallway, the glass dish on the Victorian cabinet, the cracks in the ceiling, which were going to be seen to one day – there was an air about the place that was entirely new, of fear and violence.

The shutters were closed in the sitting room. One way to tell how long they had been sitting in there and what sort of mood they were in was to see how thick the smoke had become. The air was now dark, cigar smoke most noticeable at first, while underneath it was the less powerful but more acrid smell of the Turkish cigarettes my mother liked to smoke after dinner.

They were both facing the door, Mum in her armchair, upright, a gardening magazine unread in her lap, Dad in the high-back chair at his desk. I believe they intended their faces to convey anger and disappointment, but all I saw there was fear.

'Come in and sit down,' Dad said congenially, waving a hand towards the sofa and armchairs. 'How is your grandmother?'

Alex shrugged his shoulders and said, 'Fine,' as though it was a perfectly straightforward question, and I realized then that there was something between him and Dad that I didn't understand.

'Where is it?' Dad asked him.

'I threw it away,' Alex said.

When he saw the look on Dad's face, he said quickly, 'I did – I really did. I bought it, and then by the time I got somewhere where I could have taken it I thought better of it, and I was down near the canal, so I threw it into the water. It was only then, when I saw it floating away, that I thought, "You fool, you could have sold it back to them." But it had gone and now it's too late.'

He had talked very quickly, snatching breaths like an

46

athlete to stop Dad from speaking before he had finished, but it didn't make any difference.

'I said, where is it?' Dad asked again, menacing.

'And I told you I threw it – '

'Come here,' Dad shouted. 'Come here now. I want to see your eyes.'

Alex went over to the desk and looked down at Dad. Then Dad asked him to roll up his sleeves and Alex refused.

'Don't say no to me!' Dad screamed. And again – 'Don't say no!'

Alex was standing over him, and in this atmosphere of violence he was the more threatening.

'I didn't say no to you yesterday when you rang me,' Dad said reasonably.

'Too bloody right,' Alex told him. 'Do you know what the psychiatrist told me? He said that any problems I may have are probably due to you. How do you feel about that, huh?'

'What do you mean?' Dad asked, confused.

'Just what I say – the psychiatrist said that because you've always been so desperate for me to succeed and because Mum's incapable of showing her affection in any way other than by cooking my favourite meal – because of that, he says, you've driven me to do these things. You've made me an addict.'

'What crap,' Dad said slowly. 'Just show me your arms and stop buggering about. I didn't say no when you called me yesterday and told me someone was going to beat you up unless you paid them a hundred and fifty pounds. I thought I'd rather pay than have you beaten up. And now look what's happened – I suppose that was all a lie, a way to get money, uh? And you won't even roll up your sleeves for me. What are you afraid of? That I might find new marks?'

'It's not something I'm proud of,' Alex told him desperately, still standing over the desk, but no longer threatening. 'It's not something I ever want you to see. That's past for me. Over and done with. And I won't feel very proud of myself if you see what I've done, because once you've seen those marks you'll never forget. You will never be able to put them out of your mind. Every time you look at me you will see them. But it's something I'm trying to put behind me, something I want to forget, and you're not making it any easier. God, I wish I had taken those drugs tonight – at least then I'd feel that this was justified. At least I would have deserved all this. But you won't let it drop, will you? You'll hound me like you've hounded me all my life, until I do whatever it is that you don't want me to do. And then you can say, "There – I told you he was no good," and congratulate yourselves on the power of your observation. But if it happens it'll be your creation. You can help me – and if you don't give me the chance to get it right then I'll never make it.'

Mum looked at Dad as though she thought he had gone too far this time. Alex had got through to them at last and had given them something to hold on to, something that would allow them to put away the events of the last few days.

Alex said finally, 'And if you're worried about the money, if you're angry because of that, you know I'll repay it along with the rest when I get a job. But please don't ask for it tomorrow because you know I won't have it. So if it's the money, then that's OK. But I didn't take those drugs.'

He looked upset, wrongly treated. Dad sat at his desk, cigar smoke curling across his face, looking as if he was thinking, while Alex sat back down in his chair and pulled a cigarette from his packet. But he couldn't find his matches. He looked under the magazines on the coffee table, down the back of the chair, in each of his pockets, and was crouching down on the floor looking under the chair when Mum offered him her lighter. He sat back and smoked, and then went downstairs to make us tea and coffee.

We were silent when he left the room. None of us really understood the power of heroin. We were learning a little about withdrawal and the effects that Alex was still suffering, but we didn't know then about the devious way of thinking the addict is left with even after the physical addiction is over, which makes it an instinct to lie and cheat, no matter who it's done to. We knew nothing of that.

We listened in silence to Alex down in the kitchen. When

48

they heard him coming back up the stairs, Mum and Dad braced themselves. He came in carrying a chrome tray, heavy with food and drink. He looked nervous when he saw the way they were looking at him, but they controlled themselves and said, 'How thoughtful,' and, 'Yes, please,' as he offered them drinks and cake and ice-cream.

'What's that?' Mum asked, pointing to a cream-coloured liquid in a tall glass jug.

'It's a health drink I invented in New York,' he announced proudly.

'What's in it?' Mum asked again.

'Well, there's eggs and milk and ice-cream and bananas and honey and . . . ' adopting a French accent, ' . . . a few secret ingredients.'

'Oh,' Mum said. Sighing deeply, she settled back into her chair, picked up her gardening magazine and flicked through it again without reading.

'You don't want some then?' Alex asked her.

'No thank you, dear,' she replied, not looking up, lighting another Turkish cigarette. 'I don't think so, thank you. Not today.'

I couldn't sleep that night. Back in my flat, the windows open and one of my favourite films − Hitchcock's *Strangers on the Train* − on the TV, I drank tea with lemon and set myself to doing some chores: I ironed a shirt and flicked a duster over the tape deck. I hate housework, but I needed to occupy myself because I had a creeping feeling that I had left things undone, unsaid, and that, perhaps as a consequence, something terrible was about to happen. I switched off the television when the murder took place. Later, in bed, I listened to cars passing in the street, the intervals growing between them until they seemed to keep time with the hourly chimes of the church clock at the top of the hill.

I remembered then what Alex had said about being alone − how, when he was lonely, all the things he hid from in company leapt out at him, all of the bad things, the unhappy memories. I was afraid of being alone; I wanted to call someone, in particular to talk to Katie. That was something Alex could never do in New York, for he was without friends, without his wife, and the contacts he called offered him heroin or cocaine. And after refusing – if he ever did – once or twice, who knows how many times, finally he came around and said, 'Yes, OK. Why not?' There was no one to tell him why not, or to look at him in the morning and say, 'Stop this . . . ' So the following day, when the fear got to him a little earlier, he was on the phone again, and then, very quickly, it was a ritual, more regular than brushing his teeth, and he would get up in the morning, put a needle in his arm and be able to face the world, or be able to cope with not facing it – it wouldn't really matter which way round it was by then.

So what was stopping me from losing myself like that? I considered what they would say at work if I turned up in a state. I'd give up my job, so then what could they say? I'd lock myself away; but the phone would ring or friends would come calling to see what had happened to me. Sooner or later, though, if I didn't answer, they would give up and go away. But there would still be my family: my parents would call, would come round, would get in somehow and see what was happening to me. I was sure they would. But Alex put himself outside all that. He had found it necessary to grow up without friends, to make his own family. He was wrong to leave everything behind like that, though, to cut off his past. But then I suppose he didn't expect that he'd ever need it again.

I was a little crazy during the night – not sleeping does that to me. I didn't call anyone though; it was enough to know that they were there to call. So I sat listening to the church clock, and, later, to the first trains leaving London, early trucks rattling past. I drank small shots of neat whisky – I could hear Mum's voice telling me that it would help me to sleep – and in desperation I drank one shot after the other until the curtains began to move in waves across the window, the shadows made by street-light shimmered across the floor, the smell of Katie's body lay beside me and the memory of her arms embraced me tightly. Then I clearly heard her saying, softly, 'Sshh, ssshhh . . . ' I smiled, and slept.

In the morning, after hot coffee and a cold shower, I got ready for work and went down to collect the mail – a

Barclaycard statement, a letter from the bank, a few free offers to change my life and a letter from my landlord giving me one month to vacate the flat. He had sold the building to a developer, he explained, who wanted to start work as soon as possible. He knew this would be an inconvenience for me – those were his words – but thought that we would be able to come to an agreement. Reading his letter, all I could think of was that I wanted to talk to Katie, but that evening, as I leapt up the stairs to her flat, she yelled, 'Hello!' at me, and when I reached the top she stood on the landing and bowed in a grand, theatrical gesture.

'I'm drunk, don't you know.'

In the flat she pointed to a bottle of champagne in the kitchen, which she had now drunk to below the label. I was surprised and annoyed to see her like this. Misunderstanding, she said, 'Don't worry, there's another bottle in the fridge.'

When I had poured myself a glass, she came and stood in front of me, her own glass held between thumb and forefinger, balancing on her toes as though she was going to attempt a pirouette, or fall over. Her make-up was smudged around her eyes.

'A toast,' she cried. 'A toast.'

'To what?' I asked, humouring her, laughing now.

'To my new career, of course.'

'What new career?'

'Well, exactly,' she agreed. 'It's a bit of a problem, that. But I don't have the old one any more, so we might as well toast the new . . . '

I watched her smile disappear and tears break down her face. She hid herself against my neck and I stroked her hair.

'Oh, shit,' she said quietly. 'And I was going to be so strong about this. I got the sack today. Well, not exactly the sack. But my contract has just about ended, and they aren't going to renew it.'

Pulling away and wiping her eyes, she went to fill her glass once more. A thin foam bubbled down the stem on to her fingers and, with a smile, she exclaimed, 'My contract endeth, my cup o'erflows . . . '

I held her. I wiped the tears from her eyes. Seeing her sadness made me desperate: I would have done anything for her, but she just wanted me to listen.

Later, I said, 'Well, I too have a toast to propose.' Raising my own glass and imitating her drunkenness, I declaimed, 'To the homeless, because I will be very shortly.'

When I explained what had happened, Katie looked bothered for a moment but said very clearly, 'You can come and stay here then.'

I wanted to, of course; I wanted to be with her. But I really hadn't expected her to ask and I was surprised. 'Well, yes . . . ' I replied. 'I could.'

'Listen,' her voice was business-sharp now, 'if you don't want to, then please . . . You won't be doing me any favours by staying. But I just thought that it would be very convenient for both of us – you'll have somewhere to live while you look for a flat and I'll have help with the mortgage.' She thought about it for a moment. 'Alternatively, we might just make each other completely miserable: the homeless and the hopeless.'

I didn't sleep in my flat after that. A week later, Katie came with me to help load boxes into the Healey and made space in her chest of drawers and cupboards for my clothes and papers. I exchanged the keys to my flat for a cheque from the landlord for £5,000 and a set of keys to Katie's front door. It was all so easy, and then we were living together, sharing the bed, with two toothbrushes and two brands of toothpaste on the bathroom shelf, two cups of coffee in the morning, two whiskies in the evening when I got back from work, my copies of Calvino and Primo Levi stacked beside her *Decameron* and *Divine Comedy*. We were still strangers, really, but nothing more was said about the arrangement until one night, after Katie had spent another frustrating day looking for work, when she objected to my suggestion that we go Italian in the bedroom and paint it red, white and green.

'Listen, I only invited you to stay,' she said quickly, not amused, 'so don't go getting ideas about living here with me. You're supposed to be looking for a place of your own, remember? You can rebuild Italy there.'

'OK, OK,' I told her, 'but in the mean-time, if we're

going to "stay" together, perhaps you'd better come and meet my mama and papa.'

Katie didn't want to talk much about our relationship; she'd had her fill of sweet-talking guys and was more interested in what I did than in what I said I would do.

The following Sunday, as we drove to my parents' house, she surprised me. 'Look at me,' she complained. 'I'm so nervous – this is ridiculous.'

I thought about it for a moment, and said, 'I would be too if I was meeting your parents for the first time – I'd want to make a good impression, that's all.'

Summer was over, the leaves had turned and were falling, but the day was warm, the sunlight still strong. Mum had woken us in the morning with a call to warn us we'd be having a barbecue lunch. 'Don't dress,' she said. When we reached the house we found them in the garden, kneeling round a rose bush, digging a broader bed in front of it. They stood up when they saw us, took off their gloves, smoothed down their old gardening clothes and shook Katie's hand. I was nervous for Katie and for them, kissed them both and quickly suggested that we have a drink. But before I went back into the house I asked them where Alex was.

Dad looked at Katie.

'It's OK,' I told him. 'She knows what's going on.'

Mum bent down over her flowers as though maybe I hadn't said anything after all; Dad shook his head.

'I'm sorry,' he said to Katie. 'I'm sure you don't want to get mixed up in all this.' And then, to me, 'I think he's upstairs in his room, but I really don't know.' He wouldn't look me straight in the face when he talked. 'I've had to take all the keys out of the doors – I don't want him locking himself in any more. I don't want him to think that we condone what he's doing.' He looked at Katie again and then his control slipped. 'I don't know what to do any more – I'm sure he's taking something.' There were many reasons why he thought that – because machines continued to break, food and cigarettes still disappeared, and so did money, silver, an old watch, and because Alex was always late coming home and there were hours in each day he was unable or unwilling to account for. Dad felt that this was the way in which Alex was getting back at them for the mistakes he said they'd made in his upbringing and for the ambitions they'd had for him, which he had failed to realize. 'Anyway,' he said again, 'I'm sure he's on something – you watch his eyes, you look at his pupils when he comes down – just see his behaviour and tell me if this is normal.'

'Hey – no one said he's normal – that's why he's seeing a shrink.'

Dad knelt back down beside the rose bush and we watched them digging and cutting.

'Do you like our garden?' he asked Katie in a 'Have you met my son?' sort of way. Mum walked around the beds reciting the names of the flowers that were in bloom and of those that were just coming out, insisting that we bend down to smell a new rose or rub the leaves of a scented bush. Over the budding phallic stem of a plant that might have been an amaryllis, Mum and Katie laughed together for the first time.

When Alex came out we left the plants alone. He was white with exhaustion and hadn't put on any weight. 'It's the only way I have of getting back at Mum,' he said teasingly when I mentioned it, giving her an exaggerated smile. 'I eat everything she offers – more, even – and I still don't put on weight.'

The pruning shears opened in Mum's hand, and clipped shut.

It was warm in the garden with the sun shining – the brick wall and trellis kept the breeze out – but Alex, as always, was dressed for winter, in a shirt and thick sweater. Mum and Dad watched him as he sat next to Katie and told her about New York.

'Have you been out there?' he asked after a while, and when she confessed she hadn't he said, 'You'd love it – I know I do – in fact I'm just over here to do some session work. I can't wait to get back.'

Katie, who had listened patiently, said, 'That's not what I heard from your brother.'

Alex didn't say anything, but looking at me as though I had betrayed him he got up and walked around the

garden, his movements stealthy as though he was exploring the limits of this, his latest cage. He tossed a cigarette-
end into a flower bed; Mum called out, 'Do you mind!' and,
when he ignored her and left the stub where it had landed,
went to pick it up and throw it into the far corner. Katie
tugged at my hand under the table.

We were supposed to be spending the day together so
that Mum and Dad could meet Katie, but Alex provided a
more compelling spectacle. When Dad asked him to help
with the barbecue he agreed, but by the time the charcoal
had burnt white Alex was sitting in a chair with his
headphones on and his eyes closed. When he came to he
went inside and returned carrying a colour television.
Lounging in the chair, watching a football match on the
television in the shade of an apple tree, it was obvious that
he was a greater embarrassment to Mum and Dad than
they had imagined even on their bad days. Above him,
though, the birds still sang and the sun shone on the
flowers in their garden, which gave them some return for
their labour.

We ate in silence. To begin with, Katie and I tried to start
a conversation, talking loudly and too quickly, but no one
really had the heart for it and we soon fell silent again. Alex
ignored us all; he ate the steak that was handed to him, and
then the sausages and lamb chops – I thought Mum was
going to cry – and later, after the plate had slipped off his
lap, he fell asleep.

Asleep, Alex looked like one of Leonardo da Vinci's
angels. His face was relaxed, his lips spread out into a thin
smile, his eyes were hidden behind his sunglasses. Sitting
around him, we watched for a few moments until Mum
said quietly, 'He's probably been doing it again.'

'How do you know?' I whispered, in a voice usually
reserved for visits to cathedrals.

'We don't,' Dad said, 'but we're trying to find out.' He
spoke slowly, his voice soft so that he wouldn't wake the
sleeper. 'We don't want him living here if he's still taking
heroin, but we need to be sure – '

'Oh, we know,' Mum insisted; Dad held up his hand to
silence her and then waved it in front of Alex to make sure
he was asleep.

'We don't know for sure – we found white powder on the carpet in his bedroom and I had it analysed by a friend of mine' – he laughed – 'but it just turned out to be talcum powder. I found the combination to his briefcase, too – he'd written it on a dollar bill in his wallet – and each time he leaves it behind when he goes out we check it, hoping it will be empty and at the same time afraid that we might find something . . . I've even followed him a couple of times when he's left the house. The first time he just went and sat looking out over the city. The second time he walked round the shops, looking in windows or trying on clothes. He never bought anything, though. I wondered then whether he knew I was behind him. In one arcade he stood staring in the window of a penknife shop for a long, long time . . . that worried me.'

'But we know he's on something,' Mum told us again, looking at Alex.

'We don't know' – Dad was angry now – 'and it goes against everything I stand for to act on assumptions.' Turning to us, he said, 'I even tried to talk to Simon Blake, but he gave me some rubbish about the delicacy of the relationship between a psychiatrist and his patients. He even refused to consider the possibility that Alex is back on drugs – "I would know,"' Dad said mockingly, imitating the psychiatrist's Oxbridge accent, '"or he would tell me."' Dad laughed. 'Pompous idiot. Then he suggested that maybe I myself would benefit from a few sessions with him – I tell you . . . '

At that moment Alex lifted up his arm – a supplication, perhaps? – and Dad fell silent.

'Well, I don't think he's on anything,' I whispered. 'He's just gone a bit in the head, that's all.'

After lunch, Mum and Dad went back to their gardening. There seemed nothing else for them to do, for they didn't want to go back into the house, nor did they want to sit with Katie and me, because with Alex between us there was nothing else they could talk about. So they bent down and picked up their trowels and shears to cut away at their garden, so that next year least that would be improved.

Katie and I watched them and finished off the last of the wine. They looked pale and worn-out. Mum's shoulders sagged and Dad's hair was greyer than I remembered it. For the first time I had the impression that they were in their old age, running out of time for patience and enthusiasm. Dad, once so confident of bringing Alex back and embracing him within the family, who had sat at the top of the dining table and raised his glass in welcome, had mistaken Alex's indifference for exhaustion; he had thought a rest would cure him, but he had been wrong. But Alex played along to get a roof over his head and some money in his pocket; whatever else lay between Dad's blessing and curse was of no interest to him.

While Mum and Dad were working on their new flower bed the wind blew the back door shut. Dad looked up with a start and turned protectively towards his wife; he had thought that maybe Alex had woken and gone into the house, but Alex continued to sleep in the garden chair, his breath still slow and deep.

We left them then and decided to go for a walk on Hampstead Heath. When we reached the bottom of Parliament Hill the sun was level with the grassy ridge and the figures who moved across it to fly their kites seemed to us no more than childish match-stick characters whose shadows came down the hill towards us. We left the Healey at the foot of the hill and walked up past people lying on the grass, as naked as the law allowed them to be, desperate for a last touch of the played-out sun. We were relieved then to be among fashionable parents walking their children and dogs, overtaken by kids on BMXs and mountain bikes, unseen by flushed young couples on the pathside benches. We heard model boats being raced by remote control over the lake, a crowd cheering them on and, between them, the dull bass of far-off music, drifting on the soft breeze.

Katie and I had already said what we thought about Alex – he was 'clean', Mum and Dad were over-reacting – and we walked in silence and in step until, up on the ridge, watching the kites jarring against their cords, she said, 'You know, from the moment I first saw you I knew that underneath all the shit, behind that cocaine cloud, there was someone I could get on with.'

'No more?' I asked teasingly. 'Just getting on?'

She pushed me and we ran back down the hill. Stepping back on to the road, we bumped into Eddie Mackenzie, his top lip shaved clean, a tall, blonde, red-cheeked girl in one hand and his telephone in the other.

'*My man,*' he said sternly, releasing the girl and holding out his hand. 'How have you both been?'

'Fine, fine' – his long lip made me want to laugh – 'so what dragged you from your patch today? Surely not the fresh air?'

'No,' Eddie admitted, attempting a cough, 'not that. This is Georgina – we were out eyeing up the property here. Just looking forward a little . . . it's good to have something to aim for,' he said, nodding towards one of the mansions and smiling at Georgina. 'Could've picked that one up for fifty K a few years back, I reckon.'

'We were thinking about going for a drink,' Katie lied, to get Eddie off the subject of money. 'Care to join us?'

'Mmm,' Eddie agreed. 'We were on our way to meet a contact of mine at The Flask, so let's go there.'

On the way, Eddie told us that rumours had been circulating about Katie and me. 'Seems you upset Carlos a bit,' he said, and then, lowering his voice, 'You didn't really have it off on his back seat, did you?' His eyes sparkled and I remembered again how much I disliked his voyeurism.

'What's it to you, Eddie?' Katie asked.

He waved his phone in front of us. 'This is the age of communication, dear – word gets around and you two have been out of touch for a while now.'

Watching him ordering drinks at The Flask, I remembered the guy I had become friends with seven or eight years before. He was pushy then, and eager to get on, but he was young enough for it still to be charming. Five years in the City hadn't helped him at all, but he could still mix the most effective hangover cure I've ever drunk.

He ordered a brand of rum the girl behind the bar had never heard of.

'But you can get it in Kingston.' He smiled at her.

'So why don't you go there, then?' she told him smartly.

'Because it's a long drive to Jamaica.'

He settled for a Captain Morgan's and ice and we sat

outside in the courtyard on a rotted wooden bench, Katie and me with large whiskies. Katie had just discovered that she and Georgina had friends in common when we heard a screeching of brakes, the trumpet horn of a BMW and turned to see a black man standing in the middle of the road, oblivious of the traffic around him.

'Christ,' Eddie muttered. 'That's Amigo.'

Amigo, more than six feet tall, was as thin as an anorexic. His dull brown skin matched the colour of his buffalo-hide hat. His eyes were the same shade of dried-blood brown as his worn cord trousers. It took him several minutes to sway his way across the road, and his black leather jacket creaked as he crouched down beside our table.

'My man,' Eddie tried as a greeting. Slowly, for everything about him was slow, Amigo looked up and slapped Eddie's outstretched palm.

'Yah,' he answered. He nodded vaguely around the courtyard at us.

'Amigo here,' Eddie said quietly, as the subject of his explanation tried to raise one long, slender leg up on to the bench, 'Amigo is my dealer.'

Katie and I both flinched. She said, 'Bad timing, Eddie,' and Eddie, not understanding, complained, 'Don't tell me you've been getting your drugs elsewhere? I thought we had a deal – I'm the one who supplies you.'

'No, it's nothing like that,' she explained. 'We're just off it at the moment . . . Clean livers.'

Eddie looked at me with sad nostalgia, as though he'd just heard of my death. He must have thought Katie was trying to reform me.

At that moment Amigo reached the seat beside Georgina and tried to shake her hand, offering his own, exposing a weeping sore around the knuckles of his middle finger. Georgina ignored him.

'Sorry, Eddie,' I said abruptly, standing up, taking Katie's hand, 'but we've got to go – '

'What's happened to you two?' he asked, confused, turning from us to Georgina – Amigo was fondling her knee now – 'Just wait – ' But then his phone started bleeping. Katie and I slipped away and drove home.

Katie had caught the sun. Her pale skin, reacting more

quickly than mine, was flushed red; freckles had broken out around her nose. I rubbed after-sun lotion on her and then fixed the drinks. We would not talk about Alex or Eddie. We didn't even feel like eating, so we lay on the floor in front of the television. When, later, I told her I thought we were drinking too much, she laughed at me. 'You're always worrying about something, always something wrong.'

'I'm just in pursuit of perfection,' I explained and, to make amends, mixed a jugful of stingers. We settled back down to the late movie, Katie resting her head in the pit of my arm, the dull light from the TV giving a pallid sheen to our smiling faces.

At one point Katie raised her head to say that she envied me my family, even with its problems. 'Sshh,' I told her, pulling her head back down. 'Let's not think about them now.' There were many times after that when we felt closer, but this was a sweet moment; it was as though there was no one else to consider, then, nothing in the whole world but ourselves and the enjoyment of an exquisite moment. I told her I loved her and we woke, in the middle of the night, to the white noise of the television.

One afternoon, when I was out at work, Alex telephoned Katie and, as she told me afterwards, was very talkative, witty – thoughtful, even. Then he asked if he could come to stay for a night or two. He needed to get away from Mum and Dad, to let them all cool down, because the situation was getting out of hand. He told her there was no one else he could ask; he had no other friends in London now.

Katie phoned me at work to tell me what was happening, because Alex wanted to come over that night. I was unenthusiastic. 'So you said yes?'

'Of course I did,' she replied. 'He's your brother – it wouldn't be right for me to stop you helping him.' Unsure of herself, she said, 'I only did it for you.'

'Oh.' I realized then that I didn't want Alex there. For the month and more that I had been in the flat I hadn't once looked at somewhere else to live – I didn't really want to, and each time I told Katie I was going to view a flat she suggested we go out instead. If Alex came to stay in Katie's flat, our home now, he would unsettle me. He would be the dominating elder brother and would smile condescendingly at our life. I didn't need that and I thought I could be more help to him if there were a distance between us.

'It's just for a few days,' Katie explained when I told her what I was thinking. 'It'll be OK – don't worry. We'll treat him like a favoured guest, cook him mounds of pasta and spoil him so much he won't dare to be scathing about anything.'

But when I got home that evening Alex still hadn't arrived, although he'd told Katie that he'd be there soon after lunch. She had waited in all afternoon, leaving a note on the door – 'Buying your dinner – back before you know it' – when she slipped out to the shops. He hadn't left a message, if he had called round while she was out.

With nothing else to do – the only people I could have called were Mum and Dad – we waited. At half past eight we decided to eat without him, which was a pity because he would have enjoyed the meal and been flattered by the effort Katie had made on his behalf.

When we finished I said, 'I suppose . . . something might have happened to him.'

But Katie laughed at me – 'You'll start sounding like your mother in a minute. Stop it.'

Later, just as we got into bed and put our arms around each other, the phone rang.

'Sorry,' Alex said. 'I'll explain what happened when I get there, but in the mean-time, I'm going to need your help . . . '

'What sort of help?' I asked cautiously.

'Getting over to you. Will you come over to Mum and Dad's as soon as you can? I'm going there now . . . '

On the way, I considered the fact that for the first time Alex sounded scared. When I walked up the front steps I heard Dad shouting, even before I opened the door, and I took my time putting the key in the lock – I wanted them to know I was coming in – but no one paid me any attention. Inside the house everything was white, angry, bitter.

'Don't you call me a liar,' Alex shouted.

I waited in the hallway. I would have been happy to have slipped out without anyone noticing me, but Alex had caught me once again – of course I would keep my side of our bargain.

'I am merely here to drive him to the flat,' I said out loud.

Just then Mum came rushing out of the sitting room, her teeth clenched, a white handkerchief screwed up in her hand. She went past me as though she hadn't seen me, and not for the first time I wondered at her ability to ignore me.

I followed her down to the kitchen. 'Hello?' I said.

She was dialling the police.

'What for?'

'Because we've had enough of the little . . . '

She couldn't think of a word that was suitably abusive, or if she could she still couldn't bring herself to use it. She sat for an instant with her mouth open and then began again.

' . . . Because we've had enough. I'm afraid for your father. He's already had advice from a policeman he knows and we're going to hold Alex here until they come and search his room, and if they find anything then he'll go to prison, which is just where he belongs.'

'You'd let the police search your own son? In your house?'

'That's right.'

'Don't you know if they find drugs in his room, even if they're in his cases, that you, or rather Dad, might be the one who goes to prison or pays the fine? That's the law, whatever your man told you, and it won't do Dad's reputation any good at all. He should know that . . . '

I wasn't sure she understood. For a moment she sat, her face blank, and again she looked at me as though I hadn't said anything. I was sure I had spoken, though. Then her face screwed up into a tight ball. 'Bugger,' she muttered under her breath, and slammed down the phone, her face relaxing, empty, without emotion, no longer my mother.

When we heard them shouting again, she came back to life, the anger and hatred from upstairs coursing through her.

I followed her into the sitting room.

Two men – one old, grey, the other younger, healthier –

were face to face about two feet away from each other. I wasn't sure who would strike first.

Dad looked like a stranger to me. It was Alex who had done this to him, of course, Alex, who was no more of a stranger than he had been since he first came back from America. This was his world, his own game, and I had become accustomed to seeing him in it. But I was used to seeing Dad as a father, husband and legal man in that room. What he was acting now was something out of Alex's head, something Dad had never even considered before, a vision without love or respect, a world of violence, of self, chaos.

My mother was shocked when she entered into it again. She went back to her chair and sat down without saying a word, looking around her as if to make sure that this was her house. The walls were still intact, the pictures were hanging on them – yes, everything was just as it had been before. But two men stood in front of her, close to violence, and she was right to look around her, for she was witnessing the destruction of her family, and although this would always be her house, not for a very long time would it be her home again.

We listened. They threw words like 'trust' and 'freedom' at each other. The younger man fought to protect his privacy. The older man said he had found, when he looked, what amounted to overwhelming evidence of lies, of so much deceit that he was glad to have broken the trust between them. 'It never existed anyway. You never kept your side of it.'

I don't know if he was aware of it as it happened, but when he held up a passport and talked again of freedom, there was only one possible conclusion.

'Give me my passport,' the younger man screamed. 'How dare you have broken into my case like that and stolen it? That's theft.'

'You lied to me,' the older said, calmly now. 'You've been spending money, writing cheques on an empty bank account and getting money that wasn't yours. I found your cheque-book, so don't try to deny it. That's fraud. And taking money from us as well – and for what?' he asked, not expecting a reply. 'I cannot trust you. I don't trust you.' He paused. 'Give me back the keys to my house.'

'Give me my passport.'

'What do you need it for?'

'Give it to me,' the younger man threatened. He held up the keys in front of him and the older man, snatching them, looked towards the woman as though he had just saved their lives.

'Here,' Dad said, throwing the passport on the floor between them, 'take it and get out.'

Alex picked up his passport and ran upstairs. Dad went over to where Mum was sitting and held her hand tightly. They were panting as though they had just exerted themselves; Dad looked grey. They wouldn't look at me then. I was just there to drive Alex away; I had no say; whatever had happened could not involve me – not both sons at once – and I wasn't to be associated with it.

Dad went into the hall and looked up the stairwell towards the lights at the top of the house – Alex's room. He could hear drawers being opened and banged shut, but I knew he wouldn't go up. He didn't dare.

I went past him and up to Alex's room. He was dragging all his things out of the wardrobe and chest of drawers, off the shelves, making a pile on the floor.

'Only what you need now,' I said; he looked as though I'd just whipped him and dropped the jacket he was folding, emptied the case back on to the floor and repacked it. Everything else was left where he had thrown it. I pushed him out, switched off the lights and closed the door.

When they heard us coming down, Mum and Dad walked out into the hall. Dad opened the front door and looked out. They couldn't back down now.

When Dad and Alex faced each other again there was no violence between them. Although, maybe for the last time, they were close to each other, both had already gone off into their own lives, into separate games, and in their thoughts they were far apart.

'I never want to see you again, Alexander,' Dad said. His voice was cold and court-careful.

'You are no longer my son,' Mum hissed as he passed

64

her. 'My son is dead.' She took Dad's arm and held it in both of her hands.

Alex played his own part – he walked out without saying anything, as though it really couldn't matter less to him and wasn't even worth commenting on. In his game there were no parents now.

That happened in the early autumn, and the night we stepped out into was clear, cold, star-bright. In the car, Alex reached out and took my hand, held it gently, almost caressing it; he cried just as softly, with the faintest sound. I could make out the silhouette of his face in the street-light, could see his bunched-up forehead and the glisten of tears on his cheek. He stared straight ahead.

Then he dropped my hand, picked up a tissue and blew his nose. Suddenly there was nothing about him to suggest what had happened only moments before. He reached over again, only this time he took a cigarette from the packet in my top pocket and struck a match, filling the car with white light.

The houses along the street were in darkness, but in my parents' house all of the lights had been switched on; they could have been throwing a party. As we drove away from them Alex pointed out the new shops that had opened and asked whether Katie would be up when we got back, if there was any food in the flat, because he was hungry now. Then, as though it was his first and final word on the subject, he sighed and said, 'So now I don't have any parents, either. No wife, no parents.' He said this as though the words no longer represented living people. But he patted me on the wrist as I drove and said, 'I've still got you, brother,' and that meant something.

When we got to the flat and he had carried his case up the stairs he saw Katie, and rushed to embrace her. They stood in the middle of the room like reunited lovers: he put his arms around her; she placed her hand on his head and murmured to him.

Alex explained what had happened in small, inoffensive terms, making it seem nothing more than a little disagree-ment, as though that wasn't why he had left at all. But then he shrugged his shoulders and repeated, 'But now I don't have any parents either,' and stared down at the floor as if he was trying to remember what they looked like.

Katie brought in some food and we ate and drank in silence, listening to Vivaldi. Then we got things ready, made up a bed for Alex and arranged who would use the bathroom first – it was easier by then to talk about practical things. Alex looked drained and soon went to bed.

'Now don't stay up too late,' he said as he closed the door to his room. 'We don't want you being late for work tomorrow.'

When Katie and I went to bed we lay awake in the darkness, not holding each other, not even talking, restrained by the inhabited silence beyond our chipboard walls.

I don't know how much later it was, but Katie woke me, shaking me gently. 'The phone is ringing,' she said, and I rushed, naked, to answer it.

Mum and Dad were each talking from an extension. They insisted that there was nothing else they could have done with Alex, under the circumstances, and I agreed with them. They listed their reasons all over again, and again, I agreed with them. Then they begged me not to help him.

'He *is* still taking drugs.'

'We're sure of it.'

'He'll ruin you.'

' . . . destroy you two . . . '

' . . . just like he's destroyed us, our home . . . '

' . . . get rid of him – '

Then they were quiet, as though they were realizing for the first time what it was they were saying.

Sitting naked in the darkness, I heard Alex reach and turn in his sleep.

'I never thought I'd ever say anything like that about one of my sons – ' Dad said, as he cried loudly, uncontrollably, down the phone, still trying to talk to me, ' – never.'

'I know,' I said softly, 'but it's done now and it's for the best. It'll work out somehow, and you couldn't have gone on – not like that.'

'Yes,' he told me, 'I know, but – ' His objection to the inevitable overcame him; he put down the phone.

I could still hear Mum on the line, breathing, and she too tried to talk, but all she could say was, 'I'm sorry – I can't speak now.' I heard her tears before she hung up.

Surrounded by the darkness, and now silence, Alex snored in his sleep, a bright white sheet pulled up high, completely covering his head.

II

Katie said she liked the autumn best. Winter was too cold for her and its trees reminded her of skeletons and made her sad. Spring was full of promise, but the first rich sniff of the breeze only made her want to go away. 'For what is spring in England?' she complained. 'It creeps. It drizzles. It's grey. We should go to Italy for the spring,' she suggested, 'to Tuscany, or further south where they have even more reason to celebrate.' I could only agree with her and dream.

Not even the English summer was really to her liking, for she needed to be able to depend on things and the summer here was always a matter for speculation. So it was in the autumn that she felt most at ease. On sunny days it was still warm enough for her to lie outside, and in the evenings, after the tourists had flown away, with the ducks and swallows, it was possible once again to move around town, to get seats for the theatre and a table in a Soho restaurant. We went to see the fringe plays and cabarets that came down from the Edinburgh Festival. On Sundays we walked in Holland Park, where the trees slipped from green to yellow to the colour of earth, their leaves falling around us like confetti. When it rained we sat with large espressos and hot *pains au chocolat* in the smoke-grey atmosphere of the small café on Moscow Road, the windows dripping with steam, Katie's face glisteningly damp. When I think of those days, I remember my favourite French melodrama – Claude Lelouch's *Un Homme et une femme* – for they used to play a tape of the film's soundtrack in the café. 'L'amour,' the couple sang, 'c'est bien plus fort que nous.'

But Katie was sad that autumn. In search of a job, she spent her days filling in application forms, going for

68

interviews, having lunch with anyone who could be even remotely useful to her. She had intended to use the free time she had at home to decorate the flat and catch up on some reading. But the paint cans sat in the hall and *War and Peace* lay unopened on the shelf, for she was too restless to settle down to anything. She hadn't realized how important her job had been to her, not just financially but because it had given her an easy identity. She didn't like to admit that she was unemployed.

On the few fine weekdays when she had nothing else to do she gave in to her restlessness and escaped from the city, driving the big Healey through a countryside of harvested fields and patchwork woods. She drove until she was hungry, stopped to eat in a pub, and drove on again. She wasn't going anywhere in particular; she was just desperate, then, for a sense of motion. In the evening, when she came back to the flat tired and withdrawn, she would surprise me with the smell of burnt fields and early mulch that clung to her.

But most of the time she lived beneath a pall of cloud-cover. When Alex arrived she said he could stay until he sorted himself out, for she knew that there was nowhere else he could go. 'There are certain conditions, though,' she warned him – she and I both laughed as soon as she said the words, for they reminded us of Dad and his 'reasonable conditions'. But we made it clear to Alex that neither of us would take responsibility for him. We weren't going to play his games and whatever he got up to was his business. I don't know whether he believed us, but he didn't put us to the test for a while.

As a young girl Katie had never had a home. She and her parents had moved from city to city, living in diplomatic accommodation or large rented houses filled with servants and assistants. In more exotic places, distant relatives and family friends came to stay for weeks at a time, so there were always people in and out of the guest rooms. The flat in London was her first home and she had intended to live in it alone, but circumstances had changed all that. She thought it was inevitable, and ironic, that she was following her parents' example, and seemed resigned to having Alex and me staying with her.

69

We lived quietly, then, relieved to have broken out of the cycle of loneliness and party pick-ups, which had seldom brought either of us anything more than one-week stands. With each other, we felt we had a chance to find another way. There were other reasons for living quietly, too – we were broke. Katie had a few hundred pounds in a savings account, but Alex had nothing apart from his old bank book. Every now and then he would go to cash another cheque, never returning to the same place twice because he thought they'd be waiting for him after the first time. He didn't seem to realize, in his altered state of mind, that if the bank wanted to stop him then they'd contact every branch. They wrote him letters, but he never opened them because he didn't want to know what they had to say. 'What's the point? There's nothing I can do about it now.' He would pick up a newspaper or switch on the TV to change the subject.

So we lived off my salary and the pay-off from my landlord. I thought I would find my position at *The* Agency more tolerable, now that I was working to support us all, but I was under-employed and in the end I felt more trapped than ever. On bad days I could no longer indulge in my old fantasy of walking out and driving away in the big Healey; I had responsibilities. In the morning, before I left the flat with a piece of toast and a hangover, I seldom saw Alex; Katie and I had a bath and coffee on our own. On the few mornings when I did see him, he would be sitting in the black silk bathrobe with a red dragon on the back, which he had bought on a trip to San Francisco, his face pale, a cup of tea and a full ash-tray in front of him.

'Bad night,' was all he said, and however hard I pried he would never tell me what it was that had upset him. Sometimes he looked as though he was in physical pain and I assumed that the withdrawal symptoms still hadn't gone; the memory of his wife kept him from sleeping too. But other times, when it was really bad, the whole thing must have come down on him and his life seemed impossible. When he was like that he couldn't even manage a conversation, and he'd slip back into his room before I got up, although I could tell from the warm kettle and the acrid smell of cigarette smoke that he had been up all night.

It was hard for Katie to get on with anything while Alex was in the flat. She felt bad about leaving him when she went shopping or met friends for lunch, because she knew that he would still be sitting there when she got back. Perhaps he would have gone into our bedroom and tried on my clothes; or sat in front of the long mirror brushing out his curls, changing his parting. Some days he soaked in the bath for an hour or more and shaved closely, maybe leaving just a hint of a Clark Gable pencil moustache – his appearance changed faster than the season. It was as though within these changes he was hoping to rediscover his identity, and on days when he made an effort he watched Katie's face as she came through the door to see whether she approved or not, to see whether she had even noticed. Then he would offer her a cup of coffee, and after the kettle had boiled and he'd imitated the sschush of an espresso machine, they drank black instant coffee while he told her more about his wife and their life together. Caroline was always at the centre of his thoughts, or at least of his conversation, and when he talked about her he pulled his wallet out of his back pocket and propped it open like an icon, so that he and Katie could look at her photograph while he talked. It always ended with him saying that he would return to the States and win her back – he seemed to have forgotten that she had also left New York and that he no longer knew where to find her. For a while he talked about buying another trumpet and looking for work on the London circuit – she would be proud of him if she knew he was playing again. He also wanted Katie to see that he was trying, although when he was very low he admitted to me that he didn't think he could play just then, because what had happened had taken away his confidence. Then, one day, he asked Katie to buy him a plane ticket back to the States. 'He must have been dreaming,' she told me. 'I know I'm a soft touch, and I really do like him – but not that much.'

When Mum and Dad called her during the day they begged her to throw Alex out. I suppose she did think about doing it, but she was never sure if they said it to make themselves feel better about what they had done, or because they really thought he would harm her.

71

'You don't know what you're letting yourself in for,' Dad warned her.

'Neither did you, but you still did it. And when you threw him out you knew that we would pick him up. Where would he go from here and still have a chance of getting it right?'

Of course they talked about drugs – was he still using or wasn't he?

Katie said, 'Does it matter what he does? If he wants to kill himself, then nothing we can do will stop him. But rather he does it here, where we might be able to help, than out in the street or with some other junkie.'

We tried to watch him closely, but he was so odd and inconsistent anyway that it was hard to tell whether he was using or not. At times we were both sure he was, and we'd be ready to confront him, but then something he would say or do reminded me of how he used to be, and we would no longer be certain, and didn't challenge him. Most nights, when I came back from work, Alex and Katie were sitting on the floor with coffee cups, some biscuits and a full ash-tray around them. Alex used to jump up and wrap his arms around me, or lean an elbow on my shoulder.

'Hello, dear,' he'd say. 'Did you have a good day at the office?' He would put his face very close to mine and look into my eyes until he realized that I was checking to see the size of his pupils.

Katie would sit back, amused, while Alex pulled away.

One night, when Alex was out and Katie and I had eaten and were getting ready to meet some friends for a drink in a bar down the road, the phone rang.

'Listen,' Alex said to me. 'I need to see you.'

'Well come home, then.'

'I'll meet you at the tube in Notting Hill in twenty minutes.'

When I got there he opened the car door, said, 'Brother!' in his inimitable way, slapped me on the leg. It was all too hearty and well-rehearsed. When he saw the way I was looking at him, he turned away.

'Can you buy me something to eat? A burger or anything – I haven't eaten all day. No money . . . ' he said sadly. I left him in the car and bought burgers and chips, and a Coke for each of us.

'Take me away from here,' he declaimed, with a bad stage laugh, as I got back into the Healey.

I suggested we went to the park. On the way I stopped at a phone-box to tell Katie I wouldn't be back for a while.

'Don't worry,' she said abruptly, 'I'll go on my own – see you there, maybe.'

We drove into Hyde Park, left the car and sat on a bench near the still lake. It was dark, and in the absence of stars or the moon the electric glow of the city seemed almost attractive. It wasn't late, but there was no one else around and I thought how strange we must look, two young men with hamburgers and Cokes, sitting close together on a park bench beneath an oak tree, up to our ankles in dead leaves.

When Alex finished eating he offered me a cigarette. I shivered as I took one.

'You know what's been going on, don't you,' he started, unlocking his briefcase and handing me a sweater.

'No, I don't,' I said evasively. 'You tell me.'

'It's been a bad night.' He sounded thoughtful, as though he was running over the events in his mind. 'A bad day as well, come to think of it,' he said, and laughed.

I asked him what had happened, although I knew what I expected him to say.

'I got caught again.' He looked at me as though he could see me clearly in the dark. 'I went to see a friend this afternoon, and before I knew what I was doing we'd gone and scored some cocaine.' He waited for me to say something, to do something, but I was silent. I didn't want him to hand me the responsibility so that I could say, 'You've been a bad boy,' and slap him on the knuckles. He'd only go and do it again. I wanted Alex to carry the responsibility for this, whatever it involved.

'I wish I hadn't,' he said, wringing his hands and stopping to bite a jagged fingernail.

'Tell me what happened,' I suggested quietly. I was wondering who this other person was and where they'd got the money to score cocaine. 'Tell me exactly, all of it.'

'You don't want to hear about that,' he said in an attempt to brush it off.

'I do. I need to know so that when you twist it in your mind and decide that you really didn't do anything wrong I can remind you. I can tell you exactly what happened, because otherwise it'll get corrupted.'

'That's not so. I won't forget because it wasn't fun. I knew it wouldn't be – as soon as I'd taken it I felt really sick. And then I threw up, and in the end it didn't really affect me.'

'How did you take it?' I was determined that he should tell me something he wanted to keep to himself.

'I shot it . . . ' He was irritated by the question and might as well have said, ' . . . of course, how else do you think I'd take it?'

I was silent. I had never been this close to Alex's drug-taking before. I'd been talking about it with him and everyone else for months. I'd even read books that Katie had found on drug abuse. I suppose I was obsessed by it. But I'd never been this close to the act before and I hadn't realized that it could be so much a part of the everyday: I was at work, Katie was preparing for an interview, Alex was shooting cocaine.

'Where?' I asked.

'What do you mean?'

'Where did you shoot it? In your arm? Your leg? Where?'

'In my arm.' He sounded sad now, as though he realized what he had done. But I was angry. It seemed a waste of time to have tried to help him if he could disappear and do it again, and come back and say, 'Look what I've done.' He was like a child.

But I wasn't going to reject him. I thought in a way he wanted me to, so that he could run away and have another reason for destroying himself. But I was still a long way from doing that.

The wind blew leaves around the bench while we talked. Alex raised his feet and caught some under his brown leather boots. I wanted him to remember even the smallest and least significant details – and to tell me about them – so that he would have a conscience to me; so that in future he would have one more reason to stay away from drugs. I tried to fill him with reasons not to take them, not even to want to – he needed more and more so that the next time

74

he thought about putting a needle in his arm all the reasons why he shouldn't would come rushing back to him and carry him away. That was how I thought I could help him.

A police van cruised past and Alex stopped talking. He sat, very tense, and then shuffled about on the bench. He was considering getting up and walking away, but I told him to stay where he was. The van drove past us and he let out a long, deep breath, but it came back after a moment and even my pulse was racing then.

We both had our backs to the road, so we couldn't see the van without turning round, but we heard it draw up behind us. It stopped. A door slid open. The engine was left running.

'Evening, gents,' a policeman called from the side door. Alex looked at me, terrified; I turned to the van. Another policeman, whom I couldn't see, muttered to his colleague and laughed. They probably thought we were gays or drunks or something – they could have fun with us. 'You'll have to leave now.' His voice was tired. 'We're closing the park.' He didn't want a reply and slammed the door, watching us from the van.

Alex let out a long, loud breath again. We got up quickly, nervously, and started walking towards the Healey, neither of us daring to turn around. When we reached the car Alex said, 'Hurry up,' under his breath. 'For Christ's sake, hurry up.'

I asked him if he was carrying anything.

'Of course not – you don't think I'd be stupid enough to walk around with it, do you?'

I didn't believe him at first, for from the way he was acting there was clearly something he was uneasy about. But then I thought, Maybe it's just street nature, something that becomes automatic when you're an addict and pushing drugs in a place like New York. You probably get uptight every time you see a cop or a bike or a police car. As you walk along the street you think, Do I look OK? Am I doing anything suspicious? You think about it and check yourself carefully. But the more you watch yourself, the more you think you're doing something wrong. In the end, you're walking in a really strange way, still trying to look as normal as possible, wondering if you'll be the one they

stop. And by this time, of course, it's obvious to everyone
– including yourself – that you're completely out of your
head.

We drove down to the river at Westminster and stopped
across the square from the Houses of Parliament where
there was a stand selling coffee and tea, hamburgers, hot
dogs. A dozen or more men and women squatted in
doorways within smelling distance of the stand, as spare as
the previous day's newspapers and torn plastic bin bags in
which they had wrapped themselves. They were ignored
by the customers at the stand – mostly late-shift taxi
drivers who stopped to pick up a drink and drove off again.
I bought us coffee while Alex walked over to a couple of old
men in broken boots and buttonless jackets tied round with
string.

'Buy them something as well,' he told me, and when I
did he said, 'At least we've done something for them.'

'Is that all you think it takes to help them?'

He ignored me and smiled sadly at them, to comfort
them. I realized that that was all it took for Alex to feel like
he'd done them a service. It made him feel good at least.

Back in the car, we drove to the river and stopped
half-way across Westminster Bridge. I remembered then
my fear of bridges. In Florence one year Alex and I had
walked along the arcade of shops and stalls on the Ponte
Vecchio, the muddy water of the Arno below us. We
fingered bright hundred-lire coins in the pockets of our
shorts and looked amongst the piles of cheap junk for
souvenirs to take home. In the end Alex and I bought the
same things – a gold-embossed leather wallet and a
keyring which had Michelangelo's *David*, cast in plastic,
hung from a hoop in his head. We carried them away
wrapped in pink and white striped paper bags, with the
blessings of the stall-holder upon us.

On the way back to our hotel Alex took out his keyring –
he couldn't wait any longer to play with it. He put the bag,
with the wallet in it, under his arm – I saw him do that.
Then he twirled the ring round and round his finger until
the pale plastic *David* broke away from the hoop and fell on
to the pavement. Alex was upset, but dismissed the
souvenir as a stupid toy. He didn't want it anyway, he

said, and threw the ring into the gutter after it. By the time we found Mum and Dad in the hotel restaurant Alex no longer had the wallet either. He must have dropped it on the way, but neither of us had noticed.

'Here,' I said, wanting to help him. 'Have my keyring . . . or the wallet,' but he refused them both.

When Mum and Dad discovered what had happened, they punished him. 'You must learn the value of money,' Dad told him as he sent him to bed early. He was deprived of pocket money for the rest of the holiday as well. 'It's not to be thrown away like that.' As he made his way up the staircase to our room, Alex turned and smiled at us as though this was exactly what he had wished to happen. He was apart from us again.

I could never bring myself to use the keyring or wallet after that, but nor could I throw them away. They sat in the drawer of my bed-side table and reminded me each time I saw them of the differences between us and of the souvenir stall in the middle of the old sloping bridge.

In the big Healey, on Westminster Bridge, Alex said, 'Everything I do seems designed to hurt me – I suppose I've got a masochistic streak in me. I was talking to Simon Blake about it and realized that every relationship I've had that I've really enjoyed has caused me pain. Do you remember what I told you just before my wedding? I said I was a masochist to be marrying her because she was going to drive me hard and would really hurt me if I didn't give her the things she wanted. Not quite the marriage Mum and Dad had wished for me. Well, my life has been like that. I don't seem to enjoy something unless it hurts . . . I remember a girl I went out with when I was sixteen or seventeen. When we had sex she dug her nails into my back. I don't know if she did it because I was hurting her, but she sure as hell hurt me. God . . . and I reckon ever since then I've been turned on by things like that . . . '

I didn't want to know. I caught myself frowning. I was glad it was dark because I didn't want to see his face or for him to be able to see mine. The darkness was my security, separating me from him and what he was saying.

'There must be truth in some of this,' he said gently. 'Somewhere amongst all this is the truth about me, the person I've become. Pain is a part of it . . . I suppose maybe that's why I got into heroin. It really hurt to begin with, and I was disgusted by what I was doing — that I could do that to myself — but then there was a thrill afterwards, of course, a rush that made it worth-while.' His mouth watered. 'I suppose that's why I got into it. But it's so hard to be sure about motives. Sometimes I must do things just for the sake of doing them.'

He wasn't speaking to me any more. He was thinking out loud and I just happened to be listening. Nothing was required of me. But maybe it was easier for him to have someone else present, a witness. He stripped layer after layer away and exposed things he had buried deep beneath himself, arranging them in front of us to see the extent of them, so that he could then say, 'Right — so that's all of it. Now I know just how bad it is. This must be true.'

When he stopped we looked down at the black water of the Thames and I felt the details of what he had told me drifting away. I could remember my reaction of shock and disgust, but I couldn't recall the specifics of the things he had related. Nor could I distinguish between what I thought he had told me and what I was thinking myself, for by then I had acquired some of his ugliest thoughts. In the darkness they slopped around in my mind and I talked hurriedly, trying to get them all back out into our conversation. I was afraid of being left with half-remembered rejects from his supposed past.

He must have thought I was morbid to want to go over it all again, for he had finished with it, but I insisted, and it was almost dawn by the time we drove back to the flat.

I had never been scared of sleep before, but a few nights later I had a dream that has haunted me ever since. I was lying on my back in bed and the sheet was pulled up as far as my waist. When Katie came in she danced provocatively in front of me, smiled, slipped out of her black shift and knelt naked on the edge of the bed. She stretched out beside me and I kissed her, running my fingers through her hair, down her neck, over her breasts. I moved a leg over between hers and she reached down for me below the sheet. But later, when she lay back and I climbed on top of her, she screamed in pain and pushed me away.

78

'Oh shit, my back,' she shouted, 'my spine!'

When I rolled her over I was horrified by what I saw: her vertebrae had suddenly grown out of all proportion. Some of them were now wide and very long, hanging like extended shelves in front of her shoulder blades. They were also connected vertically to each other so that they formed a grid, an outline that I recognized as the floor plan of the flat. When I looked closer between her bones I could even see into the rooms. They were furnished, intact, right down to the bare plaster walls. I could see Alex asleep in his room and there we were, lying on our bed, Katie face down on the sheet and me touching something on her back. I looked up at myself and smiled, and screamed until Katie woke me up.

I don't think it needs a genius to interpret this dream: I felt guilty about what Alex and I were doing to Katie.

She put her arms around me and said, 'Tell me what you were dreaming about,' but I wouldn't tell her. Nor could I touch her, for with my eyes open in the darkness I seemed to straddle both sleep and waking, and I was afraid of feeling her bones.

I got out of bed to drink some water and saw, on my way into the kitchen, that the bathroom light was on.

'Alex?' I whispered. 'Are you in there?' He was lying in the bath and I could hear the whine of his Walkman and smell cigarette smoke.

'Mmm,' he muttered. I tried the door but it was locked. There was no keyhole, so I knelt down to look under the door, but all I could see was the towel he had dropped.

'Alex, it's two o'clock. For God's sake go to bed. I've got to go to work in the morning.'

'I'm not stopping you,' he said. 'Anyway, I'll be out in a minute.'

I didn't wait for him, but later we heard him creeping around, trying to put the kettle down on the worktop without a sound, making sure that the tap dripped silently on to a cloth in the sink. Katie and I lay close to each other, not touching now, and listened to the care he took not to be heard.

After that night the flat never seemed the same to me. It shrank almost to the dimensions of the model I had imagined on Katie's back, and we filled it beyond comfort. I felt as though, if I reached out, I would be able to wrap my arms around the sitting room. Katie felt hemmed in too.

'We must clear this place up,' she said irritably. But we had too many things to be able to put them away so she suggested we take a stall down at Portobello Market and sell some of them.

'After all,' she said, 'most of this stuff we never use – I certainly wouldn't miss half of it. And we could do with the money . . .'

Alex was uneasy about it. 'You're not throwing things away to make room for me, are you?'

I said I thought it was a good idea. 'It's about time I got rid of some of my junk.' He seemed reassured.

Katie and I spent the next Friday evening going through cupboards and drawers looking for anything saleable, throwing them on to a pile on the floor. By nine o'clock the sitting room was littered with old clothes and unwanted objects.

'Where the hell is Alex? I thought he was going to help.'

'Don't worry,' she said calmly. 'If there's money involved, he'll be here.'

At eleven, by which time we had priced most of the things and packed them up in bags and boxes, we heard him put his key in the door. He looked absently round the room without saying anything and then threw some bags off a chair to sit down.

'I thought you were going to help,' I told him.

'And I thought you'd get on quicker without me in the way.'

'Are you still coming down to queue for the stall?'

'Oh,' he said, without enthusiasm, 'I might as well.'

'Well, we have to be out of here by half past three, so I'm going to bed.'

He said, 'No problem,' and switched on the television.

At half past three, with Katie still asleep, I was ready to go, but Alex wanted breakfast. 'We must eat,' he insisted, 'and build up our strength.'

'If you wanted breakfast, you should've had it earlier. I just want to get down there and reserve a stall. You can do what you like.' He left his bowl of cereal and followed me out of the door, stamping his feet on the way downstairs. It didn't seem worth telling him that people were asleep in the flat below.

We drove down to the market in silence through deserted streets littered with cans, bottles and discarded bags of fish and chips. The sky was still yellow, and along Portobello Road white numbered markers on the tarmac were the only indication that there would be a market in the morning. At the end of the road even the flyover, hanging above the houses and shops, was empty. Beneath it was the yellowed canvas awning of the flea market and the metal stalls left out by the Friday traders. I sat on one of the tables and waited for the supervisor to arrive, but Alex wandered off around the corner.

Rap and reggae thudded from one of the houses nearby. In the brief silences between tracks I heard people coughing, a baby crying out, a woman screaming. The sound drifted over me and I dozed off until Katie arrived with coffee. Then Alex came back, following a girl on a bicycle, who I assumed had also come to queue for a stall.

'Hi,' she said brightly.

I nodded, but Alex said, 'Hi.'

They started talking and she explained to him that she was off to New York the following week. She was wearing tight, faded jeans and a black leather jacket and it was obvious that Alex found her attractive. To keep her talking, and maybe also to impress her, he said, 'Oh, I live there – I'm just over here to meet some people. Staying with my younger brother.' The girl nodded to me again and leaned closer to Alex.

To begin with Alex sat on the edge of one of the tables and gripped its sides so hard that his knuckles went white. They talked about New York, about the music he'd been playing there – when he'd glossed over what had really happened to him he relaxed, and then, just as he regained his confidence, the girl became nervous. It was clear that he had impressed her.

'So,' he said blithely, one foot on the ground, the other swinging between them, 'what are you going to do out there?'

'Oh' – she was obviously glad that he'd asked – 'I'm

going to work in a new health club. The smartest club in town.' She described the work-out rooms and relaxation areas as though she had just bought the place. 'Lots of stars have already joined.'

When she named the club Alex said casually, 'That's right. When I was there' – he didn't see her face fall – 'I was in the sauna with Prince. What a little man he is.'

She stared at him for a moment and then said, 'Oh, really? I don't see how that can have happened – it hasn't even opened yet, jerk.'

I turned away.

Alex said nothing more, but came and sat by me. He reached into his pocket, pulled out a cigarette and then wandered off again, walking around the tables as though they were already filled, ready for business, and he had money to spend.

By nine o'clock we had set up our stall with broken clocks, chipped plates and cups, bamboo picture frames, desk accessories, a few old cameras and a pile of other junk we had collected or been given over the years. The market was already busy and people were three and four deep in front of us. I loved watching the market shoppers – if they were interested in something they picked it up, rattled, touched, knocked and even smelled it before asking the price. Then they began to haggle, looking offended when we refused to do a deal. Sometimes they walked off and then came back again, tried one more time to get the price down and eventually bought at the price we had first asked.

'Won't you just knock ten pence off it, guv?' one old man pleaded as I held up a battered table lamp that had come out of my childhood bedroom. 'Won't you do that for me? Go on – ninety p. I'm a pensioner and it's hard enough to get by on what I've got . . . ' He looked at me. He sniffed. At first I thought that if he found it so hard to survive then he shouldn't be out shopping, but then I realized that it wasn't the money; it was a matter of pride for him to get the price down. He bartered for the sake of it, not for the saving he would make.

'OK,' I said quietly, so that no one else would hear. 'Ninety it is.' He handed me the money and opened his bag, which I saw contained a pair of brass candlesticks, a travelling clock and a set of silver fish knives and forks.

'Been shopping today, eh?'

'Just a bit.' He laughed as he put the lamp into his bag. 'God bless you.'

I laughed too as he walked off. 'And God bless you,' I called after him.

We got rid of most of the saleable things early in the day and were left with a tableful of junk for the afternoon. But the people who passed in front of us changed as the day went on: the regular market shoppers and junk dealers disappeared and the place was filled with tourists looking for bargain souvenirs and young couples buying things for their flats or their new second-hand wardrobes.

Alex also changed with the day. In the morning he had been a perfect salesman, hard to bargain with, convincing people in his most persuasively reasonable voice that they really did want to buy what we were selling. But by mid-afternoon he had his back up against the corrugated-iron wall, had put on his coat and beret and was listening to his Walkman; his sunglasses hid his eyes, but I knew they were shut, and after a while his head went down. He didn't look so different then from the meths drinkers slumped on the pavement across the road.

When he woke, he smiled and said, 'Right, so what's still left to sell?' but it was drizzling by then and the regular stall-holders were already beginning to pack up. Alex stood in front of the stall and stopped a few tourists, but all they wanted was to know the direction of the tube station. Finally he picked up an old Polaroid camera – we had reduced it to a pound – loaded the film that came with it and took a picture of Katie and me. He showed it to the last of the shoppers as they walked past, but they weren't interested. 'But look,' he insisted, waving the camera in front of them, becoming frantic now. 'It works and it's only a pound.'

'Alex,' I said, taking the camera away from him, 'they don't want it. Leave it alone.' I took his picture, but he wouldn't watch as it developed. I had caught him looking desperate, and later, when we had packed up the junk, he threw the photograph under the table amongst the plastic

83

coffee-cups and half-eaten doughnuts, but I retrieved it and put it in my pocket.

Back in the flat we counted the money we had made and divided it three ways: we had each made thirty pounds. We were tired and didn't feel like eating. Katie and I settled down with a bottle of wine in front of the TV – Gary Cooper and Marlene Dietrich in *Morocco* – and fell asleep. When we woke up we found a note from Alex resting on my chest. 'Gone out. Back later.'

In the night he came into our bedroom and shook me gently. I could hear a taxi waiting with its engine running.

'Can you lend me a fiver?' he whispered.

I told him to take it from the money in the sitting room and heard him go back out into the street.

'There you are,' he said to the taxi driver, 'and keep the change.'

When he came back into the flat he went straight into the bathroom, and I was asleep before he came out. The next day, when he got up late, he came into the sitting room, said, 'Good morning,' and picked up the Sunday papers. When I asked him where he had gone last night he ignored me.

'But you must have gone somewhere,' I insisted. 'You can't have spent the money you earned yesterday if you didn't go anywhere. And your taxi cost me five pounds, so you weren't in this area.' He still said nothing.

'You can't have it all your own way,' I shouted. 'It's the least you could do – ' but Katie took me by the arm and pulled me out on to the balcony.

'It's unfair,' I told her. 'Why are we doing this?'

'Because he's your brother and you love him. He needs you – you both know that. Sometimes he must need something more for himself . . . ' She put her hands on my shoulders and looked me in the eyes. 'He's got problems, real problems, and if he's ever going to help himself then we've got to give him some space.'

'Why are you doing this?' I asked her angrily. 'You don't even really know him.'

She put her arms around my neck and pulled me close. 'Because I love you,' she whispered.

*

84

The further I go on, the more difficult it becomes to tell this story. The week after the market was a bad one for all of us. On the Tuesday morning I noticed that the money I had earned was missing, and when Katie checked in her bag she found hers had gone too.

'How could you do this to us?' I shouted at Alex.

He lay on his bed, where I had woken him, and his eyes followed the cornice around the darkened plaster ceiling.

'Shit – we're the only people prepared to help you. We're giving you a chance, but you're just making us feel stupid. If this goes on, sooner or later we'll say what everyone else has said to you – "Fuck off, you're not worth the effort." How could you . . . ?' I wanted him to get out of bed so that I could hit him. I wanted to hurt him because he was now hurting us. But he just lay there, not looking at me, his eyes closing on the gloom.

In the sitting room I said to Katie, 'Let's throw him out.' I talked loudly, knowing that he could hear. 'Why bother trying to help him if he's going to steal from us? It's not as if we're not giving him money anyway.'

But Katie said, 'No, we won't throw him out. We said we'd look after him and that's what we're going to do. If this is how he's going to repay us, then we'll just have to get used to it and not be upset. All he's doing is confirming what everyone's said about him. And if he's given every chance and still messes up, well, at least we'll know we tried . . . '

All day at *The* Agency, I thought about why he had stolen from us. He must have known we would miss the money and that it would be obvious he was the one who had taken it. Maybe he'd been stealing from us all along and we hadn't noticed before? Maybe he even thought we didn't mind? I didn't know. None of it made sense, but I began to agree with Katie that it would be wrong for us to throw him out now. He needed something solid and immutable to lean against. Still, I didn't find it easy to be treated like that by my own brother, and even now I wish I had struck him for some of the things he did to us. All day at *The* Agency I snapped at the slightest provocation, so that at the end of the afternoon my director called me into his office and suggested that maybe I needed a holiday or something. 'Take a few days off,' he told me. 'Maybe,' I replied. On the tube that evening I elbowed the grey coats and denims crowding around me into giving me some space. When I got home I was relieved that Alex wasn't there.

Up until then Katie had stayed out of Alex's room, respecting his privacy, but now that he had stolen from her she felt she had a right to intrude on him. After dinner she went in to look around and quickly came out in tears.

'The bastard's going to destroy this flat,' she shouted. She took me in and showed me what he had done to a tall palm which hung over his bed. Each one of its fronds had been burned with a cigarette and was now perforated from tip to stem. The earth in the pot was littered with cigarette-ends. Some of the leaves he had pulled off lay amongst the dirt on the floor under the bed. I said I would talk to him about it when he came back, but by one o'clock he still hadn't shown up, so we went to bed.

The next evening, when I got home from work, Katie was out seeing an early film with a friend and Alex spoke first.

'Listen,' he said, 'I've got something to tell you. You're not going to like it, but it's done now and I'm sorry. There's nothing I can do about it.'

My fists curled up. 'What?'

'I had an accident in the bathroom this afternoon. I would have told Katie about it, but she hasn't come back yet . . . I was desperate to go to the loo when I got back from the shrink, but when I sat down on the toilet the seat broke . . . '

'Alex . . . ' I said, unable to stop myself from smiling, 'how do you do these things?'

'I don't know,' he said, smiling too. 'There I was, sitting on the toilet, and then the seat broke and I was on the floor.' We laughed together. 'But the cigarette I was smoking must have fallen out of my hand, because now there's a burn on the carpet.'

He backed away quickly then and said he had to go out. That was the last time I saw him before the weekend.

While I was fixing the toilet seat, Dad called; he had just spoken to Simon Blake.

'I finally persuaded him that we had real grounds for suspecting that Alex was still taking drugs. I told him that you and Katie felt the same way too.'

'Dad – you could at least have – '

'Anyway, Simon's going away for a few weeks so he decided to put Alex through it this afternoon, and although it's impossible for him to be absolutely sure, he tells me that he's as satisfied as he can be that Alex is now off drugs.' He laughed a little.

'It's strange that Alex didn't mention it to me this evening.'

'I can't tell you how relieved I am,' Dad said, not listening.

'So what about all the signs we've been seeing for the past months? The odd behaviour? The lapses? Exhaustion? Dilated pupils? Is that just our paranoia? Seeing what we expect to see?'

'No, no,' Dad explained, 'that's all left over from the drugs he took in the States. He's still suffering the effects, and Simon couldn't tell me how long that'll go on for. But he's OK apart from that.'

'No, he's not,' I insisted. 'Nothing's changed.'

'What do you mean?'

'All that's happened is that you're now satisfied he's not taking drugs any more. But this wonderful revelation doesn't change anything for Alex. How can it? He's still the same person, with the same problems, and he seems to find it impossible to overcome them. He's still our problem, mine and Katie's, on our sofa every day, looking sorry for himself, not knowing what he's doing, or how he's going to find work, or whether he'll ever see his wife again. He's not suddenly, miraculously transformed because you discover he's been telling the truth – if it is the truth. It's just not like that.'

'I know,' Dad said quietly. 'But Simon assures me that everything will come right in the end and I believe him. He's staked his reputation on getting Alex well again.' He coughed – he had been smoking too much – and cleared his throat. 'In the mean-time, if there's anything you need . . . Are you all right for money . . . ? We'd like to see Alex some time – perhaps we could come over to you on the

weekend? We still can't have him in the house, you see . . .
your mother, she just couldn't take it. Not yet,
anyway . . . '

That night, for the first time, I had a sense that Alex had
fallen through our embrace, that we had dropped him and
he had slipped away from us. What he had left me holding
was my own anger.

There was nothing white in Eveline's flat. The walls, which
had been cream, were now more of a tobacco colour. The
thick curtains, which fell fifteen feet from pelmet to skirting, were of dulled deep burgundy. The stained wooden
floorboards had faded Persian carpets thrown over them
which Eveline always warned me to beware – 'Don't trip
on the corners, dear, they're so hard to see' – and she
would approach them like a blind person at the foot of
some stairs. Even the things that had been white once –
the pages of books, the crockery, the backing on which
some of her prints were mounted – were yellowed, or
stained with use.

Katie took to Eveline the moment she met her, unques-
tioningly. She looked like such a kind old dear, to use her
own words, with her small, fat body and wrinkled face.
But Eveline resisted Katie; she would not have things so
easy. She was wary to begin with and there was always a
'why' on the tip of her tongue.

'Why do you say you like that picture in particular?' she
asked Katie, pointing to a landscape of open fields with
hills behind, a copse of oak trees half-way up the incline.

'Because it pleases me,' Katie explained. 'It reminds me
of something, somewhere I've been, though I'm not sure
where exactly.'

'So you need to relate a picture to your own experience, do you, before you can really like it? Why can't you
just look at what the artist has put down for you? Why
must you see with experience, instead of instinct or
emotion?'

Katie was surprised by Eveline's tone, but the old
woman only laughed at her. She leaned across the sofa to
pat her arm and said, 'You mustn't mind me, my dear. I do
the same thing myself. We all do. But it's something that's

always worried me. We see what we wish to see, rather than what is there. Not just with pictures but with everything. For an artist that must be very frustrating, for what sort of reception would he meet with if he presented us with something that had no bearing whatever on anything we had either seen or dreamed of before?'

Katie was uneasy with this sort of conversation. She said she supposed contemporary art was trying to create a context where familiar objects would appear to be new. ('Exactly,' Eveline agreed.) 'But what do I know?' Katie added apologetically. 'I hardly ever go to exhibitions and I've never known an artist.'

'But anyway,' Eveline said to reassure her, 'you know what you like, so what do you make of this?' She crossed the room, walking around the carpet, and bent awkwardly to slide a stretched canvas from behind the chair I was sitting on. 'Don't tell me straight away – think about it and tell me later.' She propped up the painting in the corner of the room by the window, on an easel where she usually left new paintings while deciding where they should hang. This canvas was painted white. Layers of white oil-paint had been built up until they had a texture to them, almost a sculpted surface. The colour seemed less important than the technique, but the effect made me want to run my fingers over it, to caress it.

'Now let's eat,' Eveline said. She had cooked lamb in rowanberries. 'You always liked this when you were young and came to us for lunch,' she told me, although I didn't remember it. 'It made you feel grown up. But Alexander was the funny one. When he was ten or eleven I remember him telling us that this was not the correct way to serve lamb – or rowans. "Oh," he'd say, "don't tell me you've smothered it in those awful berries again. If you must use them, then you should serve them as a jelly, on the side of the plate." He always did know what he wanted . . . '

'Sounds precocious to me,' Katie said. 'I don't know why you put up with it.'

'I could say the same to you,' Eveline replied, 'for he's exactly the same now. But I understand perfectly why you do. Alexander has always been special. There has always been something trying to come out of him, something that will be important. People respond to it.'

'That's not it at all,' Katie said firmly. 'I'm not putting up with him for his sake – '

Eveline looked shocked. 'Well, excuse me for being so blunt, my dear, but you're beginning to sound like some sort of angel, or martyr. I suppose my white canvas over there suggests innocence to you . . . purity . . . a new beginning?'

'Eveline,' I interrupted, 'I think you're going too far . . . '

'No, she's not,' Katie insisted, 'and anyway, I can speak for myself.'

'Well, does it?' Eveline asked again.

'Yes,' Katie told her, 'in a way. But there's something more . . . '

'In this country,' Eveline said, obviously not listening to her, 'there is an alarming trend to do down exceptional people. Being British seems to mean being fair, playing safe and riding above the waves, not making them. Well, I don't see that things have ever been fair. I'm not even sure they should be – it's not as if we all have the same needs or desires. You might need more than I, Katie more than you. That,' she put in as an aside, 'is where the Communists went wrong. But I've always admired Alexander because he has an unerring ability to make waves. Now, before you two say anything, I'm going to tell you what I think about the painting over there.' She turned her chair around so that she was facing it. 'To you, it may look like one of those new minimal paintings, but it's not. This is not an empty beginning,' she said emphatically. 'It is an ending. It was painted, oh, more than fifty years ago by a very dear friend of mine, a man I might have married if your grandfather hadn't been around. He painted this for me and chose white because he wanted to represent all his feelings at once. It's not minimal or nihilistic to me – it's complete.' She sighed as though she had forgotten all this until now. 'And there's a quality to the whiteness – rich and exciting, not like the whites they use now.'

'This one is almost the colour of milk,' Katie agreed, and laughed in embarrassment at her comment.

'Well,' said Eveline, 'there's probably some dust and dirt to account for that; but I think you're right. Modern whites are sterilized – not this one, though.'

'So what made you bring it out now?' I asked, for I was surprised that she hadn't hung the picture before.

We had drunk a few chilled bottles of her favourite Beaujolais, and veins like warning lights now stood out on Eveline's cheeks. 'Your grandfather,' she said laughing, 'never approved of it. Nor of my artist friend, either, I'm afraid. Poor man, I think he was terribly jealous because although he was many things, he wasn't an artist. He thought it was an insult that someone should present me with a white canvas. It was the only time he failed to understand a picture. So we never had it on show while he was alive, but something Alexander said the last time I saw him reminded me of it . . . '

I thought it was strange that she associated this picture with Alex, for when she asked our impressions I had been reminded of him too, of the colour of heroin, or, to be more precise, of the colour I imagined heroin must look like when it has been mixed with water and is ready to be injected.

'I have been thinking of painting the flat white,' Katie told Eveline.

'Oh, but you mustn't – '

'It's a compromise,' she explained, 'the only colour we can both agree on. But I can see now that it would be a mistake.'

'Yes, it would,' Eveline insisted, 'so you'll have to think again. White is not a proper colour for a home. People think it's a neutral, a void, but in that they mistake it for black – and they certainly wouldn't paint their walls black, now would they. There's more to the colour of white than they imagine.'

When we left, as we bent down to kiss her, Eveline said, 'I like you, Katie. I know you'll excuse me for saying this, but I claim a grandmother's prerogative and I don't expect to live long enough to see whether it happens or not, but I'd be happy if you two settled down together. I think you suit each other and I know from what I've heard, and from your reaction to my white canvas here, that you respect the idea of the family. I like that. It seems to be rare now.'

Katie put her arm through mine as we walked down the road to the Healey.

'Do you suppose she had an affair with that artist friend of hers?'

'I don't know,' I told her. 'It's hard to imagine her having sex with anyone.'

'Anyway, everyone should have a grandmother like that, for all her pro-nounce-ments on Art and Colour.'

'"White is not a proper colour for a home,"' I mimicked.

Neither of us said it then, but I'm sure Katie thought, as I did, that Eveline had been right about our suiting each other, and both of us, I realized, wanted a family.

White is not a proper colour — I mocked Eveline for saying it, but she was right. It is a composite, the colour to which light-sensitive paper reverts when it has received all colour. It doesn't seem at all strange that I have no photographs from that time, except for the Polaroid we took at Portobello, for our lives then appeared to be an over-exposed white flash, originally energetic and vital, but also explosive and dangerous. I suppose it might have been possible, if I had been determined and patient enough, to break down that complete whiteness into the various colours of the spectrum from which it had been created, but it required a greater degree of concentration than I could have spared at the time. Now, as I think back on it, the whiteness of my remembered images suggests the once-white canvas roof of my Healey; the painted stucco front of the house in which we lived; the tins of paint piled up in the hallway with which we would not now cover the plastered walls; the whites of Katie's eyes and her teeth as she laughed; the sheet on which we made love. White, it appears, was the colour of my dreams and of our hopes for the future, but as I had just realized, it was also the shade of the substance which had caused Alex so much trouble.

I laughed out loud at this idea on the way back home in the Healey and Katie, smiling at me and resting a hand on my leg, must have thought I was happy at last.

*

We had invited Mum and Dad for tea on Saturday afternoon, but although they were clearly pleased to be asked
Mum couldn't make it – it was such short notice, she said,
and she had already accepted another invitation. So Dad
was going to come on his own. Alex wasn't in on the
Friday evening when we made the arrangement, so we left
a note for him on the table in the sitting room before going
to bed.

'He'll probably do a runner when he sees that,' Katie
said, and I agreed with her.

When we got up in the morning the note was still where
we had left it. I knocked on Alex's door, but there was no
answer; his bed was cold, so he hadn't come home that
night.

'Oh God, that's all we need,' I complained. 'A repentant
father and a missing prodigal son – it'll be one hell of an
afternoon.'

Before we went out shopping I wrote Alex a more urgent
note, but that too was still there when we got back. Then,
when we had given up on him and started tidying up the
flat, he appeared.

'I've got to talk to you,' he said to me.

There was no colour in his face and he looked as though
he had been up all night.

'What's wrong?'

'I need to talk to you – alone.'

Katie was cleaning her make-up off the bathroom
mirror, so Alex took me out on to the balcony. His eyes
had sunk in again and he looked ill.

I leaned against the railings. 'So what's the problem?'

He lifted one foot on to the window-box and flicked a
leaf off his gym shoe. 'I need some money.' His voice was
controlled. 'You must lend me some.'

'What for?'

He was so obviously desperate and controlled himself
only with great effort. Then, suddenly, he snapped.
'Come on,' he begged me, 'for God's sake don't put me
through all that again. I've tried everyone I can think of
this morning and no one'll lend it to me. There's just you –
you've got to . . . '

'But what for?' I asked again, barely audible over dub-noise from a tape machine that a black guy was hauling down the road on his shoulder.

'You know why I need it.'

'Why?' I screamed, violent at last. I knew what he would say, but I wanted to make it difficult for him. 'Why? Why? You tell me – '

' – because I need to buy a fix,' he said quietly. He was angry with me for making him say it. Then he shook for a few moments as though it had just turned very cold. 'If I don't get a fix I'm going to be in a bad way soon.'

I was shaking too, but with anger. It occurred to me then that with just the slightest movement I could push him off the narrow balcony. It would be so easy and would look as though he'd just lost his balance, fallen over the railings. No one would suspect me; things like that happen to addicts.

'No,' I said emphatically, shocked at myself, 'I don't care how much you want it. You can't have it.' It was like depriving him of food, and I felt savage for doing it. 'And if you leave now, you'll never set foot in this flat again. I won't lift another finger – not even this much – to help you.'

'Listen.' I recognized his dealer's voice, the 'reasonable' one he'd used down at Portobello. 'It's not just me. A woman gave me half of her supply yesterday, so now she doesn't have any – and she doesn't have money, either. I promised I'd get the cash to her by twelve.' He looked at his watch. 'By now she'll be going down fast.' He tried to make it sound dramatic, but he couldn't even summon the energy to plead her case.

'Well, let her suffer,' I told him. 'I don't care. She can die this afternoon for all I care.' I put both hands on his shoulders and was shaking him. 'What is it to me that she hasn't got money or drugs? What is it to me?'

'It's not just her,' he said softly. 'She's got children. What's going to happen to them if she collapses? How're you going to feel about them?' He was standing with great difficulty, his shoulders had slumped beneath my hands and he was fighting to keep his eyes open.

I didn't know what it was like to be on heroin. I didn't know if he was telling me the truth, nor what I should do

94

about it if he was. I knew what I wanted to do to him, though, and to her.

'How long have you been taking it?' I asked, calmer now.

'Oh, come on,' he started, but I bared my teeth. 'Since I got back here, since I started staying with Mum and Dad – '

Oh God, I thought, Dad.

'Don't move,' I warned him. He leaned against the wall and lit a cigarette, but he hardly had the energy to lift his hand to his mouth.

I went back into the flat and banged on the bathroom door. Katie trembled when I told her, as though I had just struck her.

'What can we do?' I asked.

'We have no choice. We don't have the right to put this woman or her children at risk – that's not for us.' She looked at me and I wanted to turn away, for I felt like crying. We held each other tightly. Alex had caught us again, because he knew that we wouldn't willingly endanger the children.

I was calmer, slower, after that. I didn't hurry back on to the balcony; first I had to work out what to do. After a while it became just another arrangement and it was easier to sort out my thoughts. There was money to get, although I didn't know how much; we had some in the flat, unless he'd already taken it. But we couldn't just let him go off on his own, because he'd probably never come back. Then there was Dad to worry about, always there at the wrong time. He mustn't know; not now when he thought he was coming to make things up with Alex.

Alex was still slumped against the wall, and coming upon him again I was reminded of our day at Portobello. 'How much do you need?' I asked. He didn't hear me at first, so I asked again.

'A hundred and sixty pounds,' he said easily.

'Why so much?' I was surprised, although I had no idea how much heroin that would buy, nor how long it would last him.

'I've been using "China White" – it's the best and most expensive – and I owe half of it to the woman, and I'll need the rest to get me through to Monday – I've got to see the shrink then and I don't want him to know.'

'You have to tell him,' I insisted, in control at last. 'And when we've got the money and given it to this woman you're coming back here, and you won't leave our sight until Monday . . . And when you've seen Simon Blake, whether we have to strap you down or you do it willingly, you're going to stay here until it's over and you're off it.'

The low autumn sunshine was hurting his eyes. He backed against the wall to get away from it and said, 'You don't understand.'

'Yes I do.'

'I want to stop after this . . . I need to. I can't go on doing this to myself. And I can't get money any more . . . so I've got to stop.'

When Katie came out on to the balcony, Alex turned away. It was obvious that she knew, for she looked at him as though he was an unwelcome stranger. He was ashamed in front of her.

'I want to stop,' he went on, 'but I want to tell the shrink and Mum and Dad after I've stopped. Otherwise they'll interfere. So if I can just get through the meeting on Monday OK, then I'll have two weeks to come off before Simon Blake gets back. I should be over the worst by then.'

I looked from Alex to Katie. It made sense, but then so did most of the things he told us.

He must have known that we would force him to accept our conditions, because we had something he really needed, which he couldn't get elsewhere. We had him cornered at last and we meant to take hold of him. I think it was this that convinced me to give him the money – and because he was my brother, whatever he did, for, as he had said, we're family, always.

'Dad's coming for tea today.'

'Oh fuck, no,' he swore emptily. 'Why?' Then he thought about it for a moment and said, 'You'll have to put him off.'

I shook my head. 'You'll just have to get yourself into a fit state to see him.'

'Well I'm not telling him anything today.' He looked scared again. 'I'll tell him when I'm off. When I'm ready.'

'Just don't expect us to lie for you,' Katie warned him.

He scratched his arms and legs, still shaking. 'Come on now . . . please,' he begged her. She bent down to pull a weed out of the window-box, dropped it and went inside.

'We'll have to go to the bank,' I told Alex.

'Haven't you got money here?' I didn't know if he knew that we had, but there wasn't enough anyway.

'No,' I said, 'we'll have to go and cash cheques.'

Katie got sixty pounds out of the money in the flat and then we drove to a bank on the other side of the park where we could draw cash on Saturdays. Alex sat on the back ledge of the Healey and Katie stared at him all the way. There was something pathetic about him, now that we knew he was taking heroin. Still out of touch with the seasons, he was dressed for winter, huddled in a thick coat against the wind, holding his beret in place, his eyes screwed up against the warm sun. He bore no relation then to the brother I had wanted to help. I had never seen him like this before – he was still shaking – and I never wanted to again.

Alex had been to this particular bank a few weeks before to cash one of his bouncing cheques, so he wouldn't come in with us.

'Poor boy,' Katie said as we walked along the road. 'He looks awful.'

'You're not serious? Sympathy won't help him. He'd do anything – lie and cheat and steal from us – if he thought it would get him out of having to give up. If he knows we feel sorry for him, we'll be really stuck.'

Katie disapproved.

'Come on,' I reminded her, 'he's my brother. I don't want to see him like this any more than you do.'

When we got back to the Healey, Alex had fallen asleep and didn't wake up immediately. He lay across the back ledge like a toppled dummy and snored.

'Alex,' I said loudly. 'Alex, I need to know where we're going.'

'Crouch End,' he muttered, sitting up now. Katie raised her eyebrows when he said where we were going, for we both knew that Dad had driven him up there 'to a friend's house'.

When we got to the address we gave him the money. He walked across the road and rang the bell, stood waiting, motionless, for a few minutes and then stepped back to look up at a window.

'God,' he said as he came back to the car. 'She's not answering – so either she's already collapsed or she's gone to her dealer to try and borrow some.' He looked nervous. His life-and-death story was already falling apart. 'But it's true,' he insisted, and climbed into the back.

As we drove down to the dealer's house in Highbury, Alex explained why it was that he knew this man but didn't buy from him direct. 'I know I don't pay her much over the odds for it, but the dealer doesn't want everyone ringing his bell all the time, so he sells to groups; this woman and myself and a few others make up one of his groups.'

When we got to the tree-lined street in Highbury, which, like so much of inner London, was hidden by scaffolding and edged with skips, Alex told me to drive a little way past the dealer's house. 'You can never be too careful,' he said. He walked back and rang the bell. When the door opened we were unable to see who answered it.

'Shall we call the police and get them all busted?' Katie suggested.

I looked at her quickly to see if she was serious. She must have seen from my face that I would consider doing it, and said, 'Well, why not?' She smiled again.

'Because we're not the people to do it, that's why not.'

About twenty minutes later Alex came out. 'Right,' he said easily. 'She wasn't there, so let's go back to her place and leave this little packet.'

He was smiling now and sat upright on the ledge.

'Did you get your fix?' I asked, curious to know how the whole thing worked.

'Yes.' His voice was a curious mix of shame and smugness. 'Yes, I took some there.' Katie shook her head sadly. 'It's all right,' he snapped, 'I'm not going to die just yet.'

'Don't you ever say something like that again,' I shouted at him. 'Do you hear? She doesn't deserve it. Not ever.'

He sat back, blushing, and lit a cigarette without offering us one. Then he took an envelope out of his pocket, wrote something on it and put a packet of heroin into it. He didn't say a word as he climbed out this time, nor did he appear to notice an old green Mini pull up alongside him. It only occurred to us then that we could get busted, and Katie and I slipped down in our seats.

The post-war block that Alex approached, a series of boxes stacked one on top of the other, stood between an Edwardian mansion block and a large Victorian house. It looked run-down in comparison. Alex walked back up the path and pressed several bells, hoping that someone would let him into the hall so that he could slip his packet under her front door, but there was still no reply.

Katie pointed to an emaciated woman getting out of the Mini. It was impossible to determine her age from her appearance. We thought she was about forty, maybe even fifty, but Alex told us later that she was only thirty-one. We got a better idea of her age from the two girls who followed her out of the car, both of them around four feet tall. They were obviously the woman's children, for they had her yellowing skin tone and dark, wiry hair. They stood waiting on the pavement, staring straight ahead.

Alex didn't see them until the woman called out to him. He nodded to her, but looked both ways down the road before he walked over to meet her. Alex said something to her and the two of them went into the block, while the children waited by the car, still looking neither left nor right.

They came out after a few minutes; the woman called to the girls, leaving the front door open, while Alex came back to the car.

'How do you know her?' Katie asked.

'Oh, we met through my wife. They're old friends.'

Katie said, 'Some friend – did you see the way she was acting? Those poor children. I don't give a damn what she does to herself, but those children. If she had the least concern for them – did you see them? – she'd give up whatever it is she's taking. If she can't give it up then she ought to give up the children. They look like they'd do better in care.'

Alex was going to say something but decided not to, for Katie was clearly shocked.

'Did you see? The way they stood there – those aren't

99

children,' she continued. 'God, it makes me angry. How dare she?' She huddled up in the passenger seat, lit a cigarette and said nothing more until we got back to the flat.

But later Alex said, 'At least she's not a street addict. Both she and the dealer live real lives.' We laughed. 'They do,' he insisted. 'The dealer's an addict himself, but he's also a successful architect and lives in the most beautiful house.'

'We went there, Alex,' I reminded him.

'I know it doesn't look much from the outside, but inside it's great. And he can handle it – he's happily married with a couple of kids. They all know about his addiction, but it doesn't interfere with his life.'

Alex was rather pleased with the way he'd put that.

'Come on,' I said, 'I don't believe a word of it. Maybe they're not street addicts, as you say, but don't tell me they live normal lives. What do their kids say about them at school? Or maybe he does act normally, except that half-way through a business meeting or dinner party he gets up and says, "Excuse me, I just have to go and have my fix. Do carry on without me." People aren't like that . . . you're certainly not. You don't manage very well at all. And anyway, just remember you told me what you got up to with the street addicts in New York. Remember? Getting water for your fixes from the public urinals . . . remember?'

He had forgotten about that. He forgot everything he didn't like to remember and I think that he would gladly have forgotten about his addiction too, but that was the one thing that, as regularly as the hours passed, tapped him on the shoulder and made him remember.

One of my first projects at *The* Agency had been to prepare a feasibility study on a new product called 'Just Two'. 'Just Two', we soon discovered, had an identity problem, for tests showed that people associated the name with sex aids, romantic holidays and sports cars – all very glamorous, but wide of the mark. The closest anyone came to guessing what the name really represented was a weight-watcher from Solihull, but he couldn't decide whether it was going to be a two-calorie cream dessert or a double portion of pre-cooked TV dinner. He was close, but not that close. 'Just Two' was a new night-time chocolate biscuit, 'hard on the outside, creamy within', designed as a late-night sophisto-snack 'for you to share with someone special'. The 'Just Two' campaign was killed off at the initial research stage and the lyricist adapting Noël Coward's 'Tea for Two' had to bring in his lawyers to extract his full fee. *The* Agency gave each of us a carton of a product which, in marketing terms, had never existed.

Katie wanted to make a cake for tea, but I talked her out of it – we had enough to worry about. Instead we bought one from the patisserie around the corner and filled a few plates with the no longer fresh 'Just Two's. Katie played with some flowers like a well-trained Hollywood starlet, and later, as she flicked a duster across the TV and tape deck, came out with the observation that dust always seems to show up more on black objects.

'You see what you're turning me into,' she complained. 'I'm just not cut out to be a hausfrau.'

We decided we could both do with a drink, so we put away the dusters and vacuum cleaner and poured a few large shots of whisky. I was still in the bathroom, gargling away the smell of alcohol, when the entryphone buzzed.

We stood in the hallway – 'Worse than waiting for a job interview,' Katie decided – and I dried my hands on the back of my black trousers, put a hand on her shoulder; she smiled and kissed me on the neck as we heard footsteps near the top of the stairs.

Mum came in first – 'I changed my mind,' was her only explanation – with Dad just behind her, holding a large box of chocolates. They both kissed Katie, gave me their coats and took deep breaths as they walked into the sitting room. But Alex wasn't there. They looked around the room again, in case they'd missed him when they came in. Then I explained that he couldn't make it.

Dad frowned and Mum muttered, 'No . . . oh no . . . '

'I'm only joking. He's in his room. Sit down and I'll get him.' They stood uncertainly by the small sofa, the only one in the room, and when they sat on it I understood their hesitation, for they filled it beyond comfort.

'What a nice smell,' Mum said, pointing towards a small bunch of freesias on the shelf beside her. Looking around the room she added, 'Bare plaster – how original of you, Katie.'

Katie nodded but said nothing, for she, like Dad, was watching me knock on Alex's door. I went in before he answered. They couldn't see him from where they were sitting, but he had fallen on the bed, his legs hanging off it, his eyes shut, a cigarette smouldering in the ash-tray. Two wrestlers were fighting silently on the television.

'Alex,' I whispered. I made faces at him and pointed towards the sitting room, but he waved me away as though to say, 'I'm not going in there.' I leaned down to whisper in his ear that Mum had come as well, and that if he didn't get out there and say hello, then she'd come and get him. He looked at me in desperation.

'If you do things right,' I said quietly, 'then we'll help you.' I squeezed his shoulder.

He got up and, afraid that they might hear what he wanted to say, took me out on to the balcony.

'Listen.' He was sweating again. 'There are signs they're going to be looking for – like the size of my pupils, the sniffing, and sweating.' He ran the palm of his hand across his forehead. 'I need you to get them off my back if they start, because otherwise I'm just going to walk right out of there.'

'It's all right,' I assured him. 'We'll look after you. But remember, you agreed to our conditions and one of them was that you wouldn't go anywhere without us. So don't even think of walking out, because if you do we'll all come and follow you.'

He grinned at that idea. Smoothing down his hair and rubbing his eyes, he ushered me back into the flat. I was irritated; once again he'd managed to put me firmly on his side of the game, for he knew that I didn't want to be around when Mum and Dad found out he was still taking drugs.

We walked in like a pair of conspirators and even Katie stared at us. Mum and Dad didn't stand up, but they offered Alex their cheeks and he bent down to kiss them. This was obviously something they had thought about before. They looked as though they really wanted to jump up and hug him, but they were cautious – after all, this was the first time they had seen him since he had left their house. But Mum caught him by the cheek when he bent down, shook his head from side to side and said, 'That's my boy.'

'Shall we make tea, then?' Katie suggested.

'It's OK,' Alex said, holding out a hand to stop me getting up. 'I'll do it.' He smiled at me – that confederacy again – and when I looked at Katie she told me to stay and entertain my parents.

I find it strange, as I think back on how Mum and Dad acted then, that I don't remember them talking. Undoubtedly they did talk, and more than most people, but I'm not sure that they ever said what they meant. We had too many conversations like this:

'So how is everything?' I would ask. 'Any news? Anything new . . . ?'

'No,' Dad would reply. 'No news . . . '

' . . . is good news?' Mum would say, by way of a joke.

Silence.

The problem was that for the past few months there had been only one topic of conversation: Alex. Since he was there that day I thought they would avoid talking about him, but as soon as they heard him moving about in the kitchen they both leaned forward, and Dad asked, 'Are you sure he's not on something today?'

I looked surprised, shocked, even, as though the thought hadn't even occurred to me. 'Why, no – what makes you think that?' I asked. 'I thought Simon Blake said he was clean?'

'But have you seen the size of his pupils?' Dad went on.

'No, I can't say I have.' I brushed the whole thing aside, although I felt it was obvious I was lying. I was sure that Dad would have noticed as well, but he appeared not to, or if he did he didn't comment on it. Nor did he refer to the colour that came into my cheeks. However, he did mention that I stank of alcohol and mouthwash.

'As you said before,' I told him, 'if Alex is taking anything, then sooner or later it will show. He can't hide it for ever, whatever it is.' I sat back, to end the conversation, and Mum said, 'What lovely plants.' She looked around the room again.

'Nice, aren't they. Katie takes a lot of care over them.'

'Well, I knew it must be someone else. It couldn't be you – whatever you touched always seemed to die . . . I was just saying,' she repeated when Katie came in with one of the trays, 'what beautiful plants you have.'

Katie balanced the tray, bowed a little and thanked her. 'Actually,' she said, 'they're not as healthy as they look, I'm afraid. That one,' she pointed to a small fig tree in a large terracotta pot, 'isn't at all happy. I don't think it gets enough sunlight in here.'

They talked about potting compost and plant food for a while, until Katie said, 'I'll be "mother", shall I?' and poured the tea. Alex took the cups from her and, with precise movements, passed them round. 'Thank you,' Mum said and congratulated him on not spilling any.

'Or was it you who always spilled everything?' she asked me. 'I really can't remember now.'

'I don't know – I think so – maybe it was,' I said, hoping she would leave Alex alone.

'Have you found a job yet?' Dad asked Katie. She almost dropped the teapot.

'I really haven't been looking much. I don't seem to have the time,' she lied, not wishing to discuss the difficulty she was having finding work.

'Too much fun, eh?' he joked, giving her his paternal smile. He would have nudged her if they had been closer. 'It won't do, you know.'

'Mmm, I'm just having a ball.'

'Well,' I explained, 'with so many people unemployed, if Katie really has no burning desire to get back to work, then she's doing the government a favour by staying away.'

'So you're not claiming social security?' Dad asked.

Katie, embarrassed by the question, pulled the tray with the cake and plates on it nearer to her. 'Uh, no . . . I'm not. Would you like some cake?' she asked Mum.

'Yes, please. Just a little though.'

Dad looked around the room and frowned. I could tell from the way his lips were moving that he was calculating how much it would cost to run the flat – mortgage, service charges, electricity and gas bills. He arrived at a figure, wiped the frown from his face and sat back again.

'Oh yes,' he said quickly, 'I knew you were going to ask
. . . I'd love some . . . ' He sat forward to watch Katie move
the knife across the cake, measuring up the next slice. 'Just
a little more – do you have enough there? Yes, yes, that's
perfect, thank you.'

He wedged himself back into the sofa and took a mouthful. When he'd swallowed it, he murmured his approval
and said, 'So how do you manage, then?'

Katie blushed. 'Sorry?'

'How do you manage to live, and run the flat, if you're
not working?'

Mum and I looked angrily at him, but he sat there with
the figure and a piece of cake resting on his lips.

'How bloody rude,' Alex said, too loudly. It was the first
time he'd spoken for a while and we were all surprised.
Dad was embarrassed now and said, 'I'm sorry. I didn't
mean to pry, but I was just wondering . . . ' He was hoping
that Katie would tell him without his having to ask her
again, but I knew she wouldn't.

'Damn,' Alex said, again too loudly. He was sitting
cross-legged on the floor, staring at a wedge of the straw-
berry cake, which had slipped off his plate and landed
upright on the carpet. He seemed transfixed by it.

'Ah, that's right,' Mum laughed, watching the cream cut
a trail down Alex's trouser leg, 'it was you who always
spilled things. Of course – how silly of me to forget. Do
you remember that Christmas?' she asked, turning to Dad.
'I think he was quite small then – although he's always
been clumsy, now I come to think of it,' she told Katie.
'Yes, that year we worked out that he'd managed to spill
something from each course on the tablecloth. I remember
getting a letter from the laundry explaining that they'd
have to keep the cloth a little longer because they were
having trouble cleaning it, and could we give them any
clues as to what was spilt. Clues? I just read out the
menu . . . '

Alex obviously wasn't sure what to do about the cream
and cake. He was beginning to panic, so I fetched a cloth,
moved him back out of the way and cleaned the carpet and
his trouser leg.

He was even more restrained after that and hardly

allowed himself to move, except to flick the ash from the numerous cigarettes he smoked. Mum tutted each time he missed the ash-tray. 'My boys,' she said fondly, 'what can you do with them, eh?'

'I've often wondered,' Katie agreed.

'But you've been doing so much for them,' Mum told her earnestly. She had been waiting for this moment. 'There's something myself and Dad here, we want to say. Because don't think we don't know how things have been for you here . . . ' Suddenly, in the middle of her sentence, Mum grimaced in a way that I had never seen before, as though something she had just eaten had violently disagreed with her digestion. But there was nothing physically wrong with her. She seemed to be struggling in order to find the words that would say what she truly meant. She said again, seriously, 'We know it has been hard on all of you, hardest on you, Katie – don't think we don't know . . . '

'What your mother is trying to say,' Dad interrupted, patting Mum on the knee, 'what we both want you to know is that you are the most important people in the world to us – there isn't anything we wouldn't do for you. You know that.' He looked to Mum for confirmation. 'It's not easy to put this into words . . . but we thought we had lost you, all of you, and it makes us both happy to know that we, well, that we haven't, that we can all sit here and have tea together.'

We were silent, waiting for something more to be said. I was reminded of what Eveline had told me about Alex – that she sensed something trying to come out of him; 'something that will be important,' she had said. We waited for it then, either from Alex, or from Mum and Dad.

'Would anyone like some more cake?' Katie asked. 'Or some "Just Two"s? No one's touched the "Just Two"s.'

Alex jumped up and offered them around.

When he came to Mum she moved her head back a few inches, as though she was having difficulty focusing on him. Unable to believe that her son was offering to help, she seemed about to say, 'But you only do something if you're nagged into it.' But all she did say was, 'No, thank you. It was lovely cake, though. Did you make it yourself, Katie?'

The cake, a perfect circle, had been decorated with precisely matched strawberries, which had been built up into an apex. Now that it had been cut open, the innards of sponge, cut strawberries and cream spilled out on to the plate. Katie looked at it and laughed.

Mum was a little startled and said, 'In my family, we – ' but Katie stopped the instant Mum began and said, 'Er, no . . . Obviously the fame of my kitchen has spread far and wide, but I'm afraid my cooking isn't that good. Alternatively,' she mocked, 'I could lie a little and tell you that it was just a little something I threw together before you came. Which would you prefer?'

Mum was too surprised to speak but Dad laughed at both of them and held out his plate. 'I don't mind which is true so long as I can have some more.'

Alex watched Katie cut a large slice for Dad and sighed. I frowned at him, as a parent will when he wants a child to be on his best behaviour and would rather not have to shout at him in company. Alex settled back and lit another cigarette. He wiped the sweat off his forehead with the paper napkin he'd been given with his cake, stood up and, taking the teapot from the tray, said 'I'll just go and make some more.'

When he'd gone, Dad walked out on to the balcony and called to me.

'You must be with him when Alex comes to the house,' he said bluntly. 'We don't want to have him there without you.'

He saw the look on my face and a note of pleading came into his voice. 'Well, you see, we love him, but we can't trust him just like that. Not after what he did to us.'

'But it's OK for him to be here, looked after by someone else, is it? For him to steal someone else's things? Just so long as they're not yours, eh?'

'Well,' he replied slowly, 'we did warn you not to help him.'

I couldn't listen to him any more so I went into the flat, even though he was calling me back. In the sitting room Katie was cutting stems off a couple of carnations to give to Mum and Dad. When she had wrapped a strip of ribbon around each flower she held them out to them.

'Why, thank you,' Mum replied in her most childish voice; she even curtsied. Dad took the flower and kissed her. 'Be happy,' he told her.

Katie and I stood on the balcony and watched them walk down into the street. They held hands and had a spring in their step as though they really were happy. And why shouldn't they be? As they got into the Mercedes they noticed us waving to them and gave us big, broad smiles. I put an arm around Katie's shoulder and we continued waving until they were out of sight, as though we didn't know when, or if, we would ever see them again.

There is something about the closing of a door that older people fear, irrationally, as though they might never again see what's on the other side. Each thing they end must seem like one more step towards the grave. Young people have a similar fear, but theirs is of this world. They close doors on childhood and youth reluctantly; sometimes they are afraid of growing up and away from the comforting protection of their parents. Each step they take brings them nearer to independence and responsibility.

The front door was open when we came in from the balcony, and I closed it on Mum and Dad and all they stood for, because Alex, by coming to us, needed a new game to play, not one in which there were parents like ours who searched for words to express things they had never tried to say before, but who found only, 'I told you so.' With them, for Alex, the game was already lost.

But by closing the door on them, I was also shutting us in.

Katie and Alex were on the floor in the sitting room, drinking more tea and smoking.

'Would you like some tea, darling?' Katie asked.

I settled on the sofa, rearranged the cushions and draped my feet over the end. 'Yes, I'd love some.'

When I said, 'Well, thank God that's over,' Alex looked at me in surprise, but his eyes didn't quite focus on me and he might have been seeing more than was actually there.

'Yes,' he said, with precise enunciation. The word seemed strange the way he said it. 'What's wrong?' he asked.

I remembered his drug-paranoia in the park and said, 'Oh, nothing – well, it wasn't too difficult, now was it.'

'That depends.'

'Just remember, you got yourself into it. If you'd kept on taking it for one more day without telling us, you would've come to tea and no one would have been the wiser.'

'But it is different . . . you do know.' He wanted to expose his newly confessed addiction in front of me then. He began to taunt me as he had taunted Dad, because he needed to find out how far he could go with me. I was determined that whatever happened I wasn't going to get angry; however well he played, I wouldn't fall for it.

So I watched. He paraded his addiction in front of me by rolling up his sleeves and scratching at the needle marks, but I only pretended to look, peering out of almost closed eyelids so that everything was distorted. It didn't bother me so much then.

Katie was different. She watched him and said, 'Listen, if you want to kill yourself, then that's fine. It's up to you. But if you don't, then you've got to do something about your addiction. Because if' – she stressed the 'if' – 'you don't do it now, then you are going to die.' She said it without emotion, in a matter-of-fact sort of way, and he shrugged his shoulders and replied with equal indifference, 'I know.'

We were with him all the time that weekend, because we were worried that if we gave him the chance he'd probably disappear for the evening or the night. Maybe he'd take the heroin with him and use it all. Maybe he'd leave it behind and go in search of something else. But I was sure that if we let him he would test us and discover how much we were prepared to put ourselves out for our roles in this new game.

Unlike Mum and Dad we kept on saying, 'It's nothing to us if you want to kill yourself.' But any fool could see it wasn't true, because we loved him and hated what he was doing to himself.

At about eight o'clock that evening – we were planning a late dinner – Alex decided to have a bath. 'If that's all right with you two,' he said sharply.

'Of course,' Katie reassured him. 'You've never had to ask before.'

But I knew he didn't just want a bath. 'So is it time then?'

'Time for what?' He didn't look at me.

'You know . . . ' I said awkwardly – he still didn't look at me – 'for your fix.'

He was embarrassed; I don't think he expected me to ask him straight out.

'Yes,' he admitted, deflated.

'How much do you take each time?'

'It's none of your fucking business,' he shouted.

'How often do you need it? Have you increased the dose over the past weeks? Have you just been taking heroin, or have you been using cocaine or opium as well?' There were more questions I wanted to ask him, but I didn't expect him to answer any of them. I was asking because I knew it would annoy him and I wanted to see how far I could push him before he ran away.

When he had gone into the bathroom, Katie said, 'You're too hard on him. Don't confront him like that all the time. Relax, give him room. Here,' she said playfully, pushing me back on to the floor, 'what you need is some softening up.'

She turned me over on to my stomach and, straddling me, ran her hands through my hair and over my back. A month or two before, I had longed for her to do this.

'What have I done to deserve you?'

'What has Alex done to deserve you?'

She slipped off my shirt and began massaging my back. As she eased the tendons in my shoulders I thought of how much Alex and his addiction had taken us over and changed our lives. We hardly saw our friends any more, because when we did we only thought of Alex; we were apart from the family; we no longer had the money to think of going away; and Italy was only a dream again. We were becoming as estranged from everyone as Alex.

While Katie, with her cool hands, was kneeling on top of me I realized that it made no difference to me whether it was her or someone else massaging my back. I wanted it done, now that she had started, but that was all. To her it was something caring and full of feeling, not merely a physical act. But with Alex on my mind there was no room for anything else, and even though I made appreciative noises, there was nothing personal in it for me.

I said nothing about this to Katie. When she finished I lay on the floor, silent and still thinking, while she stretched out beside me and stroked my hair. 'So serious,' she murmured, 'and so far away.' I think it was the first time that something like that had come between us. I tried not to look at her when she took her hand away, but playfully she climbed over me and looked into my eyes. What she saw there made her back away. She went into the kitchen.

'He's been in there a long time,' I said when I followed her, pointing to the bathroom. It was ridiculous for us to be making small talk. 'I hope he's all right.'

I had never thought of Alex overdosing before, but now that he was taking heroin with our knowledge – using the heroin we had paid for – the idea that he might overdose frightened me so much that I was unable to stand the silence from the bathroom. I could picture him dead on the floor.

'What do you want him to do, sing?' Katie asked. 'He's been doing it for years without our help and nothing happened to him before. Just because we know what he's up to in there doesn't change anything for him. Now,' she suggested, 'what we need is a drink.'

'I'll get it,' I said quickly, 'you sit down.' I wanted to make up for not having hidden my thoughts from her earlier; she didn't deserve them.

I took bottles of gin and Italian vermouth, and a cocktail shaker, out of the cupboard. 'I'll make you a special drink,' I told her. She looked so happy that I felt even sadder about my thoughts.

'This drink,' I explained as I measured two large parts of gin to one of vermouth and poured them into the chrome shaker, 'was reported by Robert Vermeire, the head barman of the American Bar at the Casino Municipal in Nice during the thirties. But he didn't invent it himself – "Charlie", the barman at the New York Racket Club, created it for a millionaire called Henry Payne Whitney.' I took a knife and sliced an orange. 'But Charlie's cocktail – the H.P.W. as it was known – had only half as much gin and twice as much vermouth. It was our man Robert – '

'Who?'

'Robert – Vermeire – the barman in Nice.' I lifted the shaker to the level of my right ear. 'It was Robert who changed the balance and created an altogether superior and more dynamic drink . . . There,' I said, pouring her a glass through the cocktail strainer, 'get your lips round that.'

Katie put her nose to it first, sniffed, swirled it around in the glass and then took a sip. 'Christ,' she spluttered, 'what the hell did he call this one then?'

'A "Velocity" – it works quickly and always hits the mark.'

We drank a whole shakerful, and then I tottered back into the kitchen to make us another one.

When Alex came out of the bathroom he said, 'Well, look at you two,' and laughed. We laughed back.

'And what have you two been up to while I was away?'

'Drinking,' Katie slurred.

'Well, we'll have none of that.' He wagged a finger at us. 'You two are going to end up alcoholics if you keep on like this.'

He went into his bedroom for a few minutes, and when he came out he sniffed loudly and asked, 'So where's dinner?'

'We were waiting for you,' Katie explained.

'Well, I'm here now . . . '

'So you can get on and make it.'

Alex looked uncertain. 'Are you sure?' He had never before cooked in the flat.

'If you want to make it, then please don't let me stop you,' she suggested, mockingly polite. 'The chef's off tonight.'

Alex rolled up his sleeves and approached the kitchen like a tracker in the bush. 'I'll make spaghetti,' he decided.

It wasn't until after dinner, when I had sobered up a little, that I asked him when he would start to feel the pain.

'I'll be in a bad way by Wednesday.' He looked at me as though he thought that would make me happy.

'You have been through this before, though?' Katie asked anxiously. 'When you did the methadone cure in the States?'

112

'That was different. That was something I had to do –
circumstances forced me. And methadone is an easy way
to come off. You don't really feel like you've done anything.' I thought back to the night on Westminster Bridge
when Alex had told me about his attraction to pain. 'I just
substituted one drug for another, and then it was hard to
come off the methadone. But it wasn't that hard . . . And
the symptoms I had afterwards were from the heroin, not
the methadone. But by then I'd been off heroin for some
time. Do you see how it works?' he asked urgently, as
though it was essential for him to be seen to be serious.

'Yes, yes,' Katie said dismissively. 'But what's going to
make it different this time?'

Alex looked worried. 'It'll be different because it's just
me this time. It's a test of character. They say there are two
things essential for this to work – '

'Who are "they"?' I asked.

'Other addicts I've spoken to. First, you have to want to
give up. And then you've got to feel the pain of it, so that
you know you've purged yourself. And that,' he said, 'is
what's going to happen this week . . . with your help,' he
added.

'I want one of us to be with you all the time,' I told him.
'There are bound to be times when you feel like giving in,
so I don't want you locking doors or shutting yourself up in
your bedroom.'

'But Katie's not going to want to sit with me all the time –
and I might not want her there, either.' He said this with a
smile. 'Well, not all the time, anyway.'

'But I'll be here as well. My director suggested that I take
time off work,' I told him, 'so we'll start by taking you to
the psychiatrist's tomorrow.'

'Oh,' he said, his smile fading. 'I don't want you to do
that . . . '

'So please,' I said, ignoring his reservations, 'if you're
not serious, then don't waste our time.'

'Listen, you know me – I can do this if I set my mind to
it. There's nothing I haven't been able to do when I've
really wanted to. This is my last chance; I know that and
I've got to do it now. It's OK for the other addicts I know –
they can afford private clinics and buy their way out of

113

trouble. I can't, and I'll be a loser if I keep on . . . I know this is my last chance. But I also know that I'm luckier than them.' He looked from Katie to me, and flushed. 'Because I might not have money, but I've got you two, who'll give me a real chance to get it right. You care, and you don't get that when you're paying for it. Those people can never buy what you're giving me.'

There were other things I wanted to ask him, but it didn't seem right after that. They were only details, after all, and I thought I could wait to find out the answers.

Alex never used the phrase, 'cold turkey'. Instead he talked about lying down for a week or two, about sweating it out and going through with it. He almost convinced me that there was no need for me to take the time off work. It wasn't until he went to bed that the spell he had cast was broken and we realized we were holding something other than a charm.

When we went to bed we didn't make love. Instead we lay side by side and Katie told me a story, about how she had lost her virginity.

'I was on a train from Delhi to Calcutta, one of those old trains with proper beds and room service. I was fourteen then, on school holidays, travelling out with some old family connections, the Scotts – we were going to meet up with my parents in Calcutta. God, I was excited then. It was my first time in India and the smells and crowds and colours really got to me. It was such a relief after being cooped up in school all year. It was July, and incredibly hot. We were joined at our table in the dining car by a young Indian called Rupert – not a very traditional name, I grant you. He was handsome, polite and well-spoken, and had just finished his first year of PPE at Oxford and was going home for the holidays as well. That gave us something to talk about. It was so hot that night, I remember, that I was allowed a whisky and soda. Mr Scott said it was good for the circulation or something. I don't know what it did for my blood, but it certainly loosened my tongue: I was usually quiet and shy as a girl, but I flirted with Rupert all through dinner. I thought he was wonderful, a real knight in armour, and so suave. He talked about riding over his family's estates . . . I was angling for an invitation to visit them, but he didn't take the hint. My behaviour didn't go unnoticed by Mrs Scott, though, and she insisted that we went straight back to our compartment after dinner . . . I've never liked sleeping on trains and that one was hot. It rocked a lot too. Mrs Scott was snoring, so I crept out into the empty corridor to watch the villages and fields. Then I turned around and saw Rupert. I remember breaking out into a sweat as soon as I saw him − I was wet all over. I don't remember what he said to me − something trite probably − but the whole thing was like a dream, a movie. He put his arm around my shoulder, turned me to him, kissed me and led me off to the toilet. I knew I should have said no, or pushed him off, but how could I? I'd talked so often about something like this with my girlfriends at school. But I remember crying because the dream bit was shattered − and because he hurt me. I looked around for the moonlight, listened for the music, but all I could see was Rupert's face screwed up in front of me and a cockroach climbing the wall behind him. It stank in there, too, and we were out of time with the motion of the train. I don't know why, but that bothered me. And it was over so quickly − in and out − probably the closest I'll ever get to a zipless fuck. I really couldn't work out what Erica Jong was making such a fuss about . . .

'. . . anyway, the reason I'm telling you all this is that I was reminded of it earlier, when we were talking about Alex and how different it is, now that we know he's shooting up in the bathroom − and I said that it won't have changed anything for him. After Rupert I began to have a more or less satisfactory sex life with a boy I'd been seeing from a nearby school, until my mother found out. Maybe I even told her, I can't remember. Suddenly it was a problem for her. I'd been doing fine, taking all the necessary precautions, so there was nothing to worry about there − my mother knowing didn't change anything for me. It certainly didn't stop me, anyway. But the knowledge of what I was doing changed her. Suddenly she seemed older. She had thought of herself as a young person, but then she found out that not only could I have sex, not only would I if I was given the chance − she'd worked that one out for herself − but that I had been doing it for a while. If she hadn't known I reckon she would've still thought of herself as a young mother with a young daughter. When she started seeing me as a young woman, able to do the things she did, she had to move on as well. Suddenly she saw that she had become old . . . '

'But that must happen to every parent,' I told her.

'Yes,' she agreed. 'But the point is, that listening to you worrying about Alex reminded me of your father.'

I picked up Alex from Simon Blake's just after six o'clock that Monday evening. The surgery wasn't exactly on Harley Street, but tucked away around the corner, down a side-street. Alex was waiting in the lobby, which looked more like a small, chic hotel than a medical establishment. He seemed a changed person to me: the drug inside him hadn't worn off, for he'd made sure that he was 'well stoked', as he put it, when he went to see Simon Blake, but now that I knew he had taken the last of it, he seemed different to me.

'Well,' he said as he slipped into the split-leather bucket seat, 'that went well.'

'What happened?' I asked, hoping he would tell me what he had said to Simon Blake.

All weekend he had resented my wanting to know exactly what he was doing. On Saturday he had answered my questions quickly and quietly, just to get them out of the way. By Sunday he had gone silent. Now he said, 'Just leave me alone, will you?'

But I needed to know what was going on. I turned round in my seat to face him, hoping that he would tell me something, but all he offered was a cigarette from his packet.

It was dark and the traffic was heavy as we drove west through London. It began to rain, and the noise of water on the canvas roof covered our silence. The rain became heavier, and the old windscreen wipers failed to clear it. The traffic slowed so much that we were surrounded by the red of brake lights, blurred across the windscreen. Inside, the windows misted over with condensation, and then the big Healey decided to stall.

'Bugger,' I shouted, slamming my hand down on the

steering wheel. 'Just work, will you?' It didn't, so I checked the petrol gauge, but there was enough in the tank to get us to Brighton and back. I tried the ignition again and again, but each time the engine failed to fire. By the time I stopped I had flooded it as well, so we sat and waited for the petrol to clear before I tried it again.

'Fucking car,' I hissed, as the traffic began to move around us. A man in a Ford Fiesta pulled up alongside and suggested that we push the Healey out of the way.

'Want to swap cars?' I asked, but he drove off. 'What I'd give for a Ford right now . . . '

'Why don't you two go out for the evening?' Alex suggested when we got home. 'Go on,' he said easily. 'Just the two of you. Have some fun. You both look a bit uptight tonight.'

Katie laughed at him. 'What, and leave you here all on your own? Or do you have your own plans for the evening?'

Alex shrugged his shoulders and said, 'Well, it was only an idea . . . '

After we had eaten, we switched on the television and talked over it because there was nothing we wanted to watch; we hated bad dramas as much as we loved old movies. I turned the sound down and put on some jazz – Charlie Parker on Dial, but Alex said he couldn't listen to it, so I played some classical music – anything would have done, so long as there was always something to look at or listen to apart from Alex sitting straight-faced and upright in the armchair, smoking, drinking orange juice, his face drained white. When he finally relaxed, his eyelids fluttered and closed, opened, fluttered some more and then closed again. His hand, holding a cigarette, sank quite gracefully and stopped several inches from the carpet. We watched it in case it went any further. His body was still upright in the chair, but then his head began to move down towards his chest, and after that he began to fold in the middle, his head now on course to touch his feet. Just as he was about to slide off the chair, his head jerked back into its upright position and his balance was maintained. Then it began all over again.

Katie was sitting on the floor not far from him, laughing without any sound coming from her mouth, just the facial gestures and her own head moving up and down. Then suddenly it wasn't funny any more. This wasn't someone falling asleep in his chair after dinner, but Alex beginning to run down.

The next time he nodded off his head jerked back so violently that he woke himself up.

'What was I saying?' he asked Katie, confused.

'What were you saying when?'

'Just then,' he said, irritated that she hadn't been listening to him.

'You've been asleep for a few minutes,' she told him.

'I was just talking to you.' He was angry. 'I was just talking and then I forgot.'

'That's because you were asleep,' I explained.

His face went blank for a moment. He stood up, still annoyed, and went into his room. When he came out a few minutes later, he sat down, scratched his head and laughed. 'I do seem to be forgetting things – can't remember why I went in there.'

'To go to bed?' I suggested.

'What sort of state is your room in?' Katie asked him. 'If you're going to be in there for the next few days, maybe we ought to clear it out?'

'I can't be bothered,' he said wearily. 'It'll do.'

Katie disapproved, but decided not to push it. She walked over to the window and looked out at the rain, still so heavy that the roads shone, people hurried along the pavement and cars drove slowly by. 'Well, at least it's getting my flower-boxes watered,' she said absently. She shivered.

'Are you cold?' I asked, going to stand behind her, putting my arms around her, pulling her back on to me.

'No,' she said firmly, wriggling away, 'I'm OK.' Her voice was hard and remote. She smiled at Alex as she turned around and then sat down in front of the television. 'Do you want to turn that noise off?' she said, nodding towards the tape deck.

'Don't worry,' Alex said. 'In a couple of days it'll all start happening and then you'll wish you'd never got into this.'

'I do already,' Katie muttered.

'Have you got anything left?' I asked him.

He looked at me as though I was stupid even to bother asking. Proudly, he said, 'Nope – it's all gone.'

'Hundred and sixty quid,' Katie muttered, still watching the TV.

'Any syringes left?'

'A couple,' he said evasively, and Katie turned round.

'I'd like whatever you've got,' I told him, thinking I sounded too much like Dad now and trying to change the tone of my voice. 'Is there a spoon?'

'Listen, I'll give it all to you later. OK?' he said conclusively. I nodded. 'Well, I'm going into the bathroom,' he said, and, seeing the look on my face, added, 'to have a bath.'

'Oh yeah?'

He opened his washbag for me. 'See, I'm telling you the truth. I want to give up. I'm going to. I've got to . . .'

When he'd gone Katie suggested that we search his room. 'I didn't like the way he was answering your questions about the syringes and things.' We waited until we heard him turn off the taps and lie back in the bath.

We hadn't been into his room for a couple of days. Clothes and papers were scattered all over the floor; the palm was dying, still as tall as before, but now brown and shrivelled, with more of its burned leaves on the floor. Balls of dust rolled across the carpet and collected along the skirting boards; a plate of congealed egg, with half a slice of cold toast, had been pushed under the bedside table. There were new stains on the carpet – tea or coffee or something. I shook my head at Katie. 'Don't be upset now.'

We searched through his cases and drawers, listening all the time for sounds from the bathroom. I knew when Katie had found something, because she took in a deep breath. Her eyes opened wider. She was leaning over a suitcase, a burnt spoon, which he had wrapped up in a couple of tissues, in her hand.

'Here,' I said, taking it from her and moving her out of the way, 'I'll do it.' I searched through the case, hoping I wouldn't find any drugs, feeling between the clothes and running my hand along the edge of the lining.

119

'Shit,' I swore quietly, pulling my right hand away. An old needle was sticking into my little finger. 'Quick, Katie – quick – get it out.'

She took hold of my hand and jerked the needle free. An orb of blood appeared over the hole. 'Oh God,' I moaned, not in pain but in fear. We put the needle and spoon back into the case and ran into our bedroom.

We had never talked about AIDS. We had never wanted to think about it, and since we hadn't used a condom the first time we made love there didn't seem to be much point in starting to use one later. The only reference Alex had ever made to it was that his HIV test in the States had been negative. But what about since then? Who had he been mixing with in London? Who else might have used his needles? I sucked violently at the prick in my finger, like a B-movie actor bitten by a snake. I spat out the blood into a glass of water.

Katie touched my forehead with her fingertips. Her hands were shaking and she was white around the corners of her mouth. We held each other, not like lovers or even friends, but as two scared people.

Alex knocked on our door when he came out of the bathroom. He put his head around the door. 'You can use the bathroom now if you want to.' We didn't even look at him and he went away after a moment.

When we went back into the sitting room, he was stretched out on the sofa in a black tracksuit, his hair still wet, tissue paper stuck to his chin showing thin beads of blood from a shaving cut. He smiled and pointed to the worktop in the kitchen where he had left the needles, syringes and spoon.

'Thank you,' I said, sounding like Dad again. I picked them up, if only for the sake of moving them, to emphasize that they were no longer his; I didn't really know what to do with them, though. My own hand shook as I put them up on a shelf, noticing as I did so that the spoon was hallmarked silver. How typical of Alex to indulge himself – the most expensive heroin on a silver spoon.

'Right,' he said, 'I'm going to bed – roll on tomorrow.'

'See you in the morning,' I answered quietly.

'If I'm up by then – ' but then he remembered that I

wasn't going to work and said, 'Oh yes, I'll be seeing you, kid.' He smiled, not sure what to do next, then bent down and kissed Katie near her lips. 'Thank you,' he whispered, and went into his room. Katie stared after him for a few moments before shrugging her shoulders. 'I really don't understand that guy.'

'I don't think he does, either,' I said as I went to get the syringes down off the shelf and placed them on the floor beside her. She poked them with her fingernail, as though they were hot, turning them over and over again. The spoon was burnt black on the bottom, but was sparkling clean inside the bowl. It upset us to see them again, to touch them. After a while we left them alone and I put them away in the back of one of the drawers.

When we went to bed we lay in the dark with the sound of rain falling on the balcony and splashing back on to the window – always that noise. I could picture the spoon and syringes in front of me and at last I was able to imagine what it must have been like on the other side of the bathroom door, with Alex lying on the large white towel, the headphones playing something soft and gentle, perhaps a track that made him think of his wife – a cigarette smouldering in the ash-tray on the side of the bath, a cup of tea beside it – Alex burning white powder in the silver spoon and mixing it with water in the syringe – caressing his arm, bringing the blood up to it so that the veins stood out proud above the muscle – then fingering the plunger of the syringe, running a finger over its length, touching its head and slowly pushing it down until the air had been expelled and a drop or two of the milky liquid squirted out on to his hand. And then in, gently and firmly through the flesh into the little tunnel. Right in, the liquid, still warm to feel, jetting out, perfectly soothing, all absorbing.

For an instant: images of women, of his wife. Then, images of nothing. The liquid courses around his veins and he sees, feels, thinks of nothing but the blood in his body. He can feel it most strongly in his temples and his groin. Has he reduced himself to this? A brain and a penis? He's lying on the floor, on the white towel, embraced by a perfect black nothingness, the blood still rushing.

121

Later, above the rhythm of his heartbeat, the sound of music comes through the headphones to him again. This brings him back a little and he struggles to get to his feet. He is surprised that time has passed – the bath is cold, the tea is cold, the cigarette has burned out. It doesn't matter.

Katie reached out in the darkness and touched me, but instead of touching her, I shuddered. I had put sex and drugs together and was unable to separate them straight away. I lay absolutely still, my heart racing, hoping that she wouldn't touch me again, praying that she would leave me alone – I wanted to be alone because there was nothing that I could do with her then.

'Katie,' I whispered as her hand teased along the inside of my thigh. 'Katie, I think we should be more careful.'

'We're doing all we can for him,' she said.

'Not for him – for us. That needle thing has worried me. I think we should start using a condom . . . It's not worth taking the risk. Is it? It's just not worth it.'

'Where are they?'

'I haven't got any,' I told her.

'Oh.'

'But I'll get some tomorrow.'

'OK,' she agreed. 'But hold me now, just hold me.'

I reached out and put my arms around her. The rain had stopped and it had become very quiet, but like a deaf man I could still hear the sound of rushing water. Katie rolled over on to her back, her right hand resting at the top of my thigh, just near my penis. To move it, I leaned across and kissed her on the lips. 'Good night.'

I didn't know if she believed that I didn't have any condoms, but she would have seen that I had rejected her again. She understood rejection. She probably didn't know why – maybe she thought it was something to do with her, that she didn't turn me on any more. If she did, then she had it all wrong. But how could I tell her? How could I talk to her about the things I had just seen and thought when I wanted to forget them? How could I explain to her that I had got sex and drugs all mixed up, when I didn't understand myself how it had come about?

I lay in the darkness beside the girl I could no longer touch, in silence apart from the rushing noise in my head.

It began to fade a little. She was a warm body beside mine – the fulfilment of the dream I had shared with my drinking friends, an end to my lonely nights, bringer of fine days. When she turned her back on me I moulded myself into her shape, holding her now, safe behind her back. I kissed her softly in her soap-scented hair, on her scent-smelling neck, and whispered, 'I'm sorry. I'm so sorry,' but I don't know if she heard, or, if she did, whether she understood. Then it didn't matter any more, because we were both asleep.

Katie and I were practical about preparing for Alex's cure. We spent a fortune in the supermarket, took a crate of bottles out of the off-licence and had everything we could carry washed down at the launderette. Then I cleaned the flat while Katie did the ironing and filled shelves and the mantelpiece with vases of flowers. By the time we had finished the place was as clean and well-ordered as a hospital ward – all except for Alex's room.

Heroin was an appropriate drug for Alex to choose to take. He had wanted to hide himself; heroin cut off the sensations he would normally have experienced and acted as a buffer between his nerve endings and his receptive, interpretive brain. He no longer acknowledged the world around him, and had lived in what was practically a senseless limbo. But as the drug began to wear off he once again recognized his own painful feelings. He said he wanted to be alone, and lay on his bed watching an old Western on the black and white television, listening to a tape on his Walkman. He ignored the accumulated dirt which blew around him; the skeleton of the palm which leaned over him seemed not at all out of place. When Katie went in with a vase of yellow freesias he waved her away. 'It's not a fucking funeral parlour, you know.'

He didn't want to talk to us, so we left him alone. He walked through to the kitchen when he was hungry and asked what there was to eat, or made himself something to drink, but that was all. He was still wearing the tracksuit, a little crumpled now after he'd slept the night in it. I suppose we pretended that we had made the flat a nicer place for him to be in, but I think we really did it for ourselves. We needed to do something while we waited for him to start feeling sick and dizzy. We removed all the sharp knives from the kitchen, all the razors and blades from the bathroom, any drugs and pills that he might have wanted to take if he got desperate. We were ready and it was just a matter of time before he began to suffer, time which passed slowly, the details of which I remember precisely:

Monday, 7.30 p.m.: Alex came out of his room for something to eat, a brown V-neck sweater over his tracksuit, a pair of woollen socks on his feet. With the central heating on, it wasn't cold in the flat, but he was shivering.

'Why don't you sit by the radiator if you're cold?' I suggested. He went and huddled on the floor in front of it, a plate with a chicken salad sandwich perched on his knees.

He tried several times to bite into the sandwich, but each time he pulled away and quickly drank some water. In the end he gave up and went back to bed.

10.30 p.m.: He limped into the sitting room and asked if he could have a jug of water, or some orange squash. He was sweating, but looked pale rather than flushed. Katie made it for him while I helped him back to bed. He leaned heavily on me, and it was with difficulty that I pushed back the duvet and put him under it.

Tuesday, 10.00 a.m.: Alex looked ill. Feeling sorry for himself, he lay quietly on his bed, as he had done the previous day, but he was clearly weaker. When I went into his room he looked at me without moving his head – only his eyes followed me. He reminded me of a beaten dog.

'What would you like for breakfast?' I asked. He looked down at his hands folded over the top of the duvet and said he would just like a cup of tea.

'I don't think I could manage anything else. I'd throw it up. My guts are churning at the moment.' His eyes turned a full circle in his head before settling listlessly on the wall. When I brought him his tea, he saw it as it passed in front of his line of vision, but again he didn't turn. He was like an old man – one no longer able to put up his head and smile,

124

who sits staring ahead and then adjusts himself gradually towards the cup which he knows will have been put down on the bedside table, because it is always left there for him.

2.30 p.m.: He still hadn't managed to eat anything and he was sick. At least, it sounded as though he was being sick, and he told me later that he had been, but I didn't actually see it for myself. He was still sweating and shivering, as though he had a bad fever, but now the pain was coming on as well. He rocked slowly back and forwards on the bed as though it hurt too much for him to sit or lie still. In that position, he looked as though he might be praying.

It made me feel sick to see him like that. He seemed to be in so much pain, and I was saddened by the doubts that still came into my head, that maybe he wasn't telling the whole truth. It frightened me to think that maybe he was going to such elaborate lengths to persuade us that he was in pain, that it might all be part of an elaborate pantomime, one which we had mistaken for the real thing. We watched him more closely.

9.30 p.m.: He lay on his bed with the door open, a plastic bucket beside him, a jug, and some extra blankets. There was nothing more we could do for him. During the night he staggered out on his way to the bathroom. He wasn't finding it very easy to stand upright and that added to the impression of sickness. His face, painfully thin, had lost the last of its own colour and now showed reflections of the black sweatshirt, which he was still wearing.

Wednesday, 9.30 a.m.: The telephone rang and a pukka voice, hard-nosed and arrogant, asked to speak to Alex. 'This is Simon Blake.'

'Oh, hi,' I said. 'Yes, I know exactly who you are.'

He was surprised by my enthusiasm. 'Could I speak to your brother?' he asked.

'I thought you'd gone away . . . ?'

'Yes, I was supposed to. But I have been obliged to alter my travelling arrangements. I will be in town for another two days and thought I should see Alexander again. Is he there?'

125

'Oh yes,' I told him. 'Yes, he is. I'll just get him for you.'

'Before you go,' he said, 'how is he? You see, it sounds extraordinary, but having convinced your father that the dear boy is not taking drugs, there was something Alexander said on Monday that has made me worry.'

'What was that?'

'Something about having news for me when I returned from holiday. What news? That's what I want to know.'

'I really think you should speak to Alex,' I said, and went into his room.

Alex's face fell at the same time as his body twisted violently on the bed. It wasn't the sort of movement he'd made for a while. His face was contorted with anger and his voice was filled with frustration as he swore. He hid under the duvet and said weakly, 'Tell him I'm too ill . . . yes, tell him I'm too ill to come to the phone.' Then he swore again and said, 'But he's supposed to be away.'

I told Simon Blake that Alex wanted me to tell him that he was too ill to come to the phone.

'What do you mean?'

'That's what he wants you to know,' I repeated. 'That he's ill.'

'Well, is he . . . ?'

'That's what he says.'

'Tell him I must speak to him,' he insisted.

I took the phone into the bedroom. Alex was still hiding his head under the duvet.

'Alex,' I said softly. 'Alex, he really does want to speak to you.'

'Oh, fucking hell. You know I can't talk to him like – '

His head appeared from under the pillow and there was silence for a moment as he saw the phone near his face and realized that Simon Blake would have heard him.

A distant, reedy voice called down the phone, 'Alexander. Alexander. Pick up the telephone.'

I held it out for him. He looked at me, at the phone, and snatched it out of my hand. He kicked the door shut as I went back into the sitting room.

A few minutes later he slammed down the phone, called to me and said, 'Thanks very much. He's not going away till tomorrow and wants to see me today. Why

126

couldn't you have just told him I was ill?' He stared viciously at me.

'Because I'm not going to lie for you any more,' I said firmly. 'I told you that. I've already done things for you that I wish I hadn't – I've agreed to things I shouldn't have – and I've lied to Mum and Dad. Now it's going to stop. At some point, Alex, you've got to stand up and say, "This is what I am. This is the truth." And then you have to tell the whole thing. Not just some of it. We thought you were doing that now. We thought that that was what this was all about . . . '

He stared at me, his face passive now, and sad. 'Will you help me get there?'

The phone rang again; it was Simon Blake.

'I – I want to speak to you.' He was out of breath, his voice uneven. 'Your brother's made me look an utter fool – I have staked my reputation, my whole reputation, on the fact that he is not taking drugs. I have told your father over and over again in terms that have – at times – been plainly abusive, that the boy is not taking anything. And now he tells me that he had been on heroin all along. I – I can't possibly go on seeing him. He has made me look a fool. An absolute fool,' he repeated 'A fool . . . '

'It's OK,' I explained, not quite sure why he was telling me all this, 'don't worry about it. He's done it to everyone else as well.'

'But if you knew about it, why didn't you tell someone?'

'Because unless he tells people himself, then there's really no point in their knowing. It's something he's got to do for himself, isn't it?'

'Yes,' he agreed, 'I suppose so. But you just make sure that he gets here soon.' He hung up on me.

Alex hadn't shaved since Saturday but for some reason his beard had hardly grown. He had brushed his dark, lustreless curls back off his forehead, but his hair was too long at the back and curled unmanageably round his neck.

'I can't go,' he said pathetically. 'Look at me. I don't even know if I'll be able to walk.'

'Then I'll carry you,' I told him. I bent down and lifted him off the bed. 'But first you try and walk,' I suggested.

He flinched as his feet touched the ground, and I picked him up again. There was nothing to him really, I thought, as I held him – little more than some bones in the blanket in which he had wrapped himself. He clutched the bucket as we went, as though he was likely to be sick at any moment, and said nothing to Katie as we went out. I asked him if I was hurting him, but he didn't reply, his head lolling on my shoulder. I put him carefully into the car, strapped the seatbelt around him and positioned his head over the bucket, just in case.

He said nothing on the way to Harley Street, nor when I asked him if he was going to walk into Simon Blake's office, so when we got there I lifted him up again and carried him into the building. Just inside the automatic doors a porter in a white jacket – he too could have belonged to a smart hotel – helped me get Alex into a wheelchair. I turned to go back out to the car straight away. I didn't want to be questioned. Alex smiled at me then, as another two porters, tall, muscle-bound men, wheeled the chair around and pushed him off towards the lift.

I waited for him in the Healey, running my hands around and around the steering wheel. I didn't want the radio on, for I needed space to think, but all I could do was mindlessly count the people who went in and out of the building, some in wheelchairs, others walking. I thought nothing about any of them, nor about Alex, until I saw him come through the automatic doors.

Gone were the white-coated assistants; gone was the padded wheelchair he had been taken away in. He walked carefully, reaching out a hand for the rail as the doors shut behind him; in his other hand was the plastic bucket, looking a little superfluous now.

When he saw me in the car across the road, he waved and hobbled down the steps. By the time he'd reached the bottom one I was out of the car and ready to cross over to help him. He looked so frail, with his stoop and his hair pushed back off his forehead again, the sunlight accentuating the prominent bones in his face. He smiled as he saw me coming, and I wanted to rush across and hug him. But when I did get to him I just stood close to him and held his arm, squeezing it when the road was clear to cross. He found it difficult to walk so I put his arm over my shoulder and we hobbled over together.

'Alex,' I said, 'Alex, it's going to be all right. It has to be.'

In the car he slept, with a smile on his face, and didn't wake until we were back home and I was shaking him.

Alex sat on the sofa with a cup of tea in his hand. He said he was hungry now and asked if he could have some bread or biscuits. When Katie brought him a piece of toast and butter she asked him what had happened.

He started by laughing. 'The poor man wanted to hit me, he was so angry. I admitted to him that I'd been lying all along.' Katie shook her head. 'Well, at least I was being honest with him then,' he insisted.

'Yeah,' she said. 'Go on . . . '

'It appears that Dad had been phoning him every day and sending letters saying that he knew I was taking something and that Simon should do some sort of test on me. Simon, of course, told him to get stuffed – and quite right too,' he said indignantly. 'It's none of his business.'

'Except,' I pointed out, 'that he's worried about you and he's the one who's paying Simon's bills.' Alex had shrugged his shoulders before I'd finished.

'Anyway, Simon had been telling him he was wrong, that he would've known if I was on something, that he was my psychiatrist and we had a special relationship and so on. Apparently he and Dad almost fought over it until Simon agreed – and we had that meeting. But it doesn't say much for his test, though, does it. I was out of my head at the time. But what worried him was my saying I'd have some good news for him when he got back from holiday.' He laughed easily now. 'Imagine the shock he must have had when he phoned and found I was still taking it.'

I didn't say anything, but Katie told him, 'If you ask me, I think you're a bloody idiot. It's got nothing to do with fooling the psychiatrist or your father, your brother or me – or anyone else for that matter – because we can all go to bed at night and forget about you. But you – you've got to remember. You've got to take it. If you ask me, you're only fooling yourself if you get any satisfaction out of that.'

Alex looked at her. His eyebrows shot up and down a couple of times; he squeezed his lips together. 'But it's all over,' he said, and went back to bed.

This is how it ended:

Alex stayed in bed for the rest of the day. He was fast asleep each time I looked in on him and he didn't get up until after eleven the following morning.

'I feel great,' he said as he burst in on us having breakfast. 'I feel strong . . . and good.' He took a piece of toast from my plate, flexed his biceps and stretched in front of us. He was still thin and weak. He rubbed his back and said it hurt from lying in bed for so long, and then, as though he had just remembered, he rubbed his legs and said they were hurting badly.

He sat with us all day, flicking through magazines, listening to the radio, cooking us an elaborate dinner in the evening. Katie and I watched him closely.

'How has he recovered so quickly?' I asked her. 'I don't believe in miracles.'

'Neither do I,' she said. 'I thought it would take more . . . more than a week, more pain.'

When he went into the bathroom we looked through his room again, but this time we found nothing.

'I really did expect more,' she said to me again. 'I was expecting him to be out of it for weeks. There's supposed to be more to coming off than a couple of days' sickness.'

'But we don't know how bad his addiction is. Maybe he was really off it when he came back from the States. Maybe he wasn't really hooked when he told us last week . . . He's certainly shown all the right signs of withdrawal.'

'Who knows?' Katie said finally. We didn't.

By Saturday he was up and dressed. He had washed his hair, but made sure that he didn't spend too long in the bathroom and mentioned that to me when he came out. He had shaved as well. The black tracksuit he had worn all week was stained on the back and under the arms from his sweat, but at the time he hadn't wanted to take it off, for it was a sign to him of what he was going through. On Saturday he threw it away.

'It's disgusting,' he said as he put the lid on the bin. 'I'd like to burn it, but perhaps that's a little dramatic.' He came out of his room in a pair of freshly ironed white trousers and a white shirt, cream-coloured deck shoes and a blue blazer. He could have been going to watch some cricket, except that it was the beginning of winter.

'Well, where are you off to?' I asked, for he hadn't been out alone all week.

'Just out,' he said casually. 'You guys must be really sick of spending time with me. And I feel so good today, so clean, that I thought I'd take a walk on my own. You know, look in the shops, watch the people, see what ordinary, everyday folk do with their Saturdays . . . ' He smiled at me.

'I'll come with you.' I smiled back.

Alex took off his jacket, folded it carefully over the back of the sofa and sat down. 'If you want to go out now,' he said, going into the kitchen to make himself some coffee, 'then please don't let me stop you.'

'Oh,' I said, just as carefree, 'I can wait. White – no sugar – for me, please.'

'You're beginning to hound me again,' he warned.

When he went into the bathroom Katie searched through his jacket and found a sock in the pocket. Inside there was a needle, a syringe and another silver spoon. She held them up for me to see and I went to the drawer in the kitchen; the others were still there. In his other pocket she found a small packet of heroin.

When Alex put on his jacket again and walked towards the door, I said, 'Where are you going?' I tried to hold my hands still but they both curled up into fists again. He was over near the door, but came back into the room. When he saw how I was standing, he backed off.

'I said, where do you think you're going?'

'We've been through that,' he complained, 'so why don't you just leave me alone?'

'Before you go,' I said, relaxing my hands and taking a deep breath, 'I'll have what's in your jacket.'

Alex frowned. His face fractured like glass into fragments of incomprehension, fear and frustration. When he had controlled himself again, he said, 'What . . . ? Ah, my wallet . . . but you gave it to me?'

131

'No,' I shouted at him. 'Don't fuck around – give it to me.'

He realized I knew what he was carrying and his face flushed.

I went over to him and he backed away. I felt violent, raised a fist. He had better not try anything. He stood still while I put my hand into his pocket and pulled out the sock and the packet. He slumped as I took my hand away, as though I had just lifted a huge weight off him. He seemed relieved to have been caught.

'This,' I said through my teeth, waving the packet in front of him, wanting violence now, waiting for him to deny it, or hit me, or something.

He did nothing but stare at the packet, his eyes merely registering its existence. It was nothing to him now.

'It's not how you think,' he said calmly, suddenly making me feel unreasonable, my violence inappropriate. 'I did lie to you before – I did have some left over, so I was just going to throw it away. I'd completely forgotten about it until I found it when I was cleaning up. Yesterday. I didn't really know what to do with it. I certainly didn't want to put it in your dustbins. People have been busted like that before, you know. So that didn't seem such a bright idea. I was just going to toss it into a bin in the street.' He was smiling at me again.

'I don't believe you.'

'Don't, then,' he said, and turned to go.

'Wait,' I shouted, confused. 'Where were you going with it?'

'I told you – to throw it away. Now, please, I'd like to go before it gets any later.'

'Alex!' I screamed so loudly that the people downstairs banged on their ceiling. 'Tell me the truth.'

'I have,' he said quietly, and smiled as he went.

III

Moments of separation began to scare me. No longer in control of the situation, I felt each parting like a defeat. When Alex left the flat Katie and I closed the front door after him — that was the act I had feared — and went into his room. We pulled everything out of the chest of drawers, emptied his suitcases on to the floor, tore the bed apart, checked behind the curtains, felt around inside the fireplace. Not even the police, or a discerning burglar, could have done a more thorough job of stripping the place, and when we had finished checking the pillows and sifting through the rubbish in the bin we sat on the floor with our backs against the wall, dust settling around us once again, and silently regarded our work. For a moment we almost felt contented.

In one pile, amongst dirty underwear and crumpled shirts, there was a sheaf of letters, held together by a rubber band. I reached over for them. There were a few from his wife, but most of them had been written by Alex, never sent.

'Read one to me,' Katie said.

I chose at random.

'This one's from his wife in New York — must have been before he went out there.'

I cleared my throat.

My Darling,
    Here I am under the bright lights of the big city, the city of our dreams — a fine place to be. I have been cruising down the Avenues and climbing up to lofts in search of a home for us, and have made a useful contact to help me in this, a property developer (he calls himself a 'realtor') whom I met at a party the other day. He's been acting as my chief guide and we've seen a couple of likely looking places. I'm afraid roof space

is *out* until after your gold disc.

   Besides being a bird of prey, hunting down the dream palace with four bedrooms, I've been spending time with friends – dinners, parties, a few movies. Had to go in search of some new clothes as well, since the ones I brought out from the UK really will not do here. Found some fabulous shops and, of course, spent much too much, so quickly followed it up with a dutiful daughter call to Daddy.

   The city is fun, but I must admit I'm missing you. This hotel is expensive, but a real hovel. I lie awake at night and long for you here (you know where). So come and put me right because I love you . . .

'What a woman,' Katie muttered after a moment. 'Sounds a real tough bitch with her – what did she call it? – "dutiful daughter call".' She pulled duvet feathers from her black sweater. 'What I can't understand is how Alex ever got involved with someone like that.'

'I couldn't understand it either, except that she was wild, and a big challenge. He never could resist that. "The course of true lurv" was all he said to me when I asked him if he was sure about marrying her.'

'Clothes and parties and the price of flats – wildly thoughtful type, she sounds, huh? So what's next?'

I flicked through the pile of papers. Her letters stopped when Alex arrived in New York. There were none from her after she left and went to live in Hollywood, while his were written daily, a diary of his life without her as he tried to establish himself in the music business, calling people blind, using whatever contacts he had to get him auditions. He started out taking his own tapes around the clubs and studios in the hope that he would get a chance to play them to producers. In the beginning he wrote clear, large letters with a thick black pen. I could see the confidence on the pages as he told her he was hoping to get to see the manager of the Blue Note next week . . . that someone else had promised him a hearing at a new club . . . that he had met a guy at a party who . . .

He had such bright hopes. He felt strong and brave – I could see it on the paper. But he missed his wife. It seemed to him that he was incomplete without her, and although he thought he understood why she had gone – even he

134

agreed that the deal she had been offered was too good to turn down – he wished it didn't have to be that way. 'C'est la vie,' he wrote in resignation, 'but I do miss you, miss kissin' you, yeah, yeah.' What he didn't write was that he was suffering there without her support. He probably didn't feel he could write something like that. From what I knew of her, she would have thought him weak, and weakness was one thing she could not tolerate. That was for other people; her husband had to be strong and successful.

He tried to keep up the pretence, but each day pushed him closer towards seeing his own failure. Successful people around him were already unwilling to associate with him. His letters became shorter and more definite. He no longer allowed himself to write 'I hope' or 'maybe'. Everything was settled. He was definitely making his way in what everyone acknowledged was a dangerous world. 'Jesus,' he wrote one day, 'this place is sick.' The risk was great, but he could see that the rewards would be greater.

His handwriting, however, told another story, becoming increasingly untidy; he was unable to follow a straight line. Three or four weeks after she left him, he wrote:

Hi Baby,
How are you? And, more important, where are you? I haven't heard from you for weeks now – not since we spoke on the phone. Remember me? I have a pile of letters here, but no address to send them to. Drop me a line, or better still, come over and see me sometime.
Last night I went out with your friend Mikki. Quite a guy, except that he kept on calling things 'cooky'. We did a round of the likely bars – you know how much he likes to 'hang out' – then to a party over in the Village given by some big-shot whose name I've already forgotten, who'd just moved into a new mansion or something. All that 'yeah, great', 'you look fabulous tonight, darlin'', 'loved the session' makes me sick. We didn't stay too long, then dropped in on a couple of clubs. Dig that East Coast sound. There's a song to be written behind every door in this city of sickness and sin, and I'm going to write some of them. My day's coming – hope you are too.

But his day didn't arrive, and neither did word from his wife. Alex sank lower, now no longer able to get away with introducing himself as the new arrival from England. He had been seen around, doing nothing, talking to the wrong people. He must have been marked down as a loser and shunned by people who might have been able to help him. Only the other no-hopers and a couple of small-time drug dealers were still interested. The dealers thought they might be able to do themselves some good out of him: they had the drugs, while Alex claimed to have access to some useful names in the clubs. So he started pushing drugs to the lesser stars in the mistaken belief that any contact with them was useful. He found it easier than pushing his talent. And, of course, he believed they would understand that it wasn't his real occupation – they would know he was one of them.

At this point, his letters began to read like the social column of a glossy magazine. He reeled off the big names with whom he went to this party, that dinner, a weekend on Long Island. Only his handwriting, rambling up and down the page, with words spelt in capitals or just left unfinished, gave him away. Then, after a couple of months, his wife called. She was in Hollywood but there had been no job, no large payments – just another man, a film producer. The only thing that had been irresistible was her attraction to him, his desire to have her. But it hadn't worked out and she was alone in Los Angeles. She would come home. They would sort it all out.

Alex became remote in his letters after that, as hard as the pavements of New York, on which he was obliged to walk after he sold their car to support his habit. He reported big news as he might have done to a stranger; there was no emotion left, for he was burnt out and she had torn their lives apart. He did try to get himself sorted out before she got back. He stopped dealing, stayed away from his junkie friends and spent days hawking the contents of their apartment around the second-hand shops. The television and stereo, some old clothes, a few valuable photographs – all went so that he could pay for the methadone cure for which he had now registered. But even after he'd pawned his trumpet he still didn't have enough. It was then that he called Dad and asked for money, refusing to explain further than that he was in trouble and that they

136

had always promised to help him.

When his wife arrived back in New York, Alex continued to write letters – not to her, but to the woman she had been. More letters he would never send. He was off heroin by then, but on methadone. She was disgusted by the sight of him, thin, tired of everything, and they argued over the sale of the car – that was before they even left the airport, where he had arrived, late, to meet her. She screamed when she walked into the dirty apartment, now almost empty apart from the refrigerator, bed, and a few larger pieces of furniture, which he had been unable to carry around to the junk shops. He insisted that he had needed money to pay bills and to promote himself in the city, and she believed him for a week or however long it took her to notice the pustulating needle marks on his bruised arms. When she found out what had been going on, she told him, quite calmly, that she wouldn't even stay in the same house as a junkie, much less be married to one and let him into her bed. He told her that he wouldn't have become one if she had stayed with him. A few days later she returned to LA to try again with her TV producer, and as soon after that as he could arrange it Alex flew back to London. He never heard from her again.

I tossed the letters back on to the floor.

'Poor guy,' I said, thinking aloud. 'No wonder he's in a mess. Why didn't he say anything about her cheating on him? Why couldn't he have told me that? It's hard to blame him now I know . . . '

'Maybe,' Katie said thoughtfully, moving closer and taking hold of my arm, 'he's just too proud to tell even you about that. Anyway, it makes no difference whether she was unfaithful or not – they're apart now. But it must have been easier for him to pretend to us that it all happened because of his addiction.'

'Yes, but as you say, it makes no difference – it's too late now . . . '

'What do you mean?'

'I mean,' I told her, 'that this can make no difference to us. We can't help him any more. Not now. I'm going crazy with all this . . . I keep wanting to hit him, to hurt him. I can't do more than I've already done, and that's not enough. He's breaking up our life. We don't go out – we've got no money – I'm no good at work any more. It's over, Katie.'

'No it's not. I thought we were going to support him, whatever happened.'

'But I can't go on like this. He just tried to walk out with a packet of heroin in his pocket. Remember?'

'I remember – but you said we would be solid, that what Alex needed was something immutable, to lean against.'

I remembered saying that, but it seemed long ago, and the words were no longer mine. 'The only thing that won't change,' I admitted, 'is his addiction.'

Katie flushed. 'Well, you might feel that way, but I can't stop. I can't just give up on him like that. He needs us, you and me together.'

'He needs someone, but I don't believe it's us, or Mum and Dad. Just someone.'

'That someone is us,' she insisted. 'We can't throw him out now.'

'Yes we can.' I was angry. 'I can. There's no other way out of this. He'll just go on using us if we don't. And believe me, that won't help him.'

'You do what you like,' she told me finally, standing up and leaning over me, 'but I want him to stay.'

'Of course,' I said, surprised at the bitterness in my voice. 'Because, after all, it is your flat. So you go and do what you like . . . '

'I will,' she assured me, and walked out, slamming the door behind her.

I sat on the floor amongst the heaps of Alex's clothes and papers. I smiled at the irony that I had run up against one of the qualities I most admired in Katie – her stubbornness.

In the kitchen, she was standing with her back to me, looking out of the window at the bare trees, the ice in her whisky clinking against the side of the glass as her hand shook. I tried to turn her around, but she refused to look at me, taking short breaths as though each one hurt her.

'What's happening to us?' she asked. 'I don't want to give up on Alex, and,' she said emphatically, 'I don't want to lose you,' bursting into tears. 'I don't want to lose . . . '

We didn't really expect Alex to come back that Saturday, but when he didn't show up on the Sunday we were worried. What should we do? Call the police? Try the local hospitals? Go round to see his dealers? Unable to concentrate on a book or read the papers, we spent the day watching television and getting drunk. We did nothing. By Monday, when I returned to work, we had put aside our difference of opinion as to whether we should continue to help Alex or not; we were frantic. We needed him there to sort everything out, but all that remained of him was the empty bedroom with its scattered contents, and whether we left the door open, or closed it, we still felt his presence.

When I got home from *The* Agency, Katie had gone out. She had left a note: 'Couldn't stand it here alone. Gone round to see Eddie.' At seven o'clock I heard a key in the door; Alex came in still wearing his white trousers and blazer, dirty now and crumpled. He was unshaven and looked strung out. I jumped up off the sofa as he came into the room.

'Out,' I shouted, and started pushing him away. 'I don't want you in here again.' I hustled him back towards the door, even though, without saying a word, he had already turned around and started to leave. I followed him down the stairs into the street, the heavy front door, on sprung hinges, closing slowly behind us.

Alex sat on the wall and watched me.

'So, how have you been?' he asked softly. 'I've missed you.'

Disarmed, I said, 'Fine. Fine. And you? Where have you been?'

'Oh, around.'

'And where will you go now?'

He shrugged his shoulders as though it really didn't matter, and continued to stare at me, but I was more determined to keep a distance than I had ever been. Then I heard his stomach rumble.

'Haven't you eaten?'

He shook his head. 'Not for a couple of days.'

139

I watched him for a moment – he avoided my eyes – and listened to the noise that continued to come from his stomach.

'Come on then,' I said, anxious above all to get him away from the flat. 'I'll buy you dinner.'

We walked to a small Italian restaurant that I hadn't taken him to before. The food wasn't so good, but it was quiet and seldom full. Two young couples were eating at tables on either side of the white-washed room and a solitary man in a business suit read an evening paper in the corner. The lights were low and Italian-resort muzak droned from small speakers in the ceiling. The young waiter Giorgio, his name printed on a badge which hung above his full belly, came rushing up to welcome us with a generous smile and a shortage of breath.

'Signore,' he said, his smile fading as he saw Alex, 'good evening. Due?'

I pointed to a table on its own at the back of the restaurant, beside a pair of glass doors which led out on to a darkened courtyard.

Giorgio, pleased to be able to hide us, hurried over to pull out the chairs for us. He unfurled the red-rose napkins, handed out the menus and demanded, 'To drink?'

'Later,' I told him. 'With the meal.'

When he went away, I had a chance to observe Alex. In the dim white light he looked worse than before, as bad as when he had come off the plane from New York. I wanted to ask him what he had been doing, but he looked so sad and worn-out that I decided to wait until after we had eaten.

We ordered antipasti and *penne arrabiata*. Then Giorgio brought over a bottle of his house wine. 'I drink it meself,' he said, by way of recommendation, patting his belly. The wine was thin and sharp and Alex wouldn't even taste it. Giorgio looked at him with satisfaction, as though he had been sure all along that this one wouldn't drink.

'I don't really feel like it,' Alex explained. 'And,' he said loudly as Giorgio turned away, 'I've never liked Italian wine,' although in truth he rarely drank alcohol.

'I remember pestering Mum and Dad to let us have a glass or two in Italy when we were very young, but you

140

looked so innocent and said, "Not for me, thank you. I don't drink."'

He smiled, and I thought for a moment that he was remembering the holidays in Italy. But the gesture was out of keeping with his thoughts. 'One thing that's always amazed me,' he said quietly, 'is the way you only remember what you want to.'

'What do you mean?'

He began playing with a packet of bread sticks, snapping the ends off each stick. 'This Italy you talk about – it's a dream place. I would have loved to have seen it. It's full of happy memories for you. Only happy ones . . . Don't you remember any of the bad times we had?'

'Not really,' I admitted.

'Sometimes, when I listen to you, I think it's like we went to different places, you and me. You remember us being such contented little children who got everything we wanted. There was always room on the beach and enough pocket money for another ice-cream. The sun always shone . . .'

'And did the sky look so different to you?'

'Yes,' he said, 'it did. It wasn't like that at all – what I remember are the fights we had, you and me, with each other, with Mum and Dad and the people we met. We were like caged animals – or I was, anyway. You remember me as your loving protector. Well, I tell you now,' he lowered his voice, 'it just wasn't like that. If I looked after you, it was because – because I had to. Because Mum and Dad would leave us alone, leave me alone, if I did.'

'No,' I insisted, 'that's not true. We were close. We did things together. I looked up – I loved you.'

He was embarrassed, as if he would rather I hadn't said that, but I had to tell him how it was. He seemed to have lost touch with our true past, and the version he had invented for us was coloured by his drug-damaged mind. He saw only extremes – bright colours and darkened shadows.

'Well, what about in Lerici, Venice, Camaiore?'

He shrugged, refusing to reconsider. 'You remember what you like,' he decided. 'You hold on to your memories and I'll keep mine.'

141

Giorgio brought the antipasti, banging the plates down on the gingham tablecloth and turning away without a word. We sat in silence. Alex ate only a mouthful or two of the food and then pushed the egg, tuna and olives around the plate with his fork. I watched, and felt as though, by his movements, he was reorganizing a part of me, and that however hard I tried I couldn't hold all the pieces in place. I had to go on trying, but each time I stretched out he shrank away from me, and I knew in the end I would fail.

More people came into the restaurant, and after he had served our pasta Giorgio, deciding there was now enough of an audience to warrant the extravagance, switched on the lights in the courtyard. A statue of Diana was revealed, standing in a small pool of water, bow and arrow in hand, a full quiver strapped to her back. The pump for the fountain was also turned on, but the pipe must have been fractured, for instead of spouting from the tip of the goddess's arrow water gushed out of a crack in her groin and flowed down her legs into the pool.

Alex, facing her, looked alarmed.

'Tacky, isn't it,' I suggested.

'I've just remembered – I first met Caroline in here. My God. It was here, at this very table . . . ' He looked around the room. 'They've done the place up since then, but still, how could I have forgotten?'

'There's a lot you don't remember.'

'We met,' he explained, 'after a friend's birthday party. We'd had drinks down the road at his flat. And afterwards we came here for dinner. I think there were about twelve of us, and they'd arranged the tables along the back here – three of them together.' He gestured briefly with his open hand to indicate how the tables had been placed. 'I suppose I must have been sitting more or less where I am now. The seat opposite was empty – someone was match-making – and then Caroline arrived. Even before she said anything, I was lost. She had such a smile, so much energy. God she was sexy . . . '

He stared at the statue. 'We didn't talk to anyone else. She told me about Diana the Huntress. About how she felt a sort of affinity with her. In Roman times she was associated with the moon . . . You remember I went to

142

Istanbul? When I was there I met an old man in a café – he offered me a smoke of his waterpipe – and talked about some of the women he had known. The best way to flatter a woman, he advised me, was to tell her she was beautiful "like the light from the moon when she is full". I said this to Caroline that night and she blushed, not with embarrassment but with happiness. She felt that at last she had found someone who also understood this thing, which she had thought no one else could understand. It became our secret . . . '

'Go on,' I urged him after a few minutes, pouring the last of the wine into my glass, not thinking of where this was leading us.

'Go on what? There isn't much more to tell.'

He watched the water flow from inside the statue. His eyelids became heavy, his forehead creased with wrinkles. 'I thought I knew all about women as hunters. I thought I understood something about the moon. But I didn't, did I. I found out, though,' he said slowly, now with some bitterness. 'I found out all about that. I underestimated her. I thought I knew what was going on in her mind, but really I was seeing only what she wanted me to see, what I wanted to see. I thought she would change, being with me. She wouldn't hunt . . . '

We were silent again. Alex stared at the statue. I watched him ruffle his dirty hair and then, averting my eyes, re-read the wine label. Giorgio had a faint-hearted attempt at selling us his 'especial dolci' – cassata or zabaione – but gave up and brought us grainy espressos and the bill. I didn't know what I was going to do after I had paid it.

If I had turned Alex around in the flat and, without allowing him to talk or myself to listen and watch, had pushed him out of the door, I might have been able to keep him away from Katie and me. If I had not been reminded – by something as familiar as the noise his stomach made – that he was as frail and dependent as anyone, I might have been able to turn him away. But what could I have done after I had heard that noise? If we had not sat down to dinner in the restaurant where he had first met his wife, he might not have appealed so directly and effectively to my sympathies. If I had not drunk Giorgio's cheap white wine

I might have been curious to know what Alex was carrying in his pocket that night. But all these things had happened without premeditation, and although the idea of saying goodbye to him did occur to me at the restaurant door, I shrank from it, as I shrank from the sharp wind that blew down the street. I huddled up inside my overcoat.

'Come,' I said to him after Giorgio had slammed the door behind us, 'come back to the flat tonight. We can sort out what you're going to do, tomorrow.'

I put an arm over his shoulder and, perhaps thinking that I was too drunk to walk home on my own, he put his own arm across my back. We swung along like Siamese twins and found Katie at home, her eyes wine-red, her mind numbed by the drugs Eddie had provided for her.

'Eddie says hi,' she called from the floor. 'Took me out to dinner . . . what a nice boy . . . '

'That *was* nice of him,' Alex agreed, humouring her. 'And we've just had dinner as well.'

'So you've come back to us, have you, Alexei?' she asked slowly, laughing to herself. 'We hoped you would, you know.' She tried to sit up, but collapsed again on to the floor. 'We did hope you would, didn't we?'

'Yes,' I agreed awkwardly, not sure why I was laughing with her. 'We worried when you didn't come back.'

I stretched out on the floor beside her, took her head in my hands and brushed the hair away from her eyes. 'I think you need to lie down.'

'But I am lying down . . . '

'No, not here. Come on, let's get you into bed.'

Alex watched me carry her into the bedroom, her feet banging against the door jamb.

'Weee – and over the threshold we gooo,' Katie cried out, her head lolling back. She put an arm around my neck and, laughing, pulled herself up to kiss my cheek. 'Ma man,' she whispered.

When I put her down on the duvet, she told me, 'Now, you go and put little Alex to bed. And then,' she added, purring, 'you come back here to me.' She started pulling off her clothes, kicking them on to the floor, her pale skin sallow against the white sheet, her nipples erect in the cold. 'I'll make it warm for you,' she growled. 'I'll heat you up, tiger – we'll be so hot . . . '

Alex stood in the doorway to his bedroom; he was staring at the mess we had left, but when he saw me come out of our room he pulled the door shut behind him.

'I'll clear it up tomorrow,' he said, not looking at me, 'but just now I've got to go to bed.'

I sat alone in the sitting room, my legs hanging over the arms of the sofa, a cigarette smouldering in the ash-tray. I could hear Alex putting the mattress back on to the base of the bed and throwing the sheet over it; his light went out a few minutes later.

My head hurt from the bad wine, but it was a relief to be able to sit on my own. Katie would be fast asleep by now, her mouth dry, body slick with sweat. I was relieved to be away from her and thought of nothing for a while beyond the regularity of the blood rushing through my head and the irregular shades of the bare plaster walls. Sometimes that room looked like a designer's dream disturbed in the middle of its fulfilment. At other times, as now, it felt like a cell into which Katie and Alex and I had been condemned in order to reshape our lives. In here there was no hiding.

But I could leave it. There was the door, and the Healey was parked in the street. I alone could go. It was Katie's flat, so she would stay; and Alex had given up his other options. But me, I could leave them to sort themselves out, as I had been unable to do. But what would become of my memories if I was to lose Alex? What would happen to my bright dreams of the future if I didn't have Katie with me?

I could go, as surely as the hammer struck my forehead. I could button up my coat, check I had my credit cards and wallet with me and be a long way away from them by the time they woke up. But that, I realized, would resolve all of my problems except one: if I left home, where would I go? I still refused to live without either of them.

We might have survived it if it hadn't been for my dreams. There was a chance then, but although I could control myself during waking moments and give Alex enough time to sort himself out, it required a great effort on my part. I learnt that for every action there is an equal reaction:

if I pretended not to see what Alex was up to during the day, then at night, when I closed my eyes and lay my head against the sofa or on my pillows, I saw everything. In my dreams, at least, I recognized the truth of what was happening.

But we soon slipped back into our old routine, as though it was the easiest and most natural way of the world. I went off to work in the morning with the sweet taste of Katie's farewell kiss on my lips. With my own I had given her encouragement to continue searching for a job, and she would spend the day going through the ads in newspapers, making phone-calls, arranging interviews, although she was bored with the idea of looking for work. She seemed glad, then, that Alex was there, and when she had done all she could do for the day she would lie on the sofa, a book propped up on her chest, and believe that her life had regained its old balance.

We never mentioned drugs. If Alex, supported by one of the hard-backed chairs, fell asleep over dinner, we ignored him and talked to each other as though we were alone. When he went into the bathroom we made a point of not looking at the black hands of the mantelpiece clock. We lived around him, rather than with him, and whereas before we had turned ourselves inwards, now when I came home from work we went out to the cinema or the cabaret in an upstairs room at the pub down the road. When we met friends down at the local wine bar we talked about what we had seen, the latest airline crash or rise in mortgage rates, and listened to the gossip about who had done what at the last party they had attended.

One night, a couple of weeks after Alex came back, Katie and I went out to eat at our favourite Indian restaurant and were reminded of how our life had been before he arrived. The table was filled with curries, vegetable dishes, pilaw rice and a plastic tray of chutneys. We drank whiskies and pints of lager and later confessed to our most fantastic thoughts and dreams of far-off places.

'I remember hearing a story,' Katie said, her mouth still watering at the sight of the food, even though we had started eating, 'about a couple who fell in love at first sight – '

146

' – just like us . . . '

'Yes, just like us. Their story was impossible, though. He was older than she was, and married; she was under age. Her parents wouldn't have anything to do with him. So, disgusted by what they thought was the hypocrisy of the people around them, they decided to run away. But where to go? He had a little money – not much, though – enough to get them somewhere. They planned to take a train south through Europe, as far as the money would get them – they mentioned going to the Far East and stopping at some place that neither of them had ever heard of. They wanted to get off somewhere exotic, a place where they could be together, away from all the hassles of their lives in England. The strangeness of the place would bring them even closer together. So one day they really did go . . . '

She stopped, and appeared to be following her thoughts to see where they would lead her. Her eyes moved around the table.

'I didn't think people still did things like that,' I told her. 'So where did they go?'

'I can't really remember how, but they ended up in Bombay.'

'Hardly an unknown – '

'Exactly, and what's more, they hated it. All those people living in poverty, the heat and dirt. It didn't fit into their idea of romance at all – '

'Maybe,' I interrupted, 'that's why people don't do things like that now.'

'Will you let me finish? In Bombay, he contracted dysentery. He fell down in the street and she got some people to help her carry him back to their room. They were staying in a cheap hotel, and I seem to remember that their window looked out on to a brothel. He lay in bed, and began to fade so fast that the girl thought he was going to die. She prayed to God for the first time – '

'I didn't think people did that, either.'

She stared at me, pretending to be annoyed, and then continued. 'She called for a doctor. The man who came wanted to move him to a hospital, but no – she insisted that she could do a better job of looking after him than some overworked, underpaid nurse. She turned their room into a ward, scrubbing down the walls and floor; she cooked his meals, washed the sweat off him and, when he was conscious, she read to him – from Paul Scott and *A Passage to India*. I remember that. Of course, he didn't die, and when he was well enough they left Bombay and travelled further east, to Rangoon, Bangkok, Shanghai . . . ' Her voice became as distant as the foreign cities.

'What happened in the end?' I asked, fighting off a waiter who, seeing that we had stopped eating for a moment, was trying to clear away the food.

'I can't remember,' Katie admitted.

I thought for a moment and, carried away by her story and too many whiskies, said, 'Well, maybe we should go off like that.'

She didn't seem to understand.

'Let's run away. You and me. Pack a small suitcase and get out of all this. Just go . . . '

She watched me for a minute or two. 'Go where?' she asked. 'With what? How will we live?'

I thought quickly. 'We'll rent out the flat, sell the Healey – I'll give up *The* Agency – that'll give us enough to start with.'

Katie laughed, perhaps not thinking that I was serious, but then she also started making arrangements. 'OK,' she said, 'we'll go. How soon can you leave work?'

I told her I could leave by Christmas, but something was making me feel uneasy.

'Can you just give it up? Won't you miss it?'

'No, no – I'll be glad to get out of there.'

As we talked, I remembered images from films I had seen – Clark Gable and Claudette Colbert hitching across the States in *It Happened One Night*; Humphrey Bogart and Ingrid Bergman listening to Sam playing their tune again in war-time Paris; and Bette Davis leaning on the railings of a cruise ship with the man she loved beside her and all the world a calm sea, the sky filled with a bright moon and glittering stars. I smiled at that, but my smile faded; I realized that I really wanted to go on my own. Taking Katie would be like bringing the past and its troubles along with me.

'You know what?' Katie said, smiling. 'I was just thinking about Bette Davis – '

'In *Now Voyager* – '

'Sailing in the moonlight.' She flushed and we laughed loudly, our hands touching between the chrome dishes to acknowledge the coincidence of our thoughts, sealing our future together.

'Yes,' I said, still uneasy about going with her. 'We should go – there seems to be no other way out.'

Back in the flat we sat up late. Before we went to bed, Katie kissed Alex goodnight, standing close to him, her lips near his mouth. He put his arms around her and held her for a moment.

When she closed the bedroom door behind her, she came over to where I was undressing and put her arms around my neck. Her fingertips teased my shoulders, exciting me, sliding down my back until they reached my bottom. She thrust her groin towards me, licking her lips.

'C'mon,' she urged, 'come to bed.' She moved away, left her clothes in a pile on the floor, as she usually did, and lay naked on top of the duvet.

I stood by the window and watched her.

She became uneasy. 'What's wrong?' she asked gently. 'What is it? We haven't made love for – I don't know how long. Don't you want me any more?' She said it as a joke.

'It's not that,' I said, too seriously.

'Well, what is it then? Are you sure it's not me?'

I couldn't explain it to her. I could have told her that I was confused – that sex and drugs, me, her and Alex were all getting caught up in my mind and were mixing together so thoroughly that I couldn't see clearly any more. But telling her about that would not have explained the impossibility I felt of their ever being separated again. That was what troubled me, the thought that there might be no end to it, that I would never again be able to see her as I had done when we first met. I had no words to describe that sort of eternity. It was like trying to describe the place where the wind that was blowing in through the bedroom window came from – or what the place was like where it would end up.

'Katie,' I began, walking over to the edge of the bed, 'it's not you.' This was dangerous – she sensed that, and covered herself with the duvet. 'You're beautiful to me, and as sexy as ever.'

She looked away, expecting me to reveal more, but I was silent.

'Well, what's your problem, then?' Suddenly, she was bitter. 'Gone off sex? Or do you want to go and screw someone else?'

I laughed at that idea, but by trying to laugh it off I only made her more angry.

'This isn't what I had in mind when we started living together,' she explained with a detachment that surprised me. 'Having to nurse your brother is one thing. But this is something else. What do I get out of it? I want something too, you know . . . I have needs . . . '

I knelt down, leaning my arms on the bed.

'Christ,' she hissed, 'get off your knees. You're acting worse than Alex. Just stand up, will you – I don't want to see you like this,' and in order not to witness any more, she turned to face the wall.

I tried to talk to her, but she wouldn't reply. I undressed and got into bed. She ignored me. I set the alarm clock, switched off the lamp and wished her good night, reaching out to touch her hair, but she lay motionless and even in the dark stayed away from me. Her breathing became regular and slow. Her body was warm, scented.

Then the air smelled different, damp and fertile, and I woke with a start. My heart was pounding, my face resting on dark mud, my hands covered by a thick growth of emerald creeper. The trees above me rattled in the wind – where *did* the wind come from? – and the sky above them was ash-grey. It must be early.

I didn't know why, but I was scared. My pulse was racing and now my hands began to shake. A beetle fell off the creeper. I sat up and brushed away the mud from my cheek; there was grit between my teeth, which I was unable to spit out. I didn't know where I was – I had certainly never seen this wood before – but that didn't worry me as much as the fear. I stood up, but stumbled. My left leg was numb; I must have slept awkwardly. But why was I sleeping in a wood? A blackbird flew out of the thicket and I cowered. I had to find out where I was.

I buttoned up the black leather jacket I was wearing, which I had also never seen before, and looked around. The trees were thick in all directions and nowhere could I see an end to the wood. I began walking towards the place where the undergrowth was least dense. The ground was firm, but mud clung to my boots so that before long my calf muscles began to ache. I must have walked a long way yesterday. But if so, why couldn't I remember where I had come from or why I had left?

I walked for another half an hour and then I came out into a clearing, surrounded by trees. As I stepped across tall meadow grasses, the sun shone through a circular slit in the clouds and illuminated the place where I was standing. I looked up, shielding my eyes.

'There he is.'

It was a woman's voice.

'Where?'

'Over there – '

'There.'

'There!'

The voices were shrill; there was something savage about them. Were they referring to me? I didn't know, but I felt that I ought to run. As I did so, someone blew on a hunting horn and I heard its thin notes echo through the trees, its sound rushing past me like the wind. I forced myself faster across the uneven ground, tripping over in my mud-encrusted boots, cutting my hands on briars, but the women's voices followed me. Why was I being hunted? What outrage had I committed against these women?

I had no time to stop and consider what was happening, just as I didn't dare to sit and catch my breath. Something about the voices convinced me that I didn't want to be caught.

I ran while the sun was low; I was still running when it was overhead and when its auburn rays slanted low between the trunks of the oak trees. The forest had no end. I continued to move, and the women came no closer until the twilight began to fade. Then I heard the horn again; they began to close in on me at the same time as I saw more open space beyond the trees – another clearing, perhaps, or an end. I ran faster. Ah, but then I tripped again. My feet rose high in the air and I put out my hands to cushion the fall, but I didn't touch the night-hidden ground. I was moving through darkness and had no sense of whether I was heading down, into a hole, or moving vertically along a corridor. Wherever I was, it was warm and dark, and with pleasure and an unexpected sense of relief I was able to shift from travelling head-first to leading with my feet. I went through a routine of gymnastic postures until I looked back and saw light coming from the hole through which I had fallen. Even though I had the sensation of movement, the light grew no more distant. In fact, I appeared to be going nowhere; caught in a place without gravity, I was floating.

It was there that they found me, their heads appearing around the rim of the hole, the faces of angry women, Katie's face. At least, I thought it was hers, but I had now begun to spin wildly through a vortex and it was impossible for my eyes to settle on anything. 'Katie?' I whispered, straining to look up. 'Katie? Is that you, Katie?'

'What is it?' she asked, taking a rough hold of my shoulder. 'Wake up. Come on – what's wrong? You're just dreaming . . . '

I opened my eyes and saw nothing in the darkness. I reached out for her and caught her by the neck, pushed her on to her back, her head falling on to the pillows, her nails sharp on my skin. I covered her mouth with mine. She tasted different, and the smell of her sweat had changed too. I climbed on top of her, covering her body, and thrust into her with a strength that surprised me. 'Yes,' she cried, and fought back. We bit and clawed each other, Katie cutting me with her nails, and when it was over I told her I loved her and that I was sorry.

I have only had one dream since that night, or at least if there have been others they didn't disturb my sleep, or remain with me until the morning. I must have controlled myself as thoroughly at night as I did during the day, so that at eight o'clock, when I fumbled to switch off the alarm clock, my thoughts were as dull and obscured as the bare plaster walls that surrounded me.

'My dears,' Eddie observed as he handed us each a tumbler

of whisky, 'as I am your friend I feel I must say this: you look terrible. Both of you.'

We were sitting in his studio flat, which he now referred to, in a vaguely recognizable French accent, as his *appartement*. Although there were just the three of us, the room seemed smaller than on the evening of his party. Katie and I were sitting in black leather armchairs, pushed together in one corner, which Eddie had bought at a knock-down price from one of his bank's clients. 'A little good-will gesture,' he explained.

'Why is it,' I asked, 'that every time I see you, you tell me I look terrible?'

'What else are friends for? Anyway, just look at you.' He stretched out on the only other seat in the room, a small patterned Ottoman divan, backed by a black wooden screen which hid the bed. 'You've lost weight down below. You're pale. You're carrying trunks under your eyes and you look as though you haven't had a proper meal or a good night's sleep in weeks.' He sighed. 'Passion is one thing, darlings – and believe me, I've known some in my time – but you really must look after yourselves.'

'It's not passion, you fool,' Katie laughed. 'We're still looking after Alex.'

Eddie raised a hand to his mouth. 'What I don't understand is why it was you two who got landed with him. After all, I know blood's thicker than water and all that, but he is only your brother.'

'What more could he be?' Katie asked.

'If it was your child, or,' his voice deepening, 'a lover – now that I might be able to understand. But a brother . . . ? I don't see mine from one Christmas lunch to the next and I really can't say I'm sorry about it.' His fingers sought out his upper lip, stroking the place where his moustache had been. 'Always gives me the most unwanted presents – nylon handkerchiefs and a tin of biscuits last year. I bet his wife buys in bulk at Marks and Spencer. I mean, that's not exactly what you'd call personal, now is it.' He sighed. 'I always say, you can choose your friends but your family you can only suffer.'

'Alex is more than someone I spend Christmas with,' I told him patiently. 'In fact I haven't done that with him for

153

a while, now I come to think of it. Maybe you've never been that close to your brother – but imagine if you had been once and then you separated. Imagine how you would feel if you happened to meet again after a long time and recognized yourself in him. Not just in the way he looked and talked, but also in what he said, the way he thought, the things he liked. It's shocking – like looking in the mirror.' Eddie coughed. 'And if he was a heroin addict – well . . . denying Alex would be like denying myself.'

'And by saving him, will you save yourself?'

'No,' I admitted, the drink making me morose.

Eddie fanned out his fingers, waving them in front of him like a flamenco dancer's fan. In a peculiar Spanish accent he said, 'Such a gran' gesture for a young hombre.'

'We've done everything we can,' Katie explained. 'It's up to him now. We don't even know if he's still using or not.' Then she said, with a sadness that made me want to reach out and touch her, 'We no longer bother to ask him.'

Eddie was running out of patience. 'It's not as if he's dying of AIDS or something. For God's sake. He's got arms and legs. He's not poor or paralysed. Send him out into the street – switch on the evening news – take the little bastard round a cancer ward.'

'I never knew you were so aware,' Katie teased.

'My dear,' he purred, regaining his composure, 'I'm so aware, I practically invented safe sex. But you know what I mean. This thing with Alex has got out of hand.'

Later – over the dinner which Eddie had bought in, pre-cooked, from a French restaurant but which he insisted he had prepared in our honour ('I was up early this morning to get fresh 'erbs from the market') – I told him that I was going to run away.

He was drunk by now, opening a third bottle of claret, and laughed out loud. 'Bravo – that's my boy. Pack it all in and off you go, huh?'

He surprised me, for I had thought that travel to Eddie meant taking the Underground to the City in the morning, driving along the same strip of the French Riviera each summer, skiing in Courcheval or Val d'Isère in the winter. He once told me that he had seen all he wanted to of the East from the tables of Thai and Chinese restaurants. The West he had explored through television.

'So where will you go?' he asked, filling my glass.

'Head down through France to Switzerland.' He nodded his head in approval. 'Then carry on going east − find a passage to India or China, somewhere I can get lost.'

Eddie laughed for a moment. 'Tell me you're joking,' he pleaded. 'It's a joke, right? Katie, tell me he's just drunk and doesn't know what he's saying.'

' 'fraid not.' She smiled at him.

'You can't just leave your job, your friends − and what about your good woman here? What's going to happen to her?'

'I'm going with him,' Katie told him, and again I felt uneasy.

He slapped his forehead. 'Now I've heard it all. Being a drop-out went out with the seventies − didn't any one tell you?'

'Depends what you want from life,' I said quietly.

'I know what matters,' Eddie said sharply. 'I'm not talking about feeding the poor. I value my flat, my friends, going out − '

'But you could have that anywhere,' Katie told him.

'Listen, darlings,' he drawled, 'I don't want to argue with you. Money, sex, love, work, adventure − it all ends up the same way: when you know what you want you can't have it − and when you have it you'll want something else.'

We stared at each other across the table. I had never expected him to understand. I thought bitterly that passion and love probably meant sex to him.

'Well, I see that got you thinking,' he said. 'But if you really have decided to go, then I can only wish you luck − in fact, I think this calls for a little celebration.' He pushed the empty plates away, went to the kitchen and brought over a bottle of champagne and three tulip-shaped glasses. 'The only advice Mother gave me that I have never failed to heed was when she told me always to keep a bottle of Moët on ice.' He raised his voice to a falsetto. '"You'll never know when you'll need it." It was her remedy for everything – a cure for ills, a companion to joy.'

He hit the ceiling with the cork, filled our glasses and stood to propose a toast.

'My friends.' He swayed in front of us. 'Here's to madness.'

White had been the colour of our hopes for the future, but we lived in a world of autumn brown. While the stucco front of our house was washed with white, the walls of the flat had remained the colour of cracked mud.

Once, in a time that seemed long ago, I had been able to imagine that these walls had belonged to an Italian palazzo. There were pots of this colour – the shade of lightly burnt earth – on the terrace of the place we inhabited in our dreams, in which we grew geraniums for colour, lilies for their purity, basil for its scent and rosemary to throw on the fires, which we would settle down in front of to warm ourselves on cold autumn evenings. These plain London walls, left unfinished by the developer's slapdash decorators, had belonged to our dreams in that far-off time, rich with hope and new beginnings. I remember following with my eyes the rough edges left by the plasterer's skimming board, just as I intended to run my fingers around the pinched and primitive handles of the clay pots in which we would prepare our meals each lunch-time, sliding them along a rack suspended over the open, olive-wood fire. I had longed for these things with a passion that had even allowed me to smell the herbs that grow wild in the Tuscan hills, to taste the coarseness of the red wine that we would watch being decanted from the merchant's casks into our own glass flagons. I had heard the random, far-off putt of old shotguns as farmers hunted in the deceiving twilight for rabbit or hares, felt the strength of the morning sun on my back as I bent to tend the vegetables on the land we had marked out and tilled beyond the fresh-water well, our market garden. I would have been happy there.

In the beginning I had learned to dream in this way on my own; when I met Katie we had been able to imagine that other life together with such vitality that it had begun to exist for us as convincingly as the solid walls of our London flat. It was enough for me just to look up at the bare plaster to be reminded of the place where we believed we would be happy, where we wouldn't mind the inevitability of growing old, where we might even welcome it.

But now we seemed to have abandoned both that place and our dreams for it. We had lost something of ourselves, an inner sacred part. What was left seemed to me, that night, to be little more than a defence against drear practicalities: even if we ran far and fast, I would carry the knowledge that we had lost the passion of that first innocent dream. Its memory would hang round me like an orphan's remembrance of dead parents. Maybe I was just badly drunk that night, but as we drove home from Eddie's flat, our conversation dulled by alcohol, I felt that everything had slipped away from me. I felt apart from Katie, our dreams and Alex. What was most upsetting was that I no longer even wanted to reach out and hold on to them: nothing seemed to matter very much. It could all be left behind.

Even the big Healey, on which I had lavished time and too much money, which had allowed me great pride and enjoyment in return, even the car was falling apart. I should have taken it into the garage for a service a few hundred miles before – six hundred and fifty, to be precise – and the problem with the petrol feed, which had caused it to stall earlier, still hadn't been cleared up. Now the engine began to misfire.

'This car could do with some attention,' Katie said cautiously when we were nearly home. It was an understatement, considering that as she said it the Healey, with its three-litre engine, was struggling to take us up a gentle incline. But although I appreciated her tact, I didn't say anything.

She reached over and spread her hand across my leg, squeezing my thigh. 'You're very quiet tonight.'

'I don't really have much to say,' I told her. 'I get like this sometimes . . . you know . . .'

'Are you sleepy?'

I didn't feel particularly tired, but I told her that I was because it was easier that way. When we got to the flat Alex was slumped on the sofa in front of the television, a cup of cold coffee and a full ash-tray at his feet. He took off the headphones of his Walkman when he saw us come in.

'I am tired,' I told Katie. 'I think I'll go straight to bed.'

'Stay and have a nightcap,' Alex suggested. 'I'll get you one.'

On another night I might have accepted, but when I saw his sallow face and pin-head pupils I told him I'd give it a miss.

'Thanks anyway – I'll see you in the morning.'

He stood up, uneasy on his feet, and came towards me as slowly as a cripple in need of a stick. He raised both hands to my shoulders and peered into my eyes. I looked away from him. He hugged me, pressing his slight frame on to my chest, but my own hands remained limp by my side. I remembered how firm his body had felt when he was strong, how brightly his eyes had sparkled then, what life there had been in him. I still remember it now. The memory makes me as weak as he was then. It clings to me, bitter and sweet.

I forced my hands free and held him so tightly that he fought for air. 'Brother,' I whispered in his ear, 'my brother.' Just as abruptly, I let him go and went into the bathroom to wash.

When I came out he was sitting on the sofa again and Katie was beside him, leaning against him, her lips near his, her right hand open on his chest. He had put his right arm over her shoulder. Sweet lovers, I thought, although she might have just been kissing him goodnight. Sweet, though.

I touched the plastered walls as I went through to the bedroom, and thought nothing more than that we ought to have painted them. I wished we had at least done that. I closed the bedroom door and switched out the soft light beside the bed, wishing to be asleep before Katie came in.

That night I knew I had lost everything – I, who had wanted nothing more than to find my own place in the world and someone to share it with. That night I thought of things that should not be remembered in waking moments and of which I am ashamed.

I felt ill when I lay down in the dark; I had drunk too

much. I was thinking of Alex's dark brown eyes surrounded by skin which had puckered from lack of sleep,
exercise and regular diet. A few small veins had broken
above his cheeks. His pupils made it clear that he was still
taking drugs; above them, his eyebrows no longer suggested arrogance or surprise: his face had become a barrier.
But I had imagined, when I looked at him that night, not
knowing it was for the last time, that it was a barrier he
wanted to come out from behind. He wanted me to look
over at him, but I had looked away and said nothing,
knowing there was nothing more I could do to help him.

I saw his face when I closed my eyes, and also Katie's lips
as they kissed. These two images moved together as my
head spun from the drink. They moved like figures on the
merry-go-rounds of our childhood – I could almost hear
the music – up and down and around, although unlike
with those childish moments of pleasure it was now myself
and not the world around me that remained stationary,
and my mind was the pivot which held these images in
place. When I opened my eyes and was able to distinguish
the chest of drawers, the blue curtains, the tall oak-framed
mirror I had never liked, but into which I had looked each
day, they also moved around me. There was no old man
with hard-set face and an apron of money tight across his
slack stomach, as there had been in my childhood. But at
the time I was not aware that it was myself who caused this
world of images to turn.

Katie's hair was streaming behind her, and as they
moved faster her clothes came loose to expose her beauti-
fully formed breasts, nipples erect. Alex was turning to me,
smiling, holding out a hand, not to touch me but to attract
my attention. 'Don't worry,' he seemed to call out, 'whatever happens we're family. Always remember that . . . '
They began playing music in the sitting room and I heard
them both laughing. Images swam around me in time to
the drum's beat. It slowed. 'Always remember,' Alex
mouthed. 'I love you,' Katie whispered, not looking at me,
as she eased past and moved nearer to Alex. I could neither
move nor call out to them. They were together now and I
saw them whether my eyes were open or closed. Then the
music stopped, and with it the movement. I was asleep

before Katie came to bed, and in the morning I left the flat before either of them woke up.

My family has a great capacity for suffering. Our reason tells us to avoid it, as we avoid cars in the street or contact with the flames that warm us in winter. But instinct leads us on to suffer. Some people do it in the name of God or on behalf of humanity, but we endure outrages for ourselves, for parents, brother, partner or the children. I used to think that this was entirely understandable, for it was within my family that I first felt secure. But I found it curious that there were fundamental imbalances within the structure – I would not have thought to die for my father, for instance, but there was a time, which has become irrelevant now, when I think he would have done so for me. The family, reduced to its essentials, appeared to be some kind of commune which demanded from each of us according to our abilities and gave to each of us according to our needs. I had believed that it could be perfect.

But if it is to function properly, it is necessary that the members agree to abide by a code of behaviour which, at least to begin with, is established by the parents. Our family was falling apart because Alex refused to do so, and because Mum and Dad were unable to accept a change. We were breaking up into separate units – Eveline, my parents, Alex, Katie and me. When I left the flat, I shattered the last of the fragments and was alone.

I had no idea of where I was going. Driven by a complete lack of direction, I left with a small canvas bag over my shoulder, with credit cards, cheque-book and passport in my coat pocket. I could go anywhere or nowhere.

The relief I felt at each step I took towards the front door reassured me. I hadn't even attempted to write a note to Katie to justify my departure, for I still couldn't explain it to myself. It could have been no more than a desire to be alone for a few hours – maybe I would be back home before dark. Maybe I would never return. The early morning hour – the milkman I had never met before was coming up the steps when I opened the front door – and the pain in my head from the night's alcohol made it hard to be sure of anything, but I welcomed uncertainty, for I had discovered that there was no foundation to the certainties I had honoured before. From now on, I decided, everything must be unfamiliar.

A cold mist hung over the street. Two young men, huddled in heavy overcoats, passed me on their way to work. A woman scraped sheets of frost from her car windscreen, exhaust fumes hanging heavy in the air beside her. From the flat I had often watched her going out in the early evening, with her slim legs and the greater part of her small breasts on show, or returning home late at night with men who looked both ways along the street before they went through her front door. Seeing my approach she looked up, and I spoke to her for the first and perhaps the last time.

'A fine morning.'

She stared incredulously at me as I walked on, now whistling to myself.

Out of habit, I arrived at the Underground station where a couple of girls were giving away free magazines. An older woman, crouched on the steps, also had her hand out, empty apart from dirt, but she was ignored. I gave her all the change in my pockets, a couple of pounds, perhaps, and then had to queue to buy a ticket.

When I reached the window I asked, again from habit, for a ticket to Oxford Circus, the nearest station to *The* Agency, but I had no intention of going to work. As I went down the escalator I noticed an advertisement for the boat train to Paris. Each alternate hoarding along my side of the escalator was the same – 'FRENCH LEAVE' – then women in swimsuits – 'FRENCH LEAVE' – women – 'FRENCH LEAVE' – more women – 'FRENCH LEAVE'. I took a train from Victoria and was on my way to Dover before the blonde receptionist would have taken up her position behind the matt black desk at the entrance to *The* Agency.

The sun burnt freezing mist off the Kent countryside. The bare orchards and late winter fields were crisp and desolate; I thought they were beautiful. A young couple sitting opposite me with their three children talked with excitement about everything we passed; around us there were conversations in French, German, even Flemish. I sat in silence and listened to the rhythm of the wheels on the track. The words 'French Leave' rolled again and again through my mind. I would not think of what I had left, only of where I was and of where I might be going. I gave myself up to the sense of motion, rocked from side to side and considered myself no more, that Thursday morning, than a young man on a train – without a past, and above all with no ambitions for the future.

When we passed Swanley I walked through empty carriages, looking for the buffet car, but there wasn't one on that train. When the steward came round with a drinks trolley I ordered black coffee and brandy.

'Hair of the dog, eh?' he asked, looking up at me and then down at the coffee he was pouring into a plastic cup.

I shook my head.

'Bit early to start drinking, isn't it?'

I sighed. 'Would it make you feel better if I told you that I've been working all night and that this is therefore the end of my day?'

He shrugged his shoulders. 'Takes all sorts,' he said to himself, and ignored me when, on his return from the end of the train, I asked for another brandy.

At Dover I thought about sending a telemessage to Katie – GONE TO PARIS STOP BE IN TOUCH STOP LOVE – but decided against it. On the boat I drank another brandy at the bar, bought a bottle of whisky and a carton of cigarettes in the duty-free shop and, as I had caught a whiff of Katie's scent on my jacket, hung around the perfume counter hoping that I might find a tester to spray over it. The assistant told me to buy something or go away.

I returned to the bar, rolling more than the movement of the ship justified, clutching my duty-free bag. But when the barman asked if I would like another brandy, which he called cognac, I decided not to have one. I was already soft and warm with intoxication, and since I had decided to abandon myself to coincidence I wanted to be sober enough at least to recognize where it was taking me. When I tottered down the gangway on to French soil, the harsh smell of fish and oil and stagnant water were entirely unfamiliar; I could have been anywhere.

I relished that feeling. I was looking for an adventure, something that would change my life. I would walk the streets of Paris at night, hear the even tread of my heels on the worn city streets. I would turn away from Montmartre or the boulevards of the Left Bank and lose myself in dim alleys. I had read Henry Miller and Hemingway. I knew the feasts the city of light offered those who came with a large enough appetite. I had listened to Chevalier, to hot American jazz, to Piaf and the lilting notes of the accordion. So maybe it wasn't purely by chance that I was on my way to Paris. Maybe, had I seen posters for the boat train to Amsterdam or Brussels, I would have resisted their suggestion. I put this doubt aside.

The train stopped three times between stations on the way to Paris, and each time strange images were placed before me outside the window: an empty plate of white porcelain with a blue Chinese pattern, left outside a derelict barn, steaming in the cold air. The train moved on. The next time it stopped: an old man in a blue workman's suit and beret, a fat cigarette between his lips, sitting at the wheel of a burnt-out Renault. The train moved on again through towns with names like exquisite delicacies that I could turn over in my mouth. I did so with relish and spoke one of them out loud – 'Clermont-de-l'Oise' – and the passengers opposite me looked away in embarrassment.

I waited for the train to stop again. I was sure it would, and that when it did I would see something more important than on the previous two occasions. When it came to a stand-still, I leaned forward and put my face close to the window. I could see two boys walking across a meadow, now racing each other, now stopping to pick a winter flower, which they spotted amongst the frost-crisp grasses. They reminded me of myself and Alex, and I hoped that someone had watched us walking through the innocent world of our childhood, just as I was looking at these boys. I sat back.

In another mood I might have tried to consider the significance of these images, or might not have noticed them at all. As it was, I saw, but thought no more about them – except to notice that there were three of them.

I have never been superstitious, but three has always been my special number: I was born on the third of March. I always pay attention when this number comes up. I remember the excitement I felt, for instance, when a school teacher first explained the concept of the Holy Trinity. The first time I saw triplets squashed into a pram, being pushed along the street, I was compelled to follow them until the mother, uneasy with my presence, stopped and asked me what I wanted.

'I've never seen triplets before,' I explained.

'Well now you have, so go away.'

Adherence to the number three had become one of my foibles: Katie and I lived in flat 3, my extension at *The* Agency was 33, I always backed the third horse in the Grand National and ordered a chicken masala, the third item on the menu, at our favourite Indian restaurant. I could go on. So it didn't escape my notice, as the train started off again after the third stoppage, that this would be my third stay in Paris, not counting the times I had passed through the city on my way down south. I enjoyed the coincidence and laughed out loud, again provoking the people around me. Ignoring them, I decided that if one had to live one's life according to a law, why couldn't it be to the law of three?

At the Gare du Nord I avoided the porters and taxi drivers, stepped out into the street, passed two bars and stopped at the third, where a line of men were leaning against the counter. I drank three more cognacs – it would be perverse, now, to continue to call them brandies – ordered a large espresso and tried not to think about Alex and Katie again. It was dark outside and the café window, streaming with condensation, distorted the reflections of the eight of us at the stained wooden bar. From the window we appeared to be together, but I alone was apart, the men speaking too quickly for me to understand what they were saying; I assumed it had something to do with the girl working in the kitchen, for they lowered their voices each time she came out to serve. I spent an hour, smoking and sipping the last of the cognacs. The bar was empty when I left.

I walked along the rue de Dunkerque and on into the place Pigalle. The night was icy cold, but the atmosphere around the restaurants and bars was thick with the warming reek of Gauloise cigarettes and the heavy odour of red wine and spirits. I was still flushed from the cognacs and my coat was open, my black scarf hanging loose. A man with oiled black hair caught hold of it as I walked past a sex shop.

'Venez, venez,' he ordered, his face changing from blue to red to green as signs flashed on and off across the street. 'Sexy girls,' he hissed.

I pulled the scarf out of his hand and walked away without saying anything. He swore at me, without conviction, and turned to a group of tourists being unloaded from a luxury coach.

Along a narrow street on the slope of Montmartre I found a hotel remarkable only for the smallness of its sign and the dimness of its entrance; neither seemed designed to encourage guests. Behind a mutilated reception desk an old woman, with thin hair that had been badly dyed black, was knitting what looked like a shawl and watching the television. She seemed surprised that I was alone and wanted to take a room for a few nights.

'I need to sleep,' I told her.

'Ah oui, m'sieur,' she replied, as though she was imparting wisdom, 'we all sleep at some time.'

She took the money for the first night, and handing me a key with a frayed length of string tied to it pointed towards the stairs. 'Number nine – turn left at the first floor.' She looked puzzled when I laughed at the room number.

'It's nothing,' I explained. 'Just coincidence – what you call *hazard*.'

There were no lights on the staircase, which was perhaps just as well for the place smelled bad, and I arrived at the room by a process of deduction, since the number plate was missing. Inside, the naked light bulb revealed a small double bed with a mattress which, I could see from the door, had already supported more bodies than it was created for. The walls were covered with a blue patterned paper, faded, peeling in places, and stained with the crushed bodies of bugs and spilt liquid. Yellow light came through the louvred shutters. A tap dripped slowly into a large, old-fashioned wash-basin. I threw my bag on to the floor and lay on my back on the mattress, my hands behind my head, staring up at the cracked ceiling.

I probably would have slept like that, for I was tired and still drunk, but a few minutes later there was a knock at the door and a short, dark man in his forties appeared. In his black trousers, white shirt and crimson nylon jacket he reminded me of the barber who used to hack away at my hair when I was a child. I had hated him.

'Americain?' he asked, without apologizing for disturbing me. He could have been north African, from Algiers perhaps.

I told him I was English.

'Good,' he said, and showed me his broken teeth. 'You want fun? I have friends.' His right hand began to describe a female outline. 'Have a good time, good girls. You want?'

'No,' I told him, still lying on my back, 'I don't want.'

He looked annoyed for a moment and I thought he would go away, but he tried again.

'Beautiful girls. Oh la la — vraiment les belles. Not expensive — '

'No,' I said, as finally as I could.

'You want boys? Little boys?'

'No.'

'Hashish? Cocaine?'

'No.'

'Heroin?'

'I want to sleep,' I told him. 'Alone. Here. Now.' I sat up and swung my legs off the bed.

'OK, OK,' he said quickly, 'but maybe you change your mind later. If you do, you come to room fifteen and ask — '

I got over to the door and closed it on him before he could finish.

I remembered, as I opened the bottle of whisky, that when Alex had explained how frightened he had been at discovering there was nowhere for him to hide from the demons that had haunted him in New York — dangerous things like drugs and the crimes he was prepared to commit to get them — that I had believed I was too secure to be endangered in that way. I had friends, my family, Katie. I had had them then. I had even worked in an office where people would have missed me — they would be missing me now, speculating behind doors about where I had gone to, what had happened between Katie and me, how strange I had been lately. But it already seemed long ago that I had felt so secure. I lay on the bed and listened to the sounds start up in the room next door – a girl, gentle and encouraging, but with a harsh, provocative suggestion in her voice; the man sounded tired but expectant. Probably she was one of the Algerian's girls. They got going after a while, or she did at least, sounding wild but well-rehearsed. I put down the whisky and opened the window: in the street a man was on his knees retching on to his hands. I drank some more and slept.

I woke at ten with a throbbing reminder of how much I'd had to drink the day before and with the memory of strange sounds in the hotel. Then I heard the reassuring notes of the Paris street – the engine of a 2CV, a man with a deep cough, the clip of a woman's heels. I lay in bed and attempted to identify each sound as it came to me. I became so happy occupying myself like this, experiencing the city in my imagination rather than in person, that I could have stayed in bed all day. But the pain in my stomach reminded me that I hadn't eaten since the previous morning.

I washed, changed my clothes, slipped out past the madame, with whom I had no desire to talk, and walked in the opposite direction to Montmartre's tourist haunts. I found a small café without a juke box or slot machine where I ordered *entrecôte frites* and a carafe of red wine. While I waited to be served I thought about what I was going to do in Paris and decided that I wouldn't go anywhere or do anything apart from eat, drink and sleep. I allowed myself three days of solitude. I was happy with that thought. It had been so long since I had been on my own and had time to myself that I relished the prospect of the days ahead of me as much as I savoured the taste of the cheap red wine and the smell of the meat which a thin old man brought over to me. He introduced himself as Louis and hurried away to fetch me a paper tablecloth.

The few other diners in the place left before I had finished eating, but I lingered over a second coffee. Louis came over to offer me a cognac – on the house – but I declined it. He asked me if I was on holiday and I said, 'Something like that' – he guessed that I didn't want to talk and left me alone to smoke another cigarette. I decided to return to this restaurant, to its dirty net half-curtains, tobacco-stained walls and cracked floor tiles for both lunch and dinner during my solitude.

For the next two days I was silent apart from exchanging a 'bonjour' with the madame as I paid for my room, ordering my food from Louis at the restaurant and delivering another refusal to the pimp, whose offerings became increasingly obscene.

'Eh, Americano,' he whispered down the corridor when I came back from lunch. 'You want girl and dog . . . ? Horse . . . ? Snake . . . ?'

Later, I woke in the darkness with him knocking on my door to tell me that he knew of two young girls, no more than twelve years old, beautiful virgins, he assured me, who would be happy to come and visit me. I had only to say the word, as his friend, and he would arrange it for me.

'No,' I shouted at him.

For two days I resisted the thoughts of Katie and Alex, which returned to me as regularly as hunger and thirst. If I was going to run away from them, then I must control their memory. I must be tougher, I thought, as I lay on the collapsed bed and charted the progress of the sun by the angle of the light which came through the louvred shutters. The street sounds also changed with the day; at night they were as dark and jaundiced as the Paris sky, but even these I welcomed, for they seemed to demand nothing of me. I could be silent and exist in their unfamiliarity.

On the third day, at seven o'clock in the evening, I returned to Louis' restaurant. There were a couple of men drinking at the bar, but I was the first one in the dining room and Louis had time to shake my hand and pat me on the back. I enjoyed this, just as I savoured the new familiarity of my table in the far corner from where I could watch the restaurant and the bar.

I was still reading through the menu – in no hurry, since I had the whole evening in front of me – when an attractive girl came in on her own. The men at the bar watched her, falling silent as she approached them, taking off her black gloves, slowly pulling at each finger in turn. There was something sensual about the way she did this, and the men eyed the discarded gloves as they lay on the counter as if they held the promise of intense, illicit pleasure.

The girl looked around the restaurant, and her eyes settled on me in the corner; she smiled, and I nodded in acknowledgement, for I had seen her there each time I had visited the place. Perhaps encouraged by my smile, or put off by the men at the bar, the girl picked up her gloves and walked over to me, propping her canvas bag against the table leg and pulling out the chair opposite me.

'Hi,' she said in a nasal American accent, offering her hand, 'I'm Linda from Los Angeles. I'm living in the quarter here – doing some painting.' She tossed her mass of jet-black curls with a movement I had only ever seen used on spaghetti. 'I've been watching you for a while now, over the past few days anyway, and I just love your face. Can I draw you?'

I said nothing.

If it hadn't been the third day – and if she hadn't been so attractive – I would have told her to leave me alone. As it was, I ordered a carafe of wine, which Louis brought over with a smile, placing a warm hand on my shoulder, which he squeezed as he filled our glasses.

I raised mine to her.

'Am I bothering you?' she asked.

'No, no. Not really.'

We watched each other. She was short, with a soft, well-proportioned body. There were splatters of oil-paint across her cheeks, defining the high ridge of her cheekbones. Her trousers resembled a palette, dappled with garish colours.

She didn't seem to like being watched. 'Are you always this talkative?'

'Sometimes I talk, but at the moment I don't really have anything to say.' She looked confused. I thought that a girl as pretty as her was probably used to people trying to pick her up and that maybe my lack of interest would provoke her. 'Anyway. I thought you were interested in my face, not my mind.'

She laughed. 'OK. I'll do the talking and you can look picturesque.' She bent down to reach into her bag, exposing the full curve of her unsupported breasts, and pulled out a small sketchbook and pencil.

169

I put down the menu. 'Have you eaten . . . ? I was just going to order something . . . '

'I don't usually eat in restaurants,' she explained, with a hint of embarrassment. 'I was only going to have a drink. But why not?' She smiled. 'It would be really nice.'

Linda told me about her studio at the top of a thin, dilapidated house which smelled of damp and unwashed sheets. It was a good studio, though, she assured me, and she had been lucky to find it, as the Frenchman who had helped her had been quick to point out, expecting her to reward him for his services. The place sounded exactly as I had imagined a Paris studio would look, with painted floorboards, large exposed windows, a few broken chairs, a large easel, of course. No doubt the bed was always unmade and clothes, dishes, tubes of oil-paint, sketches and canvases had been scattered around the room.

'Maybe I could come and visit you there?'

She smiled.

Maybe she thought it was too obvious a line for a pick-up. Maybe it was very English. Maybe it was exactly what she wanted to hear. She looked straight into my eyes and didn't blink. 'Sure. It's just up the road . . . '

She said no more; we were both silenced by the sudden threat or promise of a sexual encounter. Then Louis came over to take our order. I poured some wine while Linda's hand worked away over her pad, the pencil quickly darkening the white page.

'So how does a West Coast girl come to be living in Paris?'

Her hand slowed, just for a moment. 'I got messed around by a guy I was in love with.'

I nodded, to let her know I understood that these things happened, but she must have been expecting something more from me for she was silent until Louis served our dinner.

Food made us more comfortable with each other, a first shared intimacy.

'My parents warned me about him. Even my friends tried to interfere. But I wouldn't listen − not until he moved into my apartment. That's when I found out what he was really all about − came home early one day and found him in bed with two girls. He still insisted that it was me he really loved, but what sort of dumb *clutz* did he take me for? Turned out he'd even screwed a friend of mine. So I felt pretty stupid after that – and that's when I decided to leave California and start travelling.'

When Louis cleared the plates Linda picked up her pencil and started to work at her sketch again. At one point she leaned across the table and touched my face, moving my head from side to side. Her skin felt soft, her perfume a dark musk, her eyes a little moist. Her fingers caressed my cheek for a moment. When she took her hand away she left me with the impression that I had only to reach out and I could hold her.

'So what is it you like about my face?'

She rearranged her hair. 'It's morbid. You look as though everything's gone wrong in your life.'

I was silent.

'And has it?'

'Some things.'

Linda smiled at me. 'Do you want to tell me about it?'

I laughed briefly, emptily. 'There's not a lot to tell – just another of those stories of loving and losing . . . '

She leaned forward to move my head in the light, even though she was no longer sketching. If there hadn't been a table between us, she would have come close enough for me to kiss her. 'So we have that in common, do we?' She pushed her plate aside and refilled our glasses; when she spoke again her voice was as soft as her body. 'You're a real mess too?'

'That's not my story at all.' My voice was surprisingly hard compared with hers. 'I'm the one who screwed it all up. I'm the one who messed her around and walked out. And I'm the one who's still very much in love with her.'

Linda looked shocked, as though she had just woken up and found herself in a strange place. She said nothing more about love or men, but told me at length what she had seen and done in Paris. When we finished eating she declined a coffee, put on her coat and offered me her hand. Neither of us mentioned the idea of my visit to her studio.

My words had shocked myself as well as Linda. Maybe I had been silent for days because I was afraid of what I would say when I spoke. But each moment with Linda had convinced me that nothing was over between Katie and me, that we still had a chance of getting it right. I didn't know why. Maybe because however bad things had become, I still wanted to be with her more than I would ever want Linda. Maybe that was it. I drank the last of the wine, dizzy with the realization that I had walked out on Katie.

In the morning I woke early and went to the post office to call her, but just as I stepped into the phone booth I changed my mind. On the telephone, she might misunderstand what I had to say to her, so I sent her a telegram instead with the address of the hotel and the words 'I NEED YOU'.

For another two days I spoke to no one. I paid for my room, ate whatever Louis recommended, which was probably whatever he had most of in the kitchen, and walked in the streets in the daylight. At night I toured the local bars, drinking grenadines or coffee, having decided not to touch any more alcohol. So many things had gone wrong when I was drunk, and I was troubled by the thought that if I had been more intoxicated I would have tried to get into bed with Linda. I thought back over the past year and imagined the crates of spirits and bins of wine that I had drunk and the misfortunes that had followed. Now that I wanted to take control of my life I needed to purge myself of addictions, to wipe myself clean so that I could take on only the things I chose. I still smoked, though – an hourly reminder of how far I was from being perfect.

The following day I washed my clothes at the basin in the corner of the room, hung them over the cast-iron radiator to dry and started to clean the place up as best I could. In the late afternoon I went out to the street market and bought fruit and flowers – roses because they were expected of a lover, freesias, which Katie always liked, and tiger lilies because, in my strange state of mind, they reminded me of the passion I had felt. When I returned to the hotel, the madame smiled at me for the first time.

I prepared the room for Katie, since I thought that she would come, either to seal the end of our relationship or to find some way for us to start again. If she didn't . . . if she didn't come, I would have to decide whether to return to London or carry on travelling south. Either way I would have to leave Paris.

I put aside the idea of her not arriving, had an early dinner of casserole and crème caramel, a single coffee in the bar on the corner and returned to the room. She wasn't there, although she would have had time to arrange things in London and catch the morning boat train. At what hour had I arrived? I couldn't remember exactly – I had been drunk at the time. I considered going to the station so that I would be there to meet the train, but it might have already got in and I didn't want Katie to arrive at the hotel while I was out. I settled down and tried to read, but I had brought along one of those depressing books about a man who had set his heart on something and was prepared to try and try and try again to get it – he would not admit defeat. What interest could I have in a story like that when I had given up on what I wanted because I couldn't guarantee the success of my undertaking? I had lost faith in myself and my family; I had let down Alex and Katie. This realization made my heart race – I felt more alive than I had done for a long time because it occurred to me that I had no right to cherish ideals or to want to hold on to dreams. Not when I considered what went on around me. It should be enough to live and try – it was the trying that counted.

But I couldn't settle on that. I still had to insist on the dream, the whole thing, without a scent or a colour missing. I didn't want to admit that the ideal was impossible to achieve and settle with the knowledge that at least I had tried.

I lay on the bed without the will or motivation to move. The neon signs at the street corner flashed on and off like the city's heart beats, throwing bars of light on to the blue wallpaper, then leaving me in darkness. I was made stupid by the lights, a lack of alcohol and the impossibility of my thoughts. I watched the reflections come and go as adolescent lovers count the falling petals of a rose. She loves me. She loves me not. She loves me. She opened the door, and the lights in the corridor reduced her to a silhouette.

173

She was wearing a long coat, a massive scarf wrapped round her neck.

In the days since I had sent the telegram, I had often thought of what would happen when we met. Would we run into each other's arms and make wild, passionate promises? Would we both be angry at what had happened and prepare ourselves for a fight?

Katie stood by the door, apparently uncertain what to do next.

'Why are you sitting in the dark?' she asked.

I got up and switched on the light. 'I don't know. I didn't mind — I was waiting for you.' Taking her by the waist, I kissed her. 'I'm glad you've come.'

She pulled away; she was angry. 'You didn't leave me much choice. I thought I owed it to you to settle this face to face.' She looked around the room. 'Quite a place you found here.' Then she noticed the flowers. She ran her fingertips over the freesias and then raised them to her face, breathing in their scent.

I lay back on the bed — there was nowhere else to sit — but Katie paced around the room. 'Come and sit down.'

'No,' she said coldly, 'let's go out. Let's have a drink.'

I said 'OK. Did you eat?'

'No. I'm not hungry.'

It was almost midnight and the bar on the corner was closed. There were still a few lights on at Louis' place, but he had taken off his white jacket and was wiping down the last of the tables. The night was ice-cold and we buttoned up our overcoats, hiding ourselves, and started to walk towards Montmartre.

Half-way up the slope, Katie stopped. When she spoke, her voice vibrated with anger. Her hands pulled at each other as though it was only with a great effort that she could stop herself from hitting me.

'How could you just leave like that? How could you? I thought you understood — '

'Understood what?'

'I wanted to have your babies. You bastard . . . '

I couldn't look at her. 'I wanted us to have them,' I said softly, 'but everything became so impossible. You and me and Alex. I even thought there was something going on

174

between you two.'

She was shocked. 'How could you think that? Why didn't you say – '

'I couldn't explain it, not even to myself. I just felt I had to go – that's why I suggested we run away together. But then I realized that I couldn't leave with you. With you, I still had the urge to build things. When I decided to leave it was because I no longer had faith in building. What sort of things can you build when you mistrust the ground you stand on? It would have been a prison, a dungeon, not our beautiful Italian palazzo.' She said nothing. 'I always thought that the family would work – that it could contain everything – that nothing was impossible if we just stuck together. Because of Alex I saw that I'd been kidding myself. He brought things that none of us could cope with. So how could I start building, knowing that?'

'How could you be so unreasonable?' she asked. 'Why should it be different for you? Don't think that I don't dream of holding on to one pure thing in my life. But reality is always a little short of that. It's just enough to keep sight of that thing – to keep on reaching out for it.' She turned away from me. 'But not you – you had to walk out. Not even a fucking note.'

We climbed up to the Place du Tertre, where a couple of men were still hoping someone would buy the work they called art. I wondered whether Linda would be up there somewhere. The memory of her made me want to hold Katie. I was desperate to touch her.

I reached for her hand, but she slipped it out of my grasp and put it in her pocket.

'It got so that I couldn't even touch you,' I told her.

'So what's happened to change that?'

'I thought about going to bed with someone else.'

She walked ahead of me and went into a bar.

The place was crowded, the air warm and thick with smoke. A band in the middle of the room was playing jazz, so that we had to shout to be heard. We ordered coffees and large cognacs.

'So what was wrong with her?' Katie shouted.

'I wanted to be with you.'

'You're a mess.'

175

I laughed. 'That's what she said.'

'You're a mess because you're a dreamer.'

'I dream of you.'

She looked away from me.

'And you,' I shouted, 'what do you dream of?'

She wouldn't answer. There was a time when she would have come straight out with it, but she had been hurt too much and was learning to protect herself. She gestured meaninglessly with her hands and reached for the cognac.

We stayed in the bar for half an hour, not shouting any more, just listening to the band and watching the other drinkers, most of them tourists looking for the illusion of Paris. When we left we walked along the edge of the hill and came to the garish white mass of Sacré Coeur. After the noise of the bar, the silence was overwhelming. The sky was clear and star-lit. A small crescent moon hung over Paris, and below us the city spread out into a galaxy of street-lights and illuminated monuments, as much a place to wish upon as any shooting star. There was also broken glass at our feet and figures sleeping in the shadows, wrapped up so tightly that it was hard to believe they were human. A drunk urinated against a wall that existed only in his imagination.

We spoke quietly. 'I was going to give up drinking . . . ' I told Katie. 'Things go wrong when I get drunk.'

'What made you change your mind?'

'You did – I remembered that I was drunk when I met you. I really felt as though you were the person I'd been waiting for. You were the answer . . . '

'So why did you run away?' She was confused.

'You just told me why – because sometimes it's hard to reconcile the dream with what's going on around me. Everything got so mixed up . . . Alex told me that I had invented my memories of our childhood – but I decided that nothing looks the same to any two people. Everything is open to interpretation. I thought I was telling the truth.' I looked at her.

'You and me,' she said, 'I still think we see things together.'

'Yes,' I agreed.

She was silent again and stood watching the beautiful city. 'So what do you want to do now?'

'Get out of the cold,' I suggested, putting an arm around her shoulder, 'and get into bed with you.'

We both laughed, and once again I had the feeling that everything could be simple.

In the morning I woke at nine to the now-familiar sounds of the street – the hotel was always quiet at that hour. There was sunlight on the blue walls and Katie's make-up was scattered around the basin. She was still asleep, and we were holding each other in a tight embrace as we had done all night. I had missed the feel of her skin, the smell of her body. Lying on my back, her head on my chest, I buried my nose in her hair and breathed deeply. She smiled in her sleep as I stroked her hair, but when I ran my fingers over her soft back she opened her eyes. I knew I would stay with her then.

We packed our bags, put roses in the top buttonholes of our coats and left the room.

'Pssst,' said the pimp when we were half-way down the corridor. 'Americano.'

Katie and I turned round.

He nodded towards her and said, 'A real man, eh? I have a little thing to suggest – some friends, they are looking for a man like you to – '

I held up my hand. 'Please,' I begged, 'as you're my friend, please don't say it. The answer is no.'

'You leaving?' he called after us. 'You come back. Just remember, room fifteen. Or ask Madame at reception . . .'

'What is this place?' Katie asked as we went downstairs. 'A brothel?'

'Probably,' I told her.

We walked hand in hand down the street and into the Métro.

'So where are we going?' she asked.

'To the railway station.'

'We're going back to London?'

'You'll see.'

We got off at the Gare de Lyon at ten-fifteen and climbed

up the steps into the station. The place was still busy with morning commuters coming into the city. I left Katie to buy us a breakfast of coffee and croissants at the bar, while I went over to the information desk. When I got back she asked again where we were going.

'You'll see.'

We dunked bread – there were no croissants left – into the coffee and then hurried on to the platform where people were already boarding the sleek, high-speed train.

'Now it's time to be honest,' I said to her. 'And realistic.'

We climbed up into the corridor of a second-class carriage.

'Do you remember how we talked about living in Italy, in a house in the country where the hills would be covered with olive groves, the nights warm, the skies clear? How we were going to be happy doing that together, just you and me, having children, growing older, getting a little drunk each night on cheap wine and short stories? I lived with that dream. It became so real and certain that I could even smell the herbs growing on the hillside, the olive-wood and rosemary burning on the fire. But I can't live with it any more. It seems to me that we're just not being honest, thinking like that. I don't like escaping into my thoughts each time something goes wrong at home.'

Katie looked scared. 'I don't like this,' she said urgently. 'I don't like what you're doing.'

'I just want us to be honest for once.'

The train's engines revved and a guard began walking along the platform, closing the carriage doors.

'It's now or never,' I told her. 'In a minute this train is leaving for the South. If you want to go there, if you really want to do that, then let's do it now. It's time to make up your mind.'

'Why are you doing this?' she asked. 'What do you want us to do?'

'I want us to be honest about who we are and what we claim for ourselves. I need to sort this out now.' My hand was sweating on the door lever. 'I can't live with the thought that the things we dream about might never be ours. I need to know.'

She grabbed my hand off the lever.

'Do you trust me?' she asked. Her eyes were as urgent as her voice. 'If you trust me, then believe me – we're not the sort of people to run away like this. That's not for us. But believe me – we will have our family and house and all those other things. But they don't just happen like that, not to people like us. We have to work towards them, but if we really want them then we'll have them in the end.'

I let go of the door handle, took her hand and we jumped down from the train just as the guard reached the carriage we had been standing in. We held each other and kissed on the platform. The guard waited for us to finish and then asked if we were going to board the train. When I shook my head, he shrugged his shoulders. 'Les jeunes,' he muttered. 'Mais quelles folies.'

A few minutes later, at ten forty-seven, the train pulled out of the station. We stood on the platform, our bags at our feet. The few people standing nearby paid us no attention, waving to their departing friends or relatives.

'We could have been in Turin in time for dinner,' I said absently.

I watched the train shift across the rail grid outside the station shed. It took with it the desperation I had felt and the urgency of the longings I had lived with for a year and more. It would cross the continent this morning, be down in Lyon soon after lunch, cut its way through the Alps and then wander down into Piedmont where the hills sloped gently and houses were roofed over with terracotta tiles. Where one day the living would be easy for us.

'Come on,' Katie said, picking up her case and reaching for my hand, 'let's get back to London.'

I followed her with a heart as light as the breeze which ruffled her hair, brought in by trains returning to the station. But over lunch at a restaurant near the Gare du Nord I said that there was one more thing that we needed to sort out.

Katie looked anxious.

'Listen,' I said – with an ease I wouldn't have believed possible a week or two earlier – 'if we're going to go on living together in that flat, then we really do have to decide on a colour for the walls.'

179

'OK,' she agreed, 'but it can't be white because Eveline wouldn't approve.'

'And it can't be black.'

'And we should stay away from red, white and green.'

Together, we looked down at the tablecloth covered with our empty plates and the carafe with the last of the wine. It was a blue and white gingham, the same French blue as the wallpaper in the hotel room. Katie slipped one of the matching napkins into her bag.

We were tired and quiet with relief on the journey back to London, sitting side by side with our backs to the engine because Katie said that that way we would be able to see what we were leaving behind. When the light faded in the middle of the afternoon she started reading a magazine, while I switched on the Walkman. It wasn't until six o'clock, when we got on to the train at Dover, that we mentioned Alex.

'I didn't have a chance to say goodbye to him,' Katie remembered. 'He was hardly in, the last few days.'

I wondered where he went to when he went out. 'We must find some way to help him,' I said. 'Maybe we could get him into one of those self-help groups like Narcotics Anonymous.'

'So long as we're together,' she took my hand in hers, 'then we'll be able to help him.'

'I know we're not going to throw him out, but it might help if we gave him a deadline to work to, if we told him he must leave in a month or two . . . that way, maybe he'll start making plans.'

'Mmm – maybe,' Katie muttered in a tone which made me think that she disagreed. But she had obviously decided not to argue the point with me. 'I don't mind. He's your brother.'

'We'll see what happens,' I said, too tired and happy to think about him then.

But as the train pulled into Victoria Station, just after seven o'clock, I became uneasy about returning to the flat.

'Let's have something to eat first,' I suggested.

'You're always eating,' Katie teased. 'You'll get fat. And anyway, I'm not very hungry – not after that lunch. No, let's go home – I'll make you an omelette or something. OK?'

'How about some chestnuts,' I said, pointing to a man on the street corner warming himself at a brazier. Katie buttoned her coat against the cold night and followed me over to the chestnut seller.

'What is it?' she asked softly, and when I didn't reply asked again, 'What is it? What's wrong?'

'It's just that I don't want to have to worry about Alex. It doesn't seem right that I should be so concerned about my older brother. I'm going to worry if he's not there when we get back – and I'm worried now that he might be . . . '

'Well, let's go and find out.' She picked up my bag and led me, eating roasted chestnuts, down into the Underground.

When we walked along the street towards the flat we could see the light on in Alex's bedroom. Katie looked up at the clear sky and said, 'At least we have the stars,' but neither of us laughed.

When we got into the flat he didn't call out 'Hello' as he usually did. We looked in the sitting room and the kitchen, knocked on his bedroom door before going in, but he wasn't there either.

'He must have gone out and forgotten about the lights,' Katie said uneasily, for we both sensed that someone was there; the flat felt occupied. 'Maybe we should have called to warn him we were coming.'

It wasn't until I went into the bathroom that I found him. He had closed the door, but for once he hadn't locked it, not expecting to be disturbed. He was sitting on the carpet, his head propped up against the side of the bath. He must have been in there for a long time. His skin was as white as the walls around him and, in contrast, his curly hair seemed blacker than it really was. His deep brown eyes, quiet and staring, seemed to be fixed on the objects he had placed on top of the white toilet seat – his black leather wallet, propped open to display the photograph of his wife which he always carried with him; another photograph of her, which I hadn't seen before, was leaning against the cistern; on top of the cistern, a vase of dead flowers and a tape of the best jazz session he had ever played in. The

181

burnt-out candles which he had placed on the edge of the bath added an element of devotion to these objects. This was his shrine.

The short curtains had been drawn across the window above the bath and the light in the centre of the ceiling was too bright; it hurt my eyes. Alex's eyes were fixed on the shrine he had built to his marriage and his music, his impossible dream. It was very quiet in the room and it was unlikely that he would have heard if anyone had rung the bell or called on the telephone. It was unlikely that anyone would have called him – not his wife, anyway – and he wouldn't have remembered the last time he had seen anyone else. Except perhaps his dealers – he always remembered those appointments. I used to think that, apart from his dealers, he really didn't know anything or anyone, although other people knew him. The dealers and the drug they sold him were the only release he could find from a vision as bleak and inconceivable as eternity. For a long time there had been only that in his life and his head, little moments of release in a dark eternity, as brief as the movement of a shooting star across a summer sky. For those moments he had sold everything he owned – and much that he hadn't owned – and so for him there could be no tomorrow, just eternity.

He had been lying on the floor for a long time, propped up against the side of the bath, which he had filled – the water was cold now. He was sitting on a white bath towel and beside him there was an empty syringe. On the towel were a few grains of white powder, but it's unlikely that he saw them. There was also a discarded match and spoon, burned black.

The photograph in his wallet had been taken in the States. He stood with his left arm around his wife, his trumpet in his right hand: they were smiling for the camera. Behind them was an unfocused expanse of countryside, as vast as his ambitions had been. The background was the lightest shade of blue and the sun had set beyond the unseen horizon, throwing a slender but clearly defined flash of red across the sky, as slight as his chances had been of ever making his dream come true. It's possible that he was staring, with his wide-open eyes, at the

photograph and its sky. He might also have been considering the other image, the plain vase of dead flowers, the
burnt-out stubs in the candlesticks or the whiteness of the
walls. Whatever he was staring at, tears had fallen from his
eyes and run down his pallid cheeks and unshaven chin,
dropping on to the white T-shirt which covered his chest.
They seemed to be white tears, wherever they were, and
although they had now stopped falling I could easily follow
their lustrous track.

But not everything about him was so white and black.
There was a prick of red blood on his left arm where he had
injected himself, and a tiny drop of blood on the white
towel, which had come from the tip of the syringe. There
was also a large red and rust-coloured flow of blood from
his mouth, which had run down his shoulder and spread
along his arm to the floor. Even his well-trimmed nails
were now red. Like the tears, which had come from higher
up, the stream of blood from his mouth to his fingertips
had dried hard. In his mouth, along with the blood and
tears, there was also a large and glutinous clod of vomit,
also mostly red. It may be that some of the redness on his
arm and the carpeted floor was also vomit, but it seemed
blood-red in contrast to all the whiteness.

I kneeled down beside him and, with the thumb and
forefinger of my right hand, closed his eyes, hiding him
from the people who had abandoned him, from the red
flash in the sky which he could never reach and from the
room he had been unable to leave.

We cleaned him up as best we could and laid him out on his
bed. Too shocked to know what to do next, we sat on the
floor in front of him, our hands limp by our sides, resting in
each other's. I stared at him and felt a load descend upon
me that was so heavy I thought it would crush me. My eyes
felt weighed down, and at some point I must have dozed
off. I don't know for how long I was asleep, but I woke to
the smell of burning wood, to the sound of a house
collapsing around me. I had never seen that house before,
but it seemed to belong to me, a small house in the
countryside; the walls, which had been roughly plastered
and whitewashed, were now turning black with smoke.

The house burned easily, flames forking through the small shuttered windows, the low clay-tiled roof coming down with hardly a sound. I stood outside and watched it burn, calmed by the heat on my face. There was no one else around to witness its destruction and it occurred to me that maybe I had set fire to it deliberately. Then I saw that Alex was inside. 'Run,' I shouted to him, but he couldn't hear me for the noise of shattering timbers. 'Alex, get out of there. Leave it.' He disappeared behind a curtain of flames, but then came riding out on a horse, well-fed and heavy in the flanks. He rode through the front door, ducking to avoid the lintel, and appeared not to notice me. I woke up when he rode past, the horse rearing, his whip on its hide, my hand grasping at the reins. In reaching out, I also woke Katie. It was six o'clock in the morning and we could no longer avoid calling Mum and Dad.

They came quickly and saw him. Later, when the undertakers had removed the body, we went over to the house in Highgate, happy to be away from the site of Alex's death. When we entered the sitting room, Dad and Katie sat down, but Mum stood uneasily in the centre of the room, apparently unsure of what she should do next. I walked over to her and she put her arms around me, clinging as though her life depended on it.

'Crying doesn't help,' she whispered. 'It just makes me feel even emptier. There's nothing left.'

I thought that we ought to speak about Alex, but my mind was full of strange thoughts and accusations – against us, against his friends and dealers, against his wife, even against the people who smuggled drugs into the country. It seemed inexplicable that the sun was shining on poppy fields in Pakistan, or wherever the heroin Alex had used had come from. That seemed wrong. How many people would mourn because the sun was shining and the heroin crop was growing tall?

Dad came over and put his arms around us both. He said that he was tired; I understood that his tiredness – like mine – wasn't really from lack of sleep, but from having lived for so long with the immutability of Alex's addiction. We had each stood up against it in our own way – I believe even Alex tried to do that – and in the process we had become weaker, so that now it was necessary for us to hold each other. Katie also joined us.

Mum took a short breath, as though she was going to say something, but all she said was, 'Why . . . ?'

She might just as well have said 'if only' or 'we should have' or 'I wish'.

'No,' Dad told her, 'don't say that. Not now.'

'But I don't understand.' Her voice sounded like a little girl's. 'How has this happened after all we taught him?'

'One thing I remember,' I told them, speaking slowly, careful to remember exactly how it had been, 'is that when I drove Alex back from the airport − on the day he came home from New York − he stared at the old buildings and said that he wanted to die at home. Not in some hospital bed or wherever. It meant something to him, having a home and family.'

Eveline arrived while Dad was pouring us drinks. She kissed each of us in turn and then sat in an armchair near the window. Sunlight exposed every crease and wrinkle on her face and neck, making her look very old, like a cracked doll, an impression enforced by the pleated white dress she was wearing. Having said her few words about sadness and pain, she also fell silent, and we sat in a circle around the hearth, sipping our drinks, listening to the dry wood catch and crackle in the grate. Dad leaned forward and poked at the fire, more because he wanted something to do than because it needed his attention. We were silent because it didn't seem right to ask how Eveline had been or to tell them about our trip to Paris; we didn't want to mention Alex. Not that we didn't want to remember him, but that there was already something uneasy about his memory.

Then Eveline said, 'I can't help feeling that more should have been done to help him. He was fighting the devil, while we − what were we doing?'

'We tried,' Mum insisted. 'We really did try. We sup-ported − encouraged him. Gave him money, found him a psychiatrist − '

'But it wasn't enough,' Eveline said coldly. 'Never enough.'

'No. It wasn't, was it,' Dad agreed. 'It wasn't easy for us

to do what we did do, but I know I shall wake at night and think of what else we might have done for him. I feel as though I've failed him. We knew about shootings, bombs on aeroplanes, the chance of getting run down in the street. We understood about that. But this? We couldn't imagine this sort of thing, another life within our life, a diseased one. We just couldn't . . . wouldn't see it. Not really.'

We said nothing more, but sat together, listening to the reassuring sound of the fire again. We felt the weight of Alex's memory, which made it impossible for us to go and open the door, to step out of the room. So we stayed, and were hidden from each other by the shadows when the sun went down.